Elders

A Novel

Ryan McIlvain

HOGARTH
London · New York

Published in the United States by Hogarth,
an imprint of the Crown Publishing Group,
a division of Random House, Inc., New York.
www.crownpublishing.com

HOGARTH is a trademark of the Random House Group Limited,
and the H colophon is a trademark of Random House, Inc.

Portions of this work were originally published,
in somewhat different form, in *Dialogue* and *The Paris Review*.

Library of Congress Cataloging-in-Publication Data
McIlvain, Ryan.
Elders : a novel / Ryan McIlvain.—1st ed.
p. cm.
1. Mormon missionaries—Brazil—Fiction. 2. Young men—Fiction. 3. Americans—
Brazil—Fiction. 4. Brazilians—Fiction. 5. Christian fiction. gsafd I. Title.
PS3613.C535E43 2013
813'.6—dc22
2012023930

ISBN 978-0-307-95569-2
eISBN 978-0-307-95570-8

PRINTED IN THE UNITED STATES OF AMERICA

Jacket design and photograph: Ben Wiseman

10 9 8 7 6 5 4 3 2 1

First Edition

For my parents

The two friends stood for a few moments . . .

not speaking a word, as two travelers,

who have lost their way, sometimes stand

and admit their perplexity in silence.

—WILLA CATHER, *O PIONEERS!*

Elders

On an airless midsummer afternoon in Brazil, in the close, crucible heat of that country, Elder McLeod trailed his senior companion onto a street that looked just like the last one, and the last, and the last. Nothing moved. Or nothing animate, anyway—a soda can rocking on its side, dust scrims, the whites on clotheslines ghosting up above orange-brick property walls lined with beer-bottle shards. Even the gutters looked abandoned, shorn of moisture, a blond sedimentary braid running parallel to each cracking slab of sidewalk. McLeod watched Elder Passos peel off to the left of him, and for a moment all he wanted in the world was to keep walking, epically, all the way back to Massachusetts and the life he had left and the life he ached to have back. He could just ditch the last six months of his mission, light out for home—

"Elder? Elder McLeod? Hello?"

The voice came from behind him, rapid and insistent—already it grated on McLeod. He stopped. He turned his head half around, a half show of resistance, but enough to see his senior companion sidled up to yet another door, waiting, gripping the doorframe with his hand even, like a stubborn child in the toy aisle.

"It's your turn," Passos said. "Right?" He motioned his head at the door, which looked just like the last one, and the last: older than the tin it was made of, once blue (or green or yellow), but now, faded and dusted, sun-scored, a blue-gray, the color of dirty mop water. Elder McLeod stared at the door and clenched his teeth out of a sort of slow reflex. And on his Slump Day, too, he thought. That was the worst part. He thought: Five minutes. I'll knock for just five more minutes. He looked down at his wristwatch: 3:02. Ten minutes at the very most.

McLeod backed up until he stood beside Passos at the door. He rapped on the thin metal, a thin warping sound, and out of the corner of his eye he watched Passos watching. They had only been working together for a week, and the force of Passos's earnestness, his sheer newness, could still startle McLeod. Look at him now: yellow-brown, tall and lanky, his face like a tapering ear of corn, and in the center of it, a smile. Big-watted, toothy. At every door Passos smiled like that, a sort of insurance policy, McLeod thought, in the off chance that someone actually came to a door.

After several unpromising seconds at this one, Passos's smile remained bright.

"How long have you been out again?" McLeod asked him.

"Huh? Oh. Sixteen months almost."

"Congratulations," he said, but he laughed as he said it, a thin, tight laugh. *Parabéns*. He pushed air through his nose, shook his head, and stepped away from the door, not waiting to make sure no one was coming. If someone was going to come to a door, you heard it early, heard movement in the house or in the yard, someone shushing the dog maybe, someone calling out *Who is it?* Or someone rushing up to peer through the gap between the brick wall and the outer door, then calling for a parent—a mother, usually. It happened quick. You didn't need to stand around, a hopeful debutante holding a smile for full minutes. Did Passos really not know that? The Boy Wonder? The climber who had made zone leader at only eleven months out?

Elder McLeod waited, half turned again, and now he noticed the shadow of a frown on Passos's face.

"Nobody's coming," McLeod said.

"I was just making sure," Passos said.

The elders finished knocking the street, every door a no-show, and started right into the next street. More no-shows. More smiles from Passos. McLeod wanted to throw his head back and laugh. Instead, he slowed his pace, then stopped, looking down at his wristwatch: 3:08. When he looked up again the world was still the same, everlastingly the same: the dust scrims, the whites on clotheslines, the property walls bristling with colored glass, rows of sharp, bared teeth. He could hear the river in the distance now, but only just.

At a sudden gust of wind a pair of blue jeans kicked up above the property wall to McLeod's left. He thought of the old dress pants he'd laid out on his bedspread this morning, a threadbare sacrifice waiting to be burned. A tradition. A rite. Which he would duly observe tonight with Sweeney and Kimball. He hadn't seen them in a week, not since transfers and the news that they would both become senior companions, at last. He expected they would razz him, the eternal junior, and that they'd see through his good-riddance routine. It did gall McLeod that he had to take orders now from someone with *less* experience on the mission, and with no knowledge of Carinha at all, the city McLeod had served in for the last six months. But Elder Passos played the game; McLeod didn't. Passos *stooped* to the game; McLeod wouldn't.

Over the sound of the river came a different kind of coursing, much louder and nearer to McLeod. His senior companion stood to his right, upending a squeeze water bottle above his mouth. The bottle exhaled as Passos lowered it, replaced it in his bag. He wiped his lips with the back of his hand, then nodded at McLeod and started for the next door.

"Really?" McLeod said.

Passos turned around. "What?"

"Today's my Slump Day, man. And nobody's answering."

"Your 'Slump Day'?" Passos said.

"You don't know what Slump Day is? Are you really that—"

"I know what it is, Elder McLeod. It's unbecoming of a missionary. That's what President Mason said at the last zone leaders conference. No more crass names to mark so-called occasions, and no more burning perfectly good clothes either. Didn't your last zone leader communicate that?"

"He *communicated* a lot of things," McLeod said, laying emphasis on the procedural-speak he already disliked in Passos. He stared at him for a long, hard second. Then he changed his tack. "Elder Passos, we can pick this back up tomorrow, can't we? I think eighteen months on the mission is worth a little break. Don't you?"

Passos put his hands at the top of his thighs, arms akimbo, long, stick-figure limbs. He seemed to be weighing his options, which battles and when.

"How about we do five more doors?" Passos said. "Then we'll take a break, okay?"

McLeod hesitated a moment, then sighed.

The first door was Passos's. Nothing. The next was McLeod's. Also nothing. The third door triggered an explosion of barking, a big dog from the sound of it, each bark like a mortar round. After several bracing seconds of this, McLeod and Passos moved on. When they knocked the fourth door, a flutter of movement came from inside the courtyard. A door handle catching, a door scraping open. A patter of footsteps approaching the outer door. A young face through the gap. Brown eyes, shorn brown hair.

"Well hello," Passos said.

The face disappeared and the steps retreated. McLeod and Passos heard whispered voices from the open front door, a quick high alto, a dragging soprano. Then the tiny steps again.

"No one's here, okay?" said the alto voice through the outer door. *Ninguém está aqui, tá?*

McLeod snorted at the familiar phrase. It might have been the very first phrase he had learned to separate out from the rapid slur of Portuguese. *Ninguém está aqui, tá?* And that final contracted *tá*, that timidness, so typical of the local style, and so tiring. We're not interested. We're not available. We're not even here. Okay?

"But you are there," McLeod said to the boy.

"What?"

"I said *you* are there, aren't you? You're someone."

"Yeah but my mom's not here."

"Yeah? Who were you talking to just a second ago?"

The boy paused, recoursed again to his line. "Nobody's here, okay?"

"I don't believe you," Elder McLeod said.

Passos turned to him, suddenly furrowed, his dark brows combining in a long sharp V shape. *Let's go,* he mouthed, leaning away from the door.

"But listen," McLeod continued. "We're representatives of the

Church of Jesus Christ of Latter-day Saints. You may know us as the Mormons? Well, anyway." McLeod spoke in a clipped, mock-cheery tone. "I'm Elder McLeod and this is my companion, Elder Passos. 'Elder' is a title, not a name, by the way—in case you're curious. Many people are. But we've come here today with a very special message for you and your mother—"

"She's not here."

"Of course, of course. But we have a message for the two of you anyway. It's a message about liars and what happens to them in the—"

"Elder!"

A hand clamped McLeod's wrist and he was halfway off his feet. He felt the anger in Passos's grip, tried to shake himself free of it. "Let go of me!"

In the middle of the street Passos swung him loose and stared, his dark brows creased even sharper. "What do you think you're doing?"

"The kid was lying."

"Of course he was lying, Elder, but you don't say that. You never say that! Is this really how you act? Are you really this green?"

McLeod stiffened at the word. "I'm green? You think *I* am green. Who knocks doors for two hours right after lunch, when the whole damn country is asleep? And I'm green?" He turned around and started back up the street. Passos yelled after him, "Where do you think you're going?" McLeod didn't answer, didn't turn around. He shielded his eyes against the shards of light off the river as it crooked into view.

He waited at a nearby bus stop for ten minutes. Fifteen minutes, twenty. Had all the bus drivers in Carinha taken siestas too, all of Minas, the entirety of southeast Brazil? And where was Elder Passos? He had failed to follow after him, failed to turn up at the bus stop at all. He had succeeded, in other words, in surprising McLeod. Maybe there was a touch of earth in him after all. The Missionary Handbook forbade and forbade—no TV, radio, newspapers, etc., no recreational phone calls, etc., etc.—but it proscribed nothing so strongly as being separate from your companion. And yet . . . McLeod checked his watch, craned his head to see as far down the street as he could. Nothing and no one.

A touch of earth. Where was that from again? Something by Tennyson, right? Or was it Longfellow? He would have to ask Mom to look it up for him in his next letter home. Why could he never remember anything? Why could he not hold on to knowledge? Already the yield of years of effort in high school, and all the reading and memorizing he'd done on his own—it had dwindled to traces, scraps of language, and most of it floating maddeningly free of its context. Such that someone says now, at some point, and for some reason, that *who loves me must have a touch of earth, the low sun makes the color* . . . and something else. He would have to check it with his mother.

Soon enough McLeod could check things himself. He could enroll at Boston College or maybe Amherst, or maybe even one of the Ivy Leagues—he could at least apply—and then he could take history and literature classes and study facts, or study fiction, and put behind him this muddy slosh of the two. Six months more. The homestretch.

McLeod checked his watch again. Had it really been thirty minutes since he last saw Passos, and more than that without a bus? But just then he heard a low, diesel rumble: the rectangular bulk of a city bus rounding a corner, spilling its sound onto the main street. McLeod stood up from the bench with what must have been an expectant look, for by the time he saw that it was an eight bus the driver had already begun to brake for him. The bus pulled up to the curb and unfolded itself: the platform's sudden hitch downward, the hydraulic sigh of the double doors. The driver leaned on his lever and looked at McLeod. "You getting on?"

"This is the eight, right? I'm waiting for the six. Sorry," McLeod said.

"All right."

"But, hey," he said, "where is everybody?"

"Probably glued to their TVs."

"No, I mean, where are all the buses?"

"Less people to pick up, less buses." The driver studied McLeod a moment longer, a bemused little grin dawning up through his features. "The Latin American Championships, right? They started today. How do you say it?" He reached for the word in English: "Soccer?"

McLeod thanked him and stepped back from the curb as the bus pulled away, lifting a shimmering wake of dust. As it dissipated, McLeod caught sight of Elder Passos on the opposite sidewalk. He seemed apparitional, unsolid except for the green cans he carried in either hand. He started across the street.

"For a second I thought you'd got on that bus," Passos called, holding up two cans of Guaraná. "Would have been twice the refreshment for me."

"Where were you?" McLeod said.

Passos gestured at the soda as he drew close to McLeod. "I figured we needed something to cool us down. And I don't know where anything is yet. So it took a while. You'll forgive me?"

Elder Passos produced his watted smile, easy and bright, and it softened McLeod. He accepted the can from Passos, cracked the tab—the sound of barbecues, camping trips. The transporting sound of elsewhere. The elders sat on the bus-stop bench and drank in long continuous gulps, as if discovering their thirst as they tried to sate it. After a moment McLeod came up for air, broke the silence. "I'm surprised you found somebody to sell you something. Today's the start of the Latin American Championships, apparently."

"Today?" Passos said. "Seriously?" He looked off for a minute, came back. "I guess that's right, isn't it? Early January. The mission disorients you."

"Amen," McLeod said.

"Amen and amen." Passos tipped the last of his soda above his open mouth, shaking the can like a handbell, dripping it dry. When McLeod had finished his a minute later, Passos walked the two cans to a trash barrel a few feet from the bus stop. He turned around. "Better?"

Elder McLeod nodded his head, even muttered a quiet sentence about the heat and his impatience—how he was working on it, how he wasn't usually like he was back there.

"That's okay," Passos said. "We'll just knock the last door, then call it a day. We said five, right? One more?"

McLeod pushed air through his nose again, shaking his head through the disembodied laugh, a genuine sound now, almost admiring.

It was Passos's door anyway. He led them back to the street they'd been knocking earlier, and in the middle of it he put one hand to his head, another out in front of him like a seer, pretending to channel some power as to where he should knock. It was another gesture, another touch of earth. McLeod gave a grateful laugh.

"You're not quite the hard case you're made out to be," he said.

"And you're not quite the slacker," Passos said. "Not *quite*." He smiled a brief reassurance as he slowed before a faded green door about halfway down the street. He knocked it. Again there was stirring in the courtyard. There were footsteps. Just shy of the property wall a woman's voice called, "Who is it?"

Passos answered, "We're missionaries."

The metal door opened on a dark-haired woman in a sleeveless white blouse, cutoff jean shorts. McLeod noticed the shorts, the legs in them, and quickly looked down. The woman wore rubber sandals gone thin as reeds; she stood on an orange dirt walkway that led to a makeshift orange-brick house behind her, a crude box like all the other boxes on the street. McLeod looked up again, tried to match Passos's smile. The woman smiled too: a wide, simple face. Faint laugh lines, like parentheses, lifted up and fell back. Yes? she said. Could she help them?

"My name is Elder Passos," Passos began, "and this is my companion, Elder McLeod. We're representatives of the Church of

Jesus Christ of Latter-day Saints. You may know us as the Mormons. May I ask your name, ma'am?"

"I'm Josefina," the woman said. "'Ma'am' is my grandmother."

"Ah, yes." Passos lowered his eyes a moment, raised them again. "Josefina, we've come here today with a message about the restored gospel of Jesus Christ. About how families can be together forever. About peace and love and hope. The message takes about twenty minutes. May we share it with you?"

Josefina bent forward a little and peered at the missionaries' name tags, first Passos's, then McLeod's. She tilted her head. "'Elder'? How come both of you are named Elder?"

"'Elder' is a title," McLeod came in, putting on his brightest tone, his best accent.

"Are you German?" Josefina asked him.

"American."

"Really?" She looked from McLeod to Passos. "How old are you two?"

"We're both twenty," Passos said. "Would you and your family like to hear our message?"

"And what are they paying you to do this?"

"We pay our own way," Passos said.

"Really. And where are *you* from?"

"Recife."

"Is that how you do it then? A Brazilian and an American?"

"Not always."

Josefina nodded. "I've seen you guys around before, the pairs of you—white dress shirts and black pants, in this heat. But I never knew." She looked back and forth between Passos and McLeod, a wry, deliberating curl to her lips. "A northeasterner and an American come all the way down here to preach to me, huh?" Her smile broadened, her eyes narrowed. After a long silence Passos said, "Josefina?"

"Okay," she said.

McLeod perked up. "You want to hear our message?"

"Sure," Josefina said, "why not? We could use a little gospel around here. My husband especially." Josefina winked at the elders. McLeod felt a sudden blush rise up in his cheeks. He looked to Passos. The sight of him hesitating on the doorstep. Josefina said, "Oh, did you want to do it now? My husband's not here right now."

Elder Passos asked if he would be back soon. Could they come back later that night?

Josefina scrunched up her face as if tasting something sour. Then she shrugged. "Well, Leandro's on a construction job today, but what that really means is that he and the rest of his crew are holed up in a bar somewhere watching the first round of the Latin Championships. I might not see him until late, to be honest. He does have work, though. I thank God for that."

Passos said he was glad to hear it—on both counts. He removed from his breast pocket his foldout daily planner. They actually preferred to teach couples together, he said, so this would be ideal. Could they come by tomorrow?

"Better do it after six," Josefina said. "They're day games. How's seven o'clock?"

"It's perfect," Passos said, looking from Josefina to McLeod in one fluid motion. "Right, Elder?"

McLeod smiled.

Then it was night, and cool, at last. McLeod sat at his rolltop desk in the apartment's entryway that doubled, as he had described it in a letter home, as "a very, very 'cozy' living room." The light from a bare bulb overhead slanted sharply, casting shadows onto McLeod's desk and under the windowsill to the right of it, making the room appear to float in a void, the darkness outside that much darker. The open window looked out on a corner of the little cement courtyard where the elders hung laundry, where they sometimes held P-Day barbecues, and where McLeod tonight had pinned up his graying dress pants in preparation for the burning. If he leaned forward, McLeod could see the garment now. It hung like a half scarecrow, looking ominous as it silhouetted against the dull orange haze of light above their outer wall: streetlamps mostly, the occasional porch light, and the blue cathode flashing of a TV in a second-story window across the street. Second stories stuck out in the elders' neighborhood, which spread horizontally, a wide belly in the night. If he leaned a little farther forward, McLeod could look up into the sky and see stars he never knew existed. The Southern Hemisphere. A world at the bottom of the world.

Elder McLeod brought his gaze back down to earth and to the unframed picture leaning against the back of his desk, a recent black-and-white group photo of his family: his mother and sister smiling warmly, simply, his father doing his best Sean Connery, brows askew, and his dog, Buddy. A happy family. His family. He'd gotten the picture in the mail last week, on transfer day, and he'd opened it at his desk as Passos had unpacked, arranged his things, taped up pictures of Jesus to the walls. At first McLeod had laughed at his father in the picture, but then it was all he could do not to cry in front of his new companion.

Passos sat at his desk now, too, which pressed up against the wall on the other side of the window, three or four feet from McLeod's desk. Passos had an English grammar book open in front of him, though he appeared to be staring through it. Neither McLeod nor his senior companion spoke, but their silence was easy, light as the air through the window.

A banging came at the outer door, followed by Sweeney's loud "Hey-oohhh!" and Kimball's bright staccato laugh.

McLeod scraped back his chair, smiling, and looked to his companion. "You know where we'll be if you change your mind."

Passos tipped his face up: a smile of his own, thinly forbearing.

Outside, McLeod greeted his friends at the door, in English, and with unself-conscious hugs. He said their names out loud, feeling suddenly, rapturously happy. A nearby streetlamp ringed Sweeney's hair, and Kimball's too, in a sort of dirty halo.

"Come in, come in!" McLeod said. "What'd you guys do with your fancy new juniors?"

McLeod led them into the courtyard as Sweeney explained how they'd sloughed their companions off on each other, both newbie Brazilians, at Kimball's apartment. "Let them play soccer together, or play swords—whatever the natives do when they're alone."

Kimball let out a laugh-groan. "Come on, man."

"What?" Sweeney said. "I'm a little curious myself. A lot of these guys are uncircumcised, you know." He pulled up his dress collar and dipped his head. "Little sleevies."

McLeod turned to Sweeney, smiling, but with a finger at his lips. "Can you be insane a little quieter, please?" He pointed to the open window a few yards away.

"He knows English?" Sweeney whispered back.

"He must know some. I see him studying it all the time."

Sweeney lowered his voice even more. "Ah, His Highness the Zone Leader. How's that working out so far?"

"It's all right. Pictures of Jesus everywhere, even in the bathroom, but he's not as bad as you hear. I'll tell you more later."

McLeod retrieved two plastic clothespins from the far end of the line as Sweeney and Kimball pulled pairs of battered pants from their shoulder bags. They pinned the pants up beside McLeod's, then stood back to admire them. The open window was a sharp rectangle of yellow light that stretched out onto the courtyard in a long narrow corridor, some of it catching the left leg of McLeod's pants.

McLeod went to the clothesline and moved the pants out of the light—for better contrast. He took a matchbook from his pocket, lighting each pant leg in turn. The flames blackened the hems, curled them, then rolled them in a way that made the legs seem sentient, as if they were trying to outrun their death. Sweeney took a picture of McLeod standing beside the flaming legs, then he hurried over to the clothesline himself. He lit his pants, posed for his picture. After Kimball had done the same they stepped back, all three of them, and watched the flaming eddying *M*'s float on the darkness like supernatural phenomena. "Look at it, look," Sweeney said, his voice wondrous. The orange pants legs began to turn liquid, iridescent, detaching from the crotches of the pants one by one, collapsing into bluish pools of flame on the cement.

After a time Sweeney said, "Should we say a few words? A *toast*, if you will?"

Kimball gave another laugh-groan.

McLeod said, "One second," and ran into the apartment. He retrieved from the kitchen fridge three cans of Guaraná; he made a point to stock a case of it at all times. On his way back through the entryway/living room he held up the sodas for Passos to see, a little pyramid of them. His companion smiled and nodded from his desk as McLeod slowed down, hitched his step, wondering if Passos had noticed the soda on his side of the fridge, and was that the key—observation married to action? He got out to the court-yard as the fabric fires were drawing down to small, spiky flames. McLeod passed out the cans to Sweeney and Kimball. They all popped the tabs and held the cans aloft.

Sweeney went first. "To eighteen months of good people, good times. And of course to Tiff. Seven months to the wedding. You can quote me."

They drank to that. And to Kimball's hope that they could all finish strong, and that he could manage to get his band back together post-mission, and get back to his sweet Blondie, of course. His guitar. McLeod remembered the glary Polaroid of a big blond-wood Stratocaster that Kimball kept on his desk in the Missionary Training Center. He stared at the picture often, sometimes kissed it, sighed at it. These latter gestures were for Sweeney's sake, a running joke on the real shrine Sweeney really did sigh at, a whole desk full of pictures of his girlfriend Tiffany. Tiffany in a red track uniform, her long white legs in mid-stride, one straight, one bent, her dark ponytail held back as if by wires. Tiffany on horseback in a giant cowboy hat, only her chin sticking out from underneath the brim's shadow. The framed photo of Tiffany and Sweeney in formal wear, smiling, clasping hands across a giant oak trunk with a fresh carving: *TL + AS*.

McLeod's own desk at the MTC had contained a small picture of his family, and an even smaller one of his pre-mission girlfriend, Jen, but after a month in São Paulo without a letter from her, he left off the pretense and threw the photo away. The real objects of desire on his desk were books: the Bible, the Book of Mormon, the Pearl of Great Price, the Doctrine and Covenants, all of them annotated and combined into one quadruple volume, and the Missionary Classics Paperback Library: *Jesus the Christ, The Great Apostasy, A Marvelous Work and a Wonder* . . . McLeod read at night after long days of language classes, doctrinal classes, workshops on tracting and preaching. He remembered the sharp pool of yellow light from the desk lamp that made his books look like specimens under a sun-bright magnifying glass. He remembered Sweeney groaning from his bunk, "Give it a rest, Monk Boy, come on, go to sleep." But McLeod knew so little, he believed so little, and he wanted to know everything, believe everything, *now*. He felt speared on the hurtling tip of that "now," felt utterly panicked and alive, but now, in *this* now, a year and a half later, McLeod felt almost nothing.

He raised his can of soda. "To the homestretch. Here's to getting to the end of this thing in one piece. And soon."

Sweeney and Kimball hovered their cans midair.

"Very rousing," Sweeney finally said. He gave Kimball a knowing look, a little nod.

Kimball cleared his throat. "About that recent optimism of yours . . ." He laughed, a sharp, uncomfortable little laugh, more like a hiccup. "Well, no, look, seriously. Me and Sweeney here were talking and, you know, we're just a little worried about you."

"Don't be," McLeod said. "I'll survive."

"No, not like that," Sweeney came in. "Or yes, actually, just like that. It's this survival mode of yours, this watch-the-pot-till-it-boils mode. It's depressing to be around. And it doesn't work either. The days that have flown by the most for me, the months even, have been the busiest, the months I was working the hardest, really *trying*. Those were the months I grew my testimony the most, too. Knowing through doing, right? You taught me that, McLeod. 'Experimenting on the word,' 'Saint John's litmus test,' 'faith as a principle of action'—I still remember it all because you talked about it so much. You and your ten-dollar ideas, your nerdy enthusiasms. I think *that* McLeod ought to come back and tell the new McLeod a thing or two. If you're still serious about trying to believe, I mean. And if you're not, why the hell stay out here?" Sweeney paused, trying to make eye contact with McLeod. McLeod avoided the gaze. "Look, I'm just saying—we're just saying—that we sort of miss the old McLeod, you know? Mr. Monk? Mr. Ass-in-a-chair-all-night-reading?"

"Bible," McLeod said automatically, not looking up. "Keep it Bible."

"I thought we decided 'ass' was on the approved list," Kimball said, an attempt at lightness in his voice.

"Well, anyway," Sweeney said, "that's our piece. Take it for what it's worth."

The three of them inched closer to the last of the fires, the flames spreading out over the embers, squirming, all the jagged little spikes of element settled down into a strange, glowing sauce. McLeod felt the warmth of it against his shins. A slow heat in his face, too.

"Man," he said, "this senior-companion stuff has really gone to your heads, hasn't it?"

Sweeney pushed an envelope of air through his teeth, a sharp, disgusted sound.

Kimball said, "You're kidding, right?"

After a silence Sweeney walked over to the long rectangle of light and leaned his watch into it. Quarter to ten, he said. They'd better get going.

"You guys keep curfew now too?" McLeod said.

"We have for a while," Sweeney said. "The mission makes for a lousy vacation, McLeod. That's what we're saying."

At the outer door they all shook hands and made tentative plans to meet up on their next P-Day. McLeod watched his friends move away down the street: they passed under a lamppost, bright ghosts in their white dress shirts, and then passed out from under it and disappeared behind the glare.

Elder McLeod went back into the courtyard and absently pushed at the pile of embers with his shoe. Ashes now. He kept away from the light of the window; his thoughts fit better into the privacy of darkness. He remembered the blessing his father had given him in the car at Logan Airport eighteen months earlier, just an hour before he boarded a plane bound for São Paulo. "I bless you to be strong," his father said, reaching into the backseat to lay hands on McLeod's head. "I bless you with the gift of unusual strength, both spiritual and emotional." McLeod heard the quaver

in his father's voice, felt the warm weight, the tremor, of his blessing hands. "I bless you to finally learn the truth of the things you
have been taught since your early youth. I bless you to be pro-
tected . . ." He paused. The pause stretching out into a long silence,
the silence rising like a flood. In a moment his father's voice came
up again, but quieter, huskier. "Please, God, protect our boy . . .
your willing servant . . . May he know how much we love him.
May he do wondrous, wondrous things . . . In the name of Jesus
Christ, amen."

"Amen," McLeod managed to say.

His mother kept silent in the passenger seat. McLeod glanced
into the rearview mirror and noticed her posture: she sat hunched
forward, head downcast more than bowed, as dark mascara tears
ran the length of her face, the gray liquid streaks reminding
McLeod, inappropriately, of snail trails. His father had angled his
head away from the both of them, studying the car door handle to
his left. McLeod felt suddenly so bereft, so alone, even in the midst
of such obvious love (or no: he felt alone *because* of it, because
of his imminent leave-taking from it), that he had to squint back
tears of his own.

"What if I can't do it?" he said. "What if I get too homesick.
What if . . . I mean . . . I could come home, right? If things got
really bad? I could come home early and you wouldn't be ashamed
of me, right?"

"Oh sweetie," his mother said.

His father cleared his throat. "You're better than that, Seth. You
wouldn't be doing this if you weren't going to do it well. That's one
of the things I most admire about you."

"I know that, but I mean—"

"We know you'll do well, Seth. Elder McLeod, I should call you. You're an elder of the church now."

Elder McLeod came to in the courtyard as a tall lanky shadow suddenly dissected the rectangle of light on the cement. The shadow disappeared, and the light with it a few seconds later, and for a moment the darkness was total. McLeod heard Passos call out, "Sorry, hold on." The light came on through the bedroom window and another bright yellow rectangle leapt out into the courtyard, enveloping McLeod like a spotlight.

Elder Passos woke the next morning to the sounds of sweeping—brisk, purposeful strokes. They seemed to come from the courtyard outside. Who was sweeping at—what time was it? Passos strained at his bedside clock: 6:09. His alarm wouldn't sound for another twenty minutes. He slew his eyes across the room: an empty bed, and neatly made. The yolk-colored sheets hugged the mattress with military tightness, but that wasn't surprising in itself. Passos had noted well McLeod's tidiness, his zeal for symmetry. The two beds sat precisely equidistant from the window, the two stand-alone dressers, like upright coffins, equally spaced from the foot of the two beds. What surprised Elder Passos was the apparent fact of McLeod's having risen on time, early even, some twenty minutes at least. In the week they had worked together McLeod had gotten out of bed each morning around eight, sometimes later, never uttering a word of explanation or excuse as he scudded across the hallway to the bathroom.

The sounds from outside stopped for a moment. Passos thought he heard metal on cement. A dustpan? He rolled back his head on the pillow with effort, emitting a glottal, bullfrog moan, but through the bedroom window he saw only sky, a gray wash. The sun hadn't even crested the property wall.

On his way to the bathroom it occurred to Elder Passos to wonder again what had happened last night. He hadn't actually asked his companion. He hadn't dared to. McLeod had come in from his little party looking not refreshed but funereal, his eyes raw-rimmed, heavy, his mouth drawn. At his bedside he'd knelt for ten minutes at least, offering by far the longest prayer Passos had seen from him, and the first personal prayer. Then he'd climbed into bed and faced the wall.

Passos heard the sweeping again as he came out of the bathroom. He crossed into the entryway, his bare feet slapping the green linoleum as he went. Through the open front door he could see McLeod, sure enough, working a broom over the remnants of last night's fire, head down, already in his proselytizing clothes. McLeod finally looked up at the sound of Passos's laughter.

"Oh, hey," McLeod said. "What?"

"You tell me," Passos said.

They ate breakfast together at seven o'clock, held personal study from seven thirty to eight thirty, companionship study from eight thirty to nine thirty. All of it straight out of the Missionary Handbook. You would have thought God Himself had dropped in to observe. At moments Passos wanted to laugh again, but he resisted. He decided not to ask anything about anything. Whatever this was felt newborn, fragile.

As soon as the elders left the apartment, the day began to waste away in door contacting—little there because of the championships, but what else could they do? And McLeod didn't complain. At one point he did suggest they drop in and meet Maurilho, their Advocate with the Locals, as McLeod called him, and a good friend. Maurilho's blue stucco house sat just off the main street, fairly close to the elders' apartment, and very close, uncomfort-

ably close, to the neighborhood brothel, its darkened neon sign—
DRIVE-THRU—like an unlit fuse. To even pass the drive-through's
outer walls, even in the middle of the day, set Elder Passos on edge,
conjuring up images that reminded him in turn of the images he
had hidden in the back of his desk drawer. He resolved to get rid
of the magazine once and for all, and very soon.

Inside Maurilho's house Passos met the big man himself: completely bald, a smiler, with a belly that slung down from his sternum like a giant kangaroo pouch. He met Rose, too, Maurilho's
wife, a tall and elegant woman, her skin stretched drumhead taut
across high cheekbones, her hair tipping just this side of gray. Passos figured Maurilho must have drawn on a store of considerable
wit and charm to marry her. He liked them both instantly. And
their son, Rômulo, a fourteen-year-old with a buzz cut, a Ronaldo jersey, and a precocious air that reminded Passos of his little
brother.

The elders sat opposite the little family on wooden chairs.
Where are you from? How long have you been on the mission?
How did you find the church? The usual questions. After Passos
had answered each of them in brief—he gave his most basic conversion story, not even mentioning his mother's death—he followed Maurilho's eyes to his companion beside him. McLeod sat
silent, smiling.

"What are you grinning at, whitey?" Maurilho said. He ran his
palm over the high smooth dome of his head. "We look practically
alike by now, don't we?"

Rose caught Passos's eye, said softly, "He's just teasing him.
They're grand comics, these two."

"Ah," Passos said.

Elder McLeod mimicked Maurilho, smoothing his hand over his own head, the hair close-cropped and bleached almost invisibly blond by the sun. *Brancão* indeed. It occurred to Passos that McLeod was the palest companion he had had so far, by a wide margin.

"There are worse people to look like, right?" McLeod answered Maurilho. "How's your team, by the way? You still thinking of painting a flag on your head?"

"Later on, maybe. It's still early stages. Brazil beat Paraguay, four to one, in the first round. A little stroll on the pitch. It'll get harder, though."

"I assume it's just South America, right? The U.S. isn't playing?"

"No, they're not invited. You guys are too busy stockpiling for war."

"Maurilho," Rose said, a note of warning in her voice.

"What she said," McLeod said, and he smiled.

Maurilho smiled too, after a moment, and the conversation turned to other subjects. When these ran out, Rose got up and motioned for Rômulo to follow her into the kitchen, where they prepared drinks and snack plates for the rest of them. They all ate and drank in an alcove just off the kitchen. McLeod sat beside Maurilho and asked at one point how the job search was going. The big man dropped his head. McLeod chucked him, lightly, on the shoulder. They all clearly liked McLeod, and he them, but Passos felt a hanging back in himself at this intimate rapport, almost too intimate. Or was it? After the events of the last twenty-four hours Passos had reason to doubt his first impressions. Hadn't the Lord Himself established rapports? Hadn't He suffered even little children to come to Him? He might have dandled them on his knee, done magic tricks for them. Elder Passos knew he could sometimes confuse mere soberness with righteousness, and he wanted to check that in himself—that and so much else. He decided to keep an open mind about McLeod's—what to call it even? His openness? His familiarity? It was clear to him, in any case, that Maurilho and his family reciprocated McLeod's warm feelings, and that they'd missed the memos circulating through the mission about McLeod's mulishness and arrogance and sloth.

The evening drew down over Carinha in slow degrees, the light fading, dimming away the edges of the city, yet priming the color of laundry on the clotheslines, the whites ghostly blue in the almost dark. Rooftop satellites and antennae pricked the skyline like the bristled fur of a giant, sleeping animal. This was Elder Passos's favorite time of day. The air got cool and dry, the tick and whir of unthreatening insects came up, replacing for the most part the whine of motors, and also, and best of all, the people came to their doors. More often than usual anyway. They answered in the unwind after work, or with the looseness of alcohol, or out of sheer recreational curiosity. The missionaries never *reaped*, of course. The harvests of truly interested investigators in this, the most Catholic state in one of the most Catholic countries in the world, were always modest. But missionary work, at bottom, did not concern itself with quantity, or with anything finite. The three people Passos had baptized had changed their lives and hearts forever, as he himself had done four years earlier, and they, like he, had mothers, fathers, brothers, sisters, sons, daughters, some of them born, many more unborn, an infinite, waiting posterity like the sands of the sea or the stars of the sky, as the Lord had explained to Father Abraham. Passos tried to maintain an Abrahamic perspective on the hottest, barest days. He sought to persuade not all the stars in this sky but one star in a million, a golden elect, who in turn would beget numberless other stars, other *skies,* worlds without end.

Amen, Passos thought as their hour of after-dark tracting proved as fruitless as it had during the day. Amen and amen. Passos figured the flush of no-shows owed something to the championships as well. He remembered Josefina's words—*Better do it after six, they're day games*—and he smiled. Passos pictured the whole of Brazil sitting in front of a vast tentacular television, its million component screens reaching into a million different living rooms, uniting them by the same enthusiasm, the same broadcasts: the pregame shows, then the games themselves, then the postgame shows. A communal experience. He almost regretted to have to interrupt it, or have to *try* to interrupt it.

The elders approached Josefina's door, with some trepidation, at a few minutes before seven. Where did the trepidation come from? Was it fear that a promising thing might come to nothing? That a solid contact might be lost? Or was it the prospect of having to knock more doors if the appointment with Josefina fell through? Elder McLeod knocked the door—"Here goes," he said—before Passos could decide.

Josefina answered quickly, as if she'd been waiting. She opened the outer door with a smile. "Hello, what-do-I-call-yous."

"I'm sorry?" Passos said.

"Your first names," she said. "I didn't get your first names yesterday."

"Oh, well, we usually go by our titles. I'm Elder Passos." He nodded at his companion, who wore a strange, plastic smile. "And this is Elder McLeod."

McLeod took a breath. "You can just call us 'Elders' if you want. Like, 'Hello, Elders.'" He laughed a bit. "Or whatever you prefer."

Josefina smiled at the suggestion. She made a game-show sweep of her hand, said, "Please come in, Elders. It's not much, but . . ." She trailed off as they came into the dirt-packed yard. Josefina led them into the front room of her house, where a thin wiry man in a cutoff T-shirt and shorts sat in the changing light of a TV set. Josefina introduced Leandro and turned off the set. Leandro's mouth tightened, then slowly relaxed.

McLeod crossed the room, said "What were you watching?," and stuck out a hand—all too casual, Passos thought. Then he remembered his resolve to curb such thoughts.

"Postgame," Leandro said. He shook McLeod's hand, put a tentative smile on his lips.

"Your team win?"

Josefina said, "Brazil doesn't play again for a few days. Can I get you two some water? Cookies? Please, Elders, have a seat."

She directed them to a sunken plaid couch catty-corner to the love seat where Leandro sat. She went into the kitchen, reemerging a moment later with two glasses of water and a plate of white wafers. She handed them the glasses and held the plate while each of them took a *biscoito* with thanks. She placed the rest of them on a shelf of a mostly empty bookcase that stood beside the couch: a few old textbooks, magazines, a Jehovah's Witnesses tract, and two volumes of the *World Book Encyclopedia*, one marked *E–F*, the other *M–N–O*. A red throw rug in the center of the room took the edge off the poured-concrete floor. A potted plant adorned one of the corners. Passos recognized these attempts at making do—his family made them as well—and for a moment he felt exposed in front of his American companion. He looked over at him as if in fear of being caught out. McLeod sat facing Leandro and Josefina, making small talk, something about the offside rule.

"So you're the American then," Leandro said.

McLeod nodded.

"Did I hear you guys do this for two whole years?"

Another nod.

"Do you get to go home at all, see your families? Do you get to have girlfriends or anything?"

The questions were more for McLeod than Passos, who began to feel wary, as he often did, of too much conversation before a lesson. He hadn't made his teaching preferences clear to McLeod in the week they'd been together, mostly because, he now realized, they hadn't sat down for a full lesson until tonight. (A dazed, possibly homeless woman had listened to them on a bench a few days earlier, but Passos didn't count that.) He liked to come into an investigator's home and let the message, the Spirit, do the talking. He preferred to be a vessel—no more, no less.

But now Leandro was waiting for his companion to answer, and McLeod was flushing pinker than usual, eyes averted. "Well, no," he said. "We don't have girlfriends. Not during these two years at least."

"And your families?" Josefina said. "You don't get to see them at all?"

"Well, we write them every week," McLeod said. "And we call them on Christmas and Mother's Day."

"That's all?"

"It's a sacrifice, certainly," Passos interjected. He smiled and gave a firm nod as if to mark the end of one phase of the conversation, the beginning of another, the real conversation. "But we make these sacrifices"—he leaned forward in his seat, resting his elbows on his knees—"we make them because we believe very strongly in the message of the restored gospel. We'd like to share that message with you now. May we do that, Leandro? Josefina?"

Leandro looked surprised to hear his name. "What do you want me to do?"

"Nothing for now. We just wanted to ask your permission."

"Oh. Oh, sure. Go ahead."

"Please," Josefina said.

Passos looked to McLeod, nodded, and turned back to Leandro and Josefina, their faces open, a little nervous.

"Well, first," McLeod said, "just to get to know you guys better, let me ask you a few questions . . ." Passos stiffened, marveled—his junior companion had never seemed more junior—as McLeod proceeded to ask the couple how long they'd been in the area ("Our whole lives"), how long they'd been married ("Three years"), how old they were even, how *old* ("I'm twenty-nine, he's thirty-two"), and several other questions wholly irrelevant to the first missionary discussion. Passos thought of a frightened boxer, moving in too close to his opponent, leaning against him in the early rounds, stalling. Not that Josefina and Leandro were opponents, but listen to him! What was Leandro's construction job like? What did it entail? Was it hard? Was it dangerous? Did he enjoy it? Leandro answered each question at some length, and Josefina said, "I just thank God one of us has work, you know? There isn't very much of it—"

"So you believe in God," Passos cut in. "What are your thoughts on God? Do either of you belong to a church?"

He clamped his eyes on Josefina and Leandro and reached a hand over to his companion's knee as if searching for the Off button. Passos wouldn't make the mistake of inviting McLeod, open-ended, into the lesson again.

"We're both Catholics," Josefina answered, "and we believe in God, but you know . . ."

"We go every once in a while," Leandro said. He turned to his wife. "We go. Right?"

Josefina kept her eyes on Passos. "We believe in God, and we believe He's good. Merciful. Is that what you meant?"

"God is good in very deed," Passos said. "That's the first principle we teach. There is a God in heaven who loves us very much. He wants us to be happy in this life. And the greatest happiness and the greatest growth come from following His commandments, but how do we know God's commandments?"

Passos heard the inflection of his voice curl upward out of habit—too upward for now. "I meant that rhetorically," he said. He removed his Bible from his shoulder bag and opened to an underlined, age-yellowed page. "My companion is going to read a scripture from the book of Amos, in the Old Testament, that answers this question. He's just going to read it." He passed the book to McLeod and pinioned a stiff forefinger over the verse.

McLeod recited Amos 3:7 from memory, ignoring Passos's Bible.

"'Surely the Lord God will do nothing without first revealing it to His servants the prophets.'"

"Thank you, Elder," Passos said. "And that's the answer. We learn about God's will and God's commandments from the prophets He calls. He has called them throughout all human history. Noah, Enoch, Abraham, Isaac, Jacob, Moses, Aaron, Amos, John the Baptist, Jesus Himself. All these people were prophets, called to pass along messages from God to man. Does that make sense?"

It was another reflexive question, though for now he let it hang in the air, an act of faith.

"So that means Jesus," Josefina said, "was a prophet of God and the Son of God at the same time, right?"

"Absolutely," Passos said. "Absolutely."

Josefina smiled, and Leandro too—a little uncertain, Leandro's smile, but at least he seemed attentive. They both did. Engaged even. And how long had it been? How long since he had sat before two intelligent, interested investigators, and a couple at that, a young family?

"That's absolutely *right*," Passos said with sudden feeling, that old, good feeling. "God is good and God is merciful in very deed, and in His mercy He called prophets to lead us back to Him. And in the meridian of time, as it is rightly called, He rose up John the Baptist—a rude man, a locust eater—to make straight the way of the Lord, the very Son of God." Passos felt the Spirit building in him, a different energy, and he began to lift—he did it unconsciously—into the familiar registers of the charism priests of his youth, their rhythms, their bouncing cadences. This music rose in Passos at moments of excitement, heat—it rose alongside the excitement, like a bright shirt bleeding freer as the wash water warms.

"The prophet John the Baptist prepared the way for the Son of God, the Only Begotten Son, who gave His life, as we read in John, that those who believe in Him and His words, His *prophecies*, might not perish but have everlasting life. Ever. Lasting. *Life*," Passos repeated, getting warmer still, and suddenly a muted "Amen" came from Josefina, and another, a second later, from Leandro.

"Amen indeed," Passos said, "for He is life itself. He is the way, the truth, *the* life. He paid the last, the very last farthing for our sins, our waywardness, our baseness, our corruption, our lusting and groping after darkness, and can any man doubt it? No! The Lord came to earth and established His perfect church that we may know how to live worthy to return to Him. But what happened to this church? My friends, there is a 'but.' Here, sadly, tragically, there is a great and terrible 'but.' It came in the form of wicked men who drove away the pure, simple truth of that church and replaced it with the philosophies of the day, the corruptions of the day. I am sad to testify that the very truth forked away into paths choked with thorns and thistles, covered in mists of thick darkness. Every man began following after his own light, and not the Lord's light, not *the* light, until soon, and it was very soon—it was only a few generations after the Lord's ascension—soon the saving truth in all its purity and grace was lost, and the world lay in darkness for long centuries."

Elder Passos paused. He let the world lie in darkness for several seconds. He felt his companion's eyes move to him—a curious smile too, he thought, though he couldn't be sure. Passos was looking straight ahead at Josefina and Leandro, their faces arched, waiting.

"But we have come with good news," he said softly. "We have come with *the* good news. We proclaim that in the spring of 1820 the Lord saw fit to raise up a new prophet, in the fullness of times, in these the latter days. He called a young boy of only fourteen years—an American farm boy, unschooled, simple—a prophet like John the Baptist before him, rude and despised of the world. For the Lord God says He will make the weak things strong, confounding the wise and the haughty with the ignorant, confounding them even out of the mouth of babes, out of the mouth of a simple farm boy, an American. And that's just what the Lord did, my friends, in His wisdom, in His infinite, *infinite* mercy—"

"Amen," Josefina said, a little louder than before.

"Amen," Leandro said.

Elder Passos took the sudden injection of energy—energy upon energy, line upon line—and let it slingshot him down the final stretch of his speech. "In God's infinite wisdom and mercy He has given us another chance to embrace the truth, the full truth, the full and saving truth. He restored His true church through the Prophet Joseph Smith, beginning in the year 1820, and now, a hundred and eighty-three years later, we—Elder McLeod and I—we represent that very church. We are young elders of this church, down from Recife, down from Boston, and there are thousands more like us all over the world, overspreading the four corners of the earth to bring the good news once again, in all its fullness. We proclaim absolutely that God lives, that Jesus Christ paid the price for our sins, and that the latter-day gospel, the restored gospel of Jesus Christ, the gospel contained in the church we represent, the Church of Jesus Christ of Latter-day Saints—we proclaim that this gospel is true indeed! Amen!"

"Amen!" Josefina all but shouted.

"Amen and amen!" Passos did shout.

Then Leandro: "Amen!"

And Josefina a second time: "Amen!"

And Passos turned to McLeod. The curious smile gone wondering now, the blue eyes bright with amusement or Spirit or both. Too caught up to care, Passos nodded his assurances, *It's okay, it's okay to let go.* Then even McLeod, the *brancão* beside him, even he said "Amen," though he said it like an experiment, a question. And Passos answered it: "Amen!"

He rode that feeling for the rest of the night and into Tuesday morning, and Tuesday afternoon, where he needed it. The unbroken sun, the unanswered doors, the unpeopled abandoned streets—all of it tried even Passos's patience, Father Abraham notwithstanding. But at least he had something to focus on now; he could cheer himself with the thought of Josefina and Leandro. The two had agreed to a second discussion early next week, having promised to read from the Book of Mormon and pray about it.

"You know," Passos said at one point, as much to himself as to McLeod, "I think this couple might be golden."

"Which couple?" McLeod said, but then he smiled.

In midafternoon the elders went to knock a neighborhood close to downtown, passing a gauntlet of pornographic newsstands en route. Passos noticed how McLeod kept his eyes to the ground—a good technique, he observed aloud, but not ironclad. You still ran the risk of glimpsing pages rain-plastered to the sidewalk. What was best was to look straight ahead, not focusing. Passos glanced at

McLeod. He wondered if he'd said too much, rushed to judgment once again. But his junior companion nodded.

Then two more hours of fruitless knocking. The dusk still hovered an hour away, and given the championships, the postgame shows, the celebrations, Passos held out little hope for the dusk. At a few minutes before six o'clock he suggested they get off their feet, maybe stop for a restaurant dinner. Passos knew something of his own reputation in the mission, and tonight he wanted to counteract it. So how about the *rodízio* downtown, the one by the post office?

"Really?" McLeod said. "That's allowed?"

"We need to eat, don't we?"

McLeod smiled. "Okay then! I'm buying!"

Passos smiled himself, a little uncertainly, acknowledging the joke. He thought it was a joke, anyway. On the way to the restaurant he noted McLeod's buoyant stride and his light, carefree humming. Of course it was a joke. How could it matter who bought for whom? He and McLeod, all the missionaries in the mission, received the same stipend each month from the church's general missionary fund, a vast communal pot that each mission drew from, each according to its relative costs, each according to its needs. Elder Passos thought of the fund in just these terms— Marxist ones, ironic ones. The fact was that American missionaries and their families filled the coffers most of the way, and then the Americans got the same amount in the field as everyone else, even people like Passos, too poor to pay anything into the general fund. It intrigued Passos that such an anticapitalist system should count on the support of so many Americans—it originated in America, in Salt Lake City—and, really, it surprised him. He tried to bear that surprise in mind, storing it alongside Father Abraham. He thought of his teachers who had held forth on the bottom-line evils of Reagan and Bush and Clinton and Bush, and he thought *Yes, but*. Let that be his mantra. For as he sat down in a restaurant booth across from McLeod, Passos knew that America, in a sense, had already picked up the tab, for which he felt vulnerable, if also grateful, especially since McLeod had not personalized the debt. Elder Passos still burned to think of the time his only other American companion, Elder Jones, had garbled something about footing the bill for Passos and all the other freeloaders, and was it too much to ask for a simple thank-you? In the person of Jones he had hated America. In the person of McLeod—what did he feel, exactly?

McLeod rapped the restaurant table with his knuckles. "Where are you, Passos? Is the Spirit on you again?"

"Huh? Oh. Are we ready?"

They ordered drinks—Guaranás, naturally—and toasted Josefina and Leandro, their companionship, and whatever else came to mind, collecting cuts of salty meat off the spitted slabs that wheeled around the restaurant like characters in a morality play: Appetite, Pleasure, Greed . . . At the end of the night they ordered two cans of Guaraná to go and stepped out onto the street like the gluttonous princes of this world, happy, silly even, holding their bellies and groaning, ambling the sidewalks, swilling their sodas. Cars and people passed by every now and then, but Passos hardly noticed, hardly cared. How often could he claim to be truly unselfconscious, what with his uniform and his name tag and his companion at his side? The moment floated outside reality. He wanted to stay in it, cocoon-like, for as long as he could.

A car slowed down on the other side of the street until it appeared to be tracking the missionaries' movements. A man leaned his upper body out the passenger-side window, cupped his hands to his face, shouted, "Bin Laden! Boo! Bin Laden! Why don't you and your Bush go . . ." Then the car sped up again and the Doppler bent the last words out of language. The sounds of raucous laughter trailed behind.

Elder Passos turned to his companion, watched his face fill up with blood.

"Does that happen often?" he asked.

McLeod said, "Whatever."

"Since the attacks in New York?"

He nodded.

"You were in the field, right?" Passos said. "How long had you been out?"

"Three months. I was in my first area."

Out of the corner of his eye Passos noticed the muscles in McLeod's jaw gripping, ungripping.

"It happens more now, actually," McLeod said, "with all this talk about a possible war with Iraq."

The elders walked in silence for several blocks. They didn't have a destination; they simply moved.

McLeod took a sip from his can of Guaraná.

Passos shook his head and pronounced a word: *ignorantes.*

McLeod nodded.

"Do you have that word in English?" Passos said.

Another nod.

"Will you teach it to me?" Passos said.

Two weeks later the elders came home from another long, hot, unproductive day, and Elder McLeod went straight to his bed and lay down on the covers in full uniform, even kept his dusty shoes on. He hung his feet just off the bedspread and felt the blood going to them, the twin heartbeats in his soles. Tomorrow was their day off. Preparation Day, technically. They were to prepare for the coming week, according to the Missionary Handbook, by doing laundry, shopping for groceries, cleaning the apartment, writing letters home . . . Tomorrow McLeod planned to do as little as possible. The fridge was stocked with Guaraná, if little else, but he could worry about that later. The apartment was clean enough. He could set his clothes to soak tonight, hang them up in the morning. If he felt ambitious, he might head over to Sweeney's tomorrow, but for now that "if" loomed large, as large as the pain in his feet that would only get worse after he removed his shoes and the soreness expanded, in a sort of osmosis of aching, beyond its daytime confines.

"Passos?" he called out. "Companion? You ever slept in your shoes?"

No answer.

"I'm just wondering if that might be better. Forestall the pain, you know? Or no. Not really. Passos?"

Again no answer.

After a while McLeod dragged his legs to the side of the bed and placed his feet flat on the floor, bracing most of his weight on his arms. He removed his shoes, then transferred his weight, slowly, from arms to legs, like a car jack cranking down: the tires give a bit of their roundness, the pavement gives its back for support—an exchange of burdens. Elder McLeod let out a yawp as he stood up, exaggerated for effect, and loud, for Passos to hear.

He took ginger steps into the entryway/living room where his senior companion sat studying. He deposited his shoes under the blue chair by the door—the chair on the right; Passos's was on the left. When McLeod sat down in it, just a few feet from Passos's desk, his companion still ignored him. Or maybe didn't hear him? Was that possible? Elder Passos appeared to be reading, or rereading by now, the single letter he'd found in the mailbox that night. Nothing for McLeod, but he didn't worry too much. His mother wrote every week, sometimes twice a week.

"Passos?" McLeod said, more softly now. He stood up and crossed behind the desk, pausing at Passos's left, a respectful distance, though close enough to see the letter: a single page of notebook paper covered in blue, uneven scrawl. McLeod tried again. "Is everything all right, Passos?" He touched his companion on the shoulder.

"Huh?" Passos looked up quickly, brief eye contact. "Oh. Yeah." The eyes seemed to have returned from a great distance.

"What is it?" McLeod said.

"It's nothing."

Elder Passos turned his attention back to the letter. He didn't look up again. And McLeod didn't press.

———

An hour later, in bed. Lights out. Elder McLeod lay facing the wall, still awake and wondering, and annoyed, though mostly at himself. Passos kept his private affairs private. Why had McLeod expected him to do otherwise? Why had he been stupid enough to think that Passos might confide in him, share the contents of a personal letter? This was the mission, after all. What friendships cohered on the mission cohered because of the Work. You meet these people—companions, local members, investigators—and they flare up into your life like fireworks, brilliantly, and then they fade and disappear after four months, six months, a year at the outside. The final, irreducible strangeness of the mission.

How had he gotten here? How had *this* become his life? Most of McLeod's high school friends were at college now, studying, joining fraternities, going to football games, parties, having sex (lots of it, probably), living the life of the body that McLeod had only glimpsed, and forming the kind of relationships that run much deeper than a transfer or two. He thought of Sweeney again, and Tiff: McLeod used to roll his eyes at the mere mention of her name, but of course he envied them. One night in the MTC Sweeney called from his desk, "Hey Monk, you're bookish, tell me what you think of this." He quoted a paragraph from a letter to Tiffany that incorporated lines from Song of Solomon—something about the lover's neck like ivory, and her breasts like two does that feed among lilies.

"You've seen her breasts?" McLeod said.

"No comment," Sweeney said. He put down the letter and took up the framed picture of himself and Tiffany in front of the carved tree. He smiled—an impish smile, McLeod thought, though after a moment it turned tender, sad.

That same night McLeod wrote his only letter to Jen. He hadn't spoken to her in months. He had no illusions about a future with her. He kept her picture on his desk—Jen standing just inside a doorway, in a winter coat, brown bangs slanting down into one eye, a smile of surprise on her reddened face—but mostly he kept it out of habit, or to keep up appearances. *Dear Jen,* he began the letter,

> *You remember me? The doubter? The foul-mouthed blasphemer? Well, I'm here in the MTC now, in São Paulo, Brazil. Had you heard? I must have slipped through the cracks in the screening process. I suppose it helps when the bishop is your father. You can always bribe him with the promise of yard work. In seriousness, I hope this letter finds you well.*

They had met through youth group, gone to church dances together. One day in the spring of their junior year she invited him over to her house for a swim. They stood in the shallow end of her inground pool, just the two of them, lathing their arms, adjusting to the water. Jen wore a simple, one-piece bathing suit, modest, and all the more alluring for it. They must have talked about something or other, but McLeod had forgotten the conversation. All he remembered now was the inverted triangle of shadow that hovered like a keystone over her swimming suit. He remembered how she put three fingers under his chin, lifting his head. "I'm up here, okay?"

A year passed. A year and a half. They kissed a lot. They didn't go further. McLeod reached for her breast over her shirt one night in his Cavalier, idling at the edge of her cul-de-sac. Jen's breathing caught, then quickened. They kissed deeper. McLeod pressed and rubbed and after a time moved his hand down to the bottom hem of Jen's shirt, tucking under it. At the first touch of his fingers on her stomach—he felt her muscles grab—Jen turned away. She stared at the blackness beyond the window. She whispered, "Seth, I've told you. What have I told you?"

McLeod pushed quavering air through his nose. He flushed red in the driver's seat, was glad of the darkness, was suddenly eager for his girlfriend to leave.

"I've told you I'm not comfortable with that," Jen said.

"Okay."

"It's not okay," she said. "It's not. I'm really not comfortable with it, Seth."

He heard a plaint in her voice, not anger but concern, an edge of fear even. He hated it. He felt dirty, predatory, and he hated it. Something ruptured in the center of his chest and poured out of him and he hated it. "You're not comfortable?" he said. "*You* are not comfortable!" He drew tight the crotch of his jeans against his erection. "Look at this! Look! I'm eighteen years old! *We* are eighteen years old! We should be fucking right now! We should be clawing at each other! What is wrong with us, Jen? What is wrong with us?"

Jen reached for the passenger-side door. McLeod grabbed her shoulder. "I wasn't finished."

"Don't touch me," Jen said, jerking away. "Do *not* touch me."

"Why not? Give me one good reason why I shouldn't? Why *we* shouldn't! It's not like we don't love each other. You've said it yourself. Why should we need more than that? Why should we be so afraid of everything? Have you ever noticed that? How fucking *afraid* we are of everything?"

"Do you hear what you're saying, Seth? Can you hear what you're saying? You're supposed to be preparing for your mission!"

"Give me one good reason. One!"

"Because chastity is important! Because you're supposed to protect my virtue!"

"Says who?"

"Says God!"

"Fuck God! Fuck! God! Do you know how fucking *sick* I am of God? What if he's a story, Jen? What if he's a cipher? What if he's complete and utter and total bullshit?"

> . . . *I've been meaning to apologize about that night for a long time—to really apologize, I mean, to try to get at the reasons. That was my father's "assignment," actually. But the truth is, I still don't know the reasons. I was a different person then, I think. Just in the last six months I've changed so much. I've had long and deep and probing conversations. About the nature of knowledge. About faith. And now here I am in the MTC. I'm a missionary, Jen. I'm experimenting on the word. I hope you can forgive me. Anyway, I'm sorry.*
>
> *Yours,*
> *Elder McLeod (Seth)*

In the morning McLeod's equilibrium returned, but the taste of his memories still lingered: coppery, bitter. He told himself things had changed. He was experimenting on the word again. He was different. He thought of Josefina. Certainly Josefina was different. If only Josefina, then—wasn't that something? His bedside clock read 7:32. Passos's bed was empty, unmade. Had McLeod slept through his alarm, or forgotten to reset it? Why hadn't Passos gotten him up on time? He remembered it was P-Day. Maybe that explained it. Did the 6:30 rule really matter on P-Day?

McLeod jumped out from under his sheets at the thought. It mattered! Things mattered again. Move. Let him move. The cool tile underfoot like the reassuring end to a dream: he had only been falling in his sleep, he was here now, and with two feet on the ground.

Crossing the hallway to the bathroom McLeod noticed his companion, in P-Day clothes, already at his desk in the entryway/living room. He thought to call out to him, thought better of it. In the bathroom he threw cold water on his face and noticed a new picture of Jesus in the corner of the bathroom mirror: it looked like a cutout from one of the church magazines: Jesus in the dark purple glow of Gethsemane. In the shower his thoughts returned to that night with Jen, and he tried to replace them, his whole past, with Josefina. She really was different. Josefina and Leandro, but especially Josefina. In the last lesson he had watched her as she answered his nervous follow-ups. Did that make sense, what they'd said? From the corruption of death to the incorruption of life eternal? "Yes, of course," Josefina said. "I believe that." Not a breath of hesitation in her voice, not a wrinkle of doubt in her face. Was she for real? What did she know that he didn't? How did she do it? How can I do it? Lord, let her faith be real, and let me follow her example. Let her justify the message.

A chill came over McLeod, an uncertainty. When he tried to

dispel it, it only thickened, changed, coating him like a sort of weightless film, a feeling that only resolution, sudden resolution, could lift. Thirty seconds later McLeod was in the bedroom changing into his proselytizing clothes. He went out to the entryway/living room and stood over Passos. His senior companion was still deep in concentration at his desk—there was the blue-scrawled letter, and there was his response to it; he hunched over a second letter now—but McLeod, for once, felt bold in the Spirit. He felt inspiration watering his mouth.

"Elder Passos, listen to me," McLeod said. "Passos?" He laid a hand on his companion's shoulder, as he had last night.

Passos looked up with last night's eyes, except now a trace of annoyance shot through the distance. "Why are you dressed like that? It's P-Day."

"I think we should pay Josefina and Leandro a visit," he said. "I know it's unscheduled, but I think we should."

"We can try tonight, I guess, after P-Day's over."

"I think we should do it this morning—that's why I'm dressed like this."

"What are you talking about?" Passos said. "We're off until six. And you can see I'm busy. We can try tonight or tomorrow."

Elder McLeod shook his head. "You have to trust me on this, Elder. I had a feeling. During my shower. Just . . . Please, we'll stay in tonight. We can make up the lost time then."

Passos stared at him for a long moment. "You had a feeling?"

"Just trust me, Elder. Have I ever done this before? Have I ever once in my entire mission done something like this? I know I'm the junior companion, but I'm telling you—"

"Okay," Passos said, getting to his feet. "Okay, okay. We stay in tonight."

A short twenty minutes later the elders rounded the corner onto Josefina and Leandro's street, having taken the bus to within a few blocks and walked the rest at pace, Passos leading, head down. When he arrived at the outer door he quickly rapped the metal.

"Wait," McLeod said.

"Wait?"

"Well, I mean—"

The door opened on Josefina in another sleeveless blouse, a jean skirt this time, rather short, and the same worn sandals. She looked surprised. "Elders! What are you . . . I wasn't expecting you this morning."

Elder Passos turned to McLeod, raised his eyebrows.

"Well, we just wanted to stop by and check in on you," McLeod said. "We just wanted to see how you were doing."

In truth Elder McLeod wanted to make sure Josefina really existed; he wanted her to *matter,* but how to say that? Some five months earlier he and a previous companion, Elder Oliveira, had baptized a ten-year-old boy who lived on the far outskirts of town. Zé. Zézinho, Oliveira nicknamed him. Zézinho who loved Oliveira so much more than the message. Zézinho who had hardly heard the message. When Oliveira learned of his imminent transfer, he and McLeod traveled to Zé's sprawling *favela* of a neighborhood after dark, to break the news in person. Elder McLeod still remembered the conversation that night ("You'll still be able to visit, right?"

RYAN McILVAIN

"I'm afraid not, Zé. I'll write you letters, though." "Letters?"). He remembered the sudden silent tears down Zézinho's cheeks. But mostly he remembered the sense of foreboding he had felt as he and Oliveira made the trek to Zé's house. They'd taken the cross-town bus to its terminus, and since the *kombes* had stopped running they had to walk an hour more along the grass-lined dirt road. The insects sounded menacing that night, like static on the radio, loud. The stars burned overhead, a few trash-can fires in the distance. The fires got larger and larger as the elders ascended the broad hill that marked the entrance to the neighborhood. At the top of the hill, a twine-tied banner spanned two telephone poles: WHERE'S OUR ASPHALT, TOWN HALL?

Elder McLeod felt a similar foreboding as he followed Josefina into her living room. Leandro had already left for work ("Well, 'work,'" Josefina said, making air quotes. "Argentina plays today") and the room felt that much bigger for his absence. She sat down on one side of the love seat—the side closest to the couch, McLeod noticed, the side Leandro usually sat on. She invited the elders to sit, too.

"Actually," Elder Passos said, "could I use your bathroom?"

Josefina showed Passos to the doorway of the kitchen and pointed him to the right. McLeod sat down in the middle of the couch. When Josefina came back she took the same spot on the love seat, though McLeod thought she might have hesitated a second. She adjusted her skirt, her knees together, dully shining. She noticed McLeod noticing, or he worried that she had. He studied the rug underneath his shoes.

At length Josefina said, "Everything all right, Elder?"

"Great, great." He looked up into her face, laughed a little. "The better question is how are you? How are you liking the lessons?"

"Well, I forgot to read in the Book of Mormon last night—"

"Oh, that's okay, that's okay. I didn't mean to . . . I just wanted to make sure everything was all right with you two? Make sure you didn't have any questions or concerns? Missionaries just get these feelings sometimes, and we figure better safe than sorry, you know?"

Josefina's smile faded, slowly. Her face went flat. Her eyes widened.

"Josefina?" McLeod said.

"Who told you?" she said. "How did you . . . Our neighbor came by last night, our Pentecostal neighbor, and I guess she'd seen you guys coming here because she brought some literature about you. About the Mormons."

"Oh."

"I didn't read the whole thing—it was mostly Leandro. But he said it said the Mormons had plural wives and that they—"

"*Had* plural wives. In the past."

"That's right, that's right. I think it said that. But it said Joseph Smith had more than twenty wives. Is that true? Leandro just told me about it, I didn't read it myself. I felt scared to, actually. For some reason I felt I shouldn't read it." She looked down. Elder McLeod searched for something to say. When the silence grew accusing, Josefina looked up in a sort of quiet panic that made McLeod want to reach out and touch her. "Look," she said, "to be honest, in the beginning I wanted you guys to teach both of us, but mostly Leandro. I thought it would help him. And he *has* been drinking less, even with the championships. But last night when Leandro was telling me about the pamphlet, I wanted him to stop. I realized I was afraid he would ruin what you've taught us." Another silence. "And I know that's bad. Not about last night—I mean what I said about the beginning."

McLeod gave a series of quick shallow nods. "I understand what you're saying. But it's not bad. Not bad at all. I think it's probably very normal. We're just grateful we've gotten to know you." He paused. "And you don't have to be afraid of anything. If what we're saying is true, it's true, and nothing will change that. And the fact is that, yes, Joseph Smith had plural wives, many of them. The church stopped the practice in the late eighteen hundreds, but yes, what Leandro said is true."

Josefina held her face like a paper lantern, her eyebrows pinched, her look flickering, fragile. She started a sentence and stopped, prodding at an idea. "I guess," she said, "I guess I do have a concern then. You've been teaching how Joseph Smith was a modern prophet, how he was the vessel for restoring the pure church of Christ. How could he do that if he was—and please don't take offense at this, Elder—but how could he do that if he himself was impure?"

Elder McLeod felt his face betray a grimace. He wished for Passos. He nodded, said, "Well, look, I think, first, that an impure vessel can still bear a pure message. I think . . ." He trailed off. "Or I don't know. Maybe I should let Elder Passos answer this question."

"No," Josefina said. "Please. I want to know what you think."

"Well," McLeod said, "I guess I don't know what the missionary answer would be. I can just say that, whatever Joseph Smith was or wasn't, I can say that I was raised in the Mormon Church, and I think I had a very happy childhood . . . I mean, we spend a lot of time in these lessons learning the doctrine—of course—but the heart of the church, for me at least . . . it's that, but it isn't, you know? And like I said, we should get Passos's opinion. What's taking him so long anyway? We should ask him when he gets back."

"That's okay," Josefina said. She gave a tight, quick smile. "I think I know what you mean. And maybe Elder Passos wouldn't be so happy to hear that Leandro and I were reading a pamphlet like that. Maybe that could stay between us?" She looked away from McLeod in the direction of the bathroom, then down at the empty coffee table in front of her.

"I haven't even offered you anything!" she said suddenly, standing up. "How terrible of me! I'm afraid I don't have any snacks, but can I get you something to drink? Juice? Water?"

McLeod felt breathless under the weight of Josefina's confidence. He wanted to reassure her that her secret, *their* secret, would be safe with him. Instead he said, "Water," and he barely got the word out.

Josefina smiled and turned toward the kitchen. She gave her back to McLeod. He looked down.

Elder Passos stood over the sink in Josefina's bathroom, running the water. He looked up from the envelope he held in his hand and caught a glimpse of himself in the cloudy mirror: heavy-lidded, drawn, wax-yellow, as if the last dozen hours had aged him a dozen years. The immediate thought had occurred to him just as he entered Josefina's house: he needed to check on his little brother, needed to be sure, and sure enough: the envelope showed a Morro Verde postmark, at ten fifteen on the previous Friday. A school hour on a school day, exactly as he'd feared. He rubbed and rubbed his thumb over the pink circular time stamp, slightly raised, Braille-like. He knew Nana usually sent her letters with Tiago to mail on his way to school, in Fortuna, clear on the other side of town. Who had sent it from the closer post in Morro Verde? Had Tiago skipped school that day? Since when did Tiago skip school? First his grandmother twists her ankle, and now his star-student brother plays truant? Could his middle brother have delivered the letter? Passos doubted it. Felipe was not the errands type. He had his own day school to go to, besides, and it wasn't in Morro Verde. Unless he'd changed schools without telling Passos or his old school had changed schedule. He knew some of the vo-techs taught upperclassmen in the evenings. If Felipe ever wrote him, of course, he'd have a better idea, but Felipe wasn't the writing type either.

When was the last time Tiago had sent him a letter? Not for a while—at least a month. Elder Passos wondered if the advent of the teenage years made everyone less mindful, or just a loud unrepresentative few. What had Passos been like at thirteen? He couldn't access it any longer, not really. But he knew he had started at the city middle school that year, the same middle school Tiago now went to. He'd started taking his studies more seriously, excelling in his marks, making his mother proud. "My little scholar," she used to say, smiling down at him—large brown eyes, her face framed in curls. Passos felt expansive, full of promise, in the warmth of that smile. He redoubled his efforts at school. A few years later Passos started to note something of himself in the way Tiago took time out from the store or pickup football games to do his homework or study for his tests. And now in Tiago's letters, however brief, he found other echoes of his younger self: the small, careful penmanship, the serious tone, the adult phrasing. "In regards to your recent letter . . ." he'd write. "Things continue as usual here . . ." he'd write. The familiar motions of precocity. Passos felt certain that Tiago could go on to college, either in Brazil, or, lately he thought, in America. But why was he skipping school? And where were the precocious letters lately? Where was Tiago?

The water still ran in the bathroom sink, a lulling sound, and Passos still circled and circled the raised postmark with his thumb, like a stuck machine. He only noticed the movement now, and stopped it, on account of a building muscular tension at the base of his palm. He tucked the envelope back into his shoulder bag, turned the water off. How long had he been in here? It must have been at least five minutes. More? He looked in the mirror to arrange his face in an expression of listlessness, or extra listlessness. He flushed the toilet again for good measure.

Out in the living room Elder McLeod and Josefina sat quietly, not quite looking at each other, sipping from glasses of water. Passos's glass sat on the coffee table in a hoop of settled liquid. He took a seat beside his junior companion, took a long draft of the drink. He showed a weak, apologetic smile to Josefina.

"Are you feeling all right?" she said.

"I'm okay," Elder Passos said in a voice meant to suggest he really wasn't, was merely bearing up well.

"Well," Josefina said, "drink up. This summer heat can test even you northeasterners, can't it?"

Passos smiled, put the glass of water to his lips again, finishing most of it.

"Anyway," McLeod came in, "as I said, we just wanted to drop by for a few minutes and make sure that you're doing okay, Josefina. Is there anything you need? Anything we can do for you?"

"Just keep doing what you're doing." She smiled. "Our next lesson is Saturday, right? Should Leandro and I read anything in specific? Which number is it?"

"Nothing specific," Passos said. He paused. He had the impression that Josefina wanted them to leave, though at the moment he didn't actually mind. An unannounced visit in the middle of the morning? A P-Day morning at that? It must be as inconvenient for her as for them. What had gotten into McLeod anyway? Had Passos created a monster? Josefina looked at him, still waiting. "No, nothing specific to read. Just keep reading the Book of Mormon every night. We'll start in on the fourth discussion this Saturday. That's the green pamphlet we gave you, if you want to preview it."

"We already have," Josefina said. "We read all the preview pamphlets together. The green pamphlet is all about how alcohol and drugs defile the body, right? How the body is a temple? Lean-dro and I read that again just recently."

"That's excellent," Elder McLeod said. "We love to hear about that kind of initiative."

"Yes," Passos said, "yes, we do."

The elders finished their waters and thanked Josefina for her time, leaving her with a prayer. On the way back to the bus stop McLeod thanked Passos for indulging him. "I just wanted to make sure things were going all right for them, you know? Josefina said everything was fine, and that was all I needed to hear. I just got nervous, I guess."

"You had a 'feeling,' you said. In the shower."

"It came to me there. I guess it was a prompting."

"A prompting? That doesn't sound like you, Elder. No offense."

"Well what about you?" McLeod said. "What's gotten into you in the last, I don't know, the last fourteen hours? What was in that letter last night?"

"Complications."

"You can tell me, Passos. I'm your friend, right?"

"Maybe later."

"How about now, Elder? Before I lose you to your letters again."

He did need to get back to them, Elder Passos thought. Nana. Tiago. Felipe. Dos Santos. They hummed in his head like heated molecules. The elders took a left onto the main street just as the six bus pulled away ahead of them. "Hey!" Passos ran after it, waving his arms, but it didn't slow down. A few seconds later his companion caught up to him at the bus stop. McLeod sat down on the bench, patted the spot beside him. "It's okay, right? We're staying in tonight. You can write letters to your heart's content, but while you're here why don't you explain to me all the radio silence. I know something's worrying you, and I think that's why you should tell me. At the very least I'm your companion, and we're supposed to support each other, right? 'Succor' each other? Doesn't it say that somewhere?"

Passos dropped down beside McLeod, still breathing hard. He wasn't exactly stalling, but after a moment McLeod added, "I can offer some collateral vulnerability, if that sweetens the deal."

Passos laughed. "Where did you learn a phrase like 'collateral vulnerability'?"

"You're not the only one who studies another language, you know."

"Ah, yes, very good," Passos said in English. "Very good."

Just then another six bus turned onto the main street and Passos stood up and started waving it down like a taxi, to make sure.

He realized he didn't even know which ankle Nana had sprained, and he'd neglected to ask in his letter, now sealed. It lay on the desk in front of him in a fanned-out pile: long letters to Tiago and Felipe, his letter to Nana, and a brief update to Elder Dos Santos, whom he'd meant to call João. He'd been meaning to for months. Passos didn't *think* Nana had mentioned which ankle. Had she? For the fourth time he took up the letter, the sheet sharp-creased at three places, unevenly spaced apart. The overhead bulb bchind him could only hold back the darkness so much. The letter's creases caught shadows, cradled them, like little dark pools that Passos had to tip this way and that to empty out so he could see to the words underneath.

Cristiano, meu filhinho, Nana's letter began, though Passos was not her little son and not Cristiano, either, at least not for these two years. He considered his title of "Elder" a privilege, and a temporary one at that; he wished his grandmother would use it, referring to him the way he referred to himself: *Love, Elder Passos.* But of course he couldn't out-and-out tell Nana, make more demands on a woman whose whole life was demands. He also feared she might take it the wrong way. She wasn't a member of the church, after all. So much of the life of a missionary, of any Mormon, must have seemed strange to her, cultish even, as he knew her parish friends used to whisper.

I pray every day and night that you are well and with God. I believe He strengthens the poor and the downhearted and we are all that but this week especially. Things are a struggle for us this week especially. I am sorry to tell you that I have sprained my ankle. This was Tuesday. I did it on a rutted part in the street out front of the store.

Passos paused, reread the first lines, for the fifth time now, as if he hadn't already memorized them. The standard salutation, the talk of a "struggle," Nana's inevitable word. Then the news of the ankle. No mention of which one. She moved straight to the politicians, another inevitability.

If the town paved the road like they keep saying they're going to then I wouldn't have done it would I? They're always talking, the politicians, the scoundrels who talk and talk. Criminals. Promise promise, don't deliver, and then when it comes time for reelection, why they build some bridge or some useless park downtown for the rich people to walk across or sit in. I have a mind to sue the city. Or the state or whoever. I can't walk on it. I can't hardly stand up anymore. It's all swelled up and it's a nasty color I don't even want to describe to you my little son. Little Tiago says I should go to the hospital but they're scoundrels too, most of them are, and if I'm going to sit in a waiting room forever and a day I might as well sit and wait right here like I'm doing. I'm in the bedroom now.

Tiago is helping out with the store and sometimes Felipe. Business is slow as usual of course. We were promised paved roads more than a year ago. That would help keep the dust down and out of the store. Poor Tiago spends half his time hosing down the sidewalk out front and even still we've had to lay down wax paper on top of the pastries and cheese bread. It looks unappetizing like that as I'm sure you can imagine.

    Anyway I hope and more than that I pray I'll be back on my feet soon. I pray to God my ankle will feel better. Will you pray for me, Cristiano? You are a man of God now and the Lord hears the prayers of His faithful servants. Pray for Felipe too, I hardly see him anymore, just a little in the mornings, the late mornings, and then he leaves the house without a word. I don't know where he goes, Tiago says it is to the football fields, but he won't hardly listen to me anymore. He is very headstrong like his father was.

Passos stopped, as he had every time he'd read the line. It set his jaw on edge, perhaps more so now as he saw how close it came to the end of the letter. A gratuitous add-on—a slap, and a sort of brag. Elder Passos knew, if only for a pained illumined instant, that he hated Nana's mention of his father because she had known him and he really hadn't. In Passos's memory his father was a big loud man enveloped in an alcoholic cloud, then a ghost, a memory even in his memory. Tiago knew him only through photographs, which Elder Passos imagined must be easier. He envied that purity—the purity of blankness. Tiago held in his head no half-formed memories to swirl into the mix at the mention of their father, or at the suggestion that one or all of them might be like him in some way, this ghost, this faded man who had gone out of state in search of work, or so their mother had said for a long time. Passos must have been twelve or thirteen when she finally abandoned the story and started dating again. He was fourteen when she got sick.

I pray that God will bless you, Cristiano. We all love you and miss
you very much. Pray for my ankle and I know God will heal me.
    A great big hug,
    Nana

Elder Passos held the letter above his desk, dropped it, watched it waft down in two swinging arcs to the wood. It depressed as it settled back against the desk. Not a single mention about his brothers' schooling, not a word about church. Passos tried again to worry if they were going to either; he worried out of a kind of thin hope, for worry relies on at least the possibility of good outcomes; it needs that to tauten the line. But the line couldn't hold. His brothers were in free fall. Nana couldn't catch them. Neither could Passos, of course. He was here. Two thousand kilometers from home while his earthly house sank into the sand. What was he doing here? What was he *really* doing? Why was he dabbling in English, angling for the assistantship, when his own family needed him more than ever? It all seemed so suddenly petty and small and dislocated, the mission—or his did, anyway. It felt like a springboard, a means to some worldly end. He felt ashamed of himself.

Passos was sixteen when the missionaries knocked on his door. It was a Saturday afternoon, almost a month to the day since the funeral. The fact of that. The unyielding fact. The smell of cancer still seeping from the walls of the house, like spoiled food, and riding on top of it a trace of stale flowers from the homeopathic experiments of the final withering months. The little house felt cavernous to Passos, oppressive, and though a knock came at the front door instead of a clap from behind the barred front gate, Passos got up and answered it right away, if only to reprieve the gloom. The sun flooded in, bright white, such that Passos had to shield his eyes as they adjusted to the two tall silhouettes in the doorway. They must have let themselves in past the outer gate, or maybe Felipe had left it open en route to the dirt field where he played more football now than ever.

Passos's eyes adjusted all the way as the silhouettes resolved into two young men, in business clothes, not much older than Passos, in fact—one of them pale, the other dark. They smiled like salesmen. They looked briefly behind him.

"Good afternoon," the darker one said, a Brazilian, though from his accent clearly not a northeasterner.

Passos knew he looked younger than his sixteen years, so he put on his adult voice, a bit cagey, a bit suspicious. "Yes? Can I help you?"

The Brazilian introduced them—they were missionaries, they taught about the restored gospel of Christ. Then the paler one spoke for the first time, his words thick as fists. "Is your mother here? Your father?"

Passos felt the air go out of his chest. "What?"

"Is your mother or father home? Can we speak with one of them?"

"My mother?"

"Yes."

"My mother?"

"Well . . . yes."

And all of a sudden he was covering his face, bent forward, feeling his shoulders convulse up and down. The moment rushed over Passos like a sickness, a sudden surge, as if his body were poised to empty out its toxins but nothing came out and nothing came out. He felt an involuntary tightness in his stomach, heard the Brazilian, "Hey, are you all right, hey, we're sorry . . ." and it was all Passos could do to close the door.

The next morning he stayed home from Mass, Tiago too. Of course Felipe stayed home. Felipe had been at the pickup field since sunup. On weekends now he barely left that field. He'd come home for a quick lunch bearing bloody dirt stains on his calves, his shins, since he didn't wear guards. Last Saturday he had showed up with a thick streak of dried blood running from his nostril all the way to his chin. He said he'd left it like that, all morning, as a message. He'd slide tackle anybody, the biggest kid on the field. He didn't care, and didn't back down from a sucker punch.

Passos and Tiago sat on the couch now, playing a card game in the dim grainy light of the floor lamp. The metal blinds let in sunlight that lay on the concrete floor in slowly broadening pinstripes. Passos could tell from the sharpness of the lines how bright and hot the morning must be. The sound of clapping came at the outer gate. Tiago went to the door and opened it into the glare and after a moment Passos could recognize, even from the couch, the missionaries, their white shirts and dark slacks, their smiles. Felipe had closed the gate behind him, apparently, or maybe Nana had on her way to the parish. In any case the two young men had respected it. The Brazilian one lifted his voice from across the dirt courtyard, making the same introduction to Tiago that he'd made to Passos the day before. Then the gringo asked if anyone else was home with him. His older brother maybe? They'd met yesterday.

Tiago turned around with a sudden tightness in his face, but a look at Passos seemed to reassure him.

Inside the house the missionaries sat opposite Passos and Tiago on chairs brought in from the kitchen. The paler missionary introduced himself as Elder James, an American from Salt Lake City. And Elder Dos Santos and his accent came from Porto Alegre, about as far from Recife as the country allowed. Passos introduced himself and Tiago, only nine then, shy and wounded, skittish. He mentioned Felipe, too, out on the pitch.

"Can I ask," Elder James said when Passos had finished, "can I ask where the adults are?"

"Our father left and our mother died last month—of breast cancer," Passos said, surprising himself with his directness. "Our grandmother takes care of us now. She's at Mass this morning."

The two elders nodded, grim little nods, their mouths going tight, their eyes soft, as if they'd prepared for this moment, like everybody else had. Then Elder James nodded to Dos Santos and Dos Santos's face changed from sadness to a sort of pained urgency. He looked to Passos and his little brother, leaned forward in his chair, placed his elbows on his knees. "Cristiano, Tiago, we can't imagine how hard this time must be for you. But we felt we needed to come here today and testify to you—to give you our word—that the Lord has provided a way for families to reunite in the next life, and to reunite *as* families, to be together forever. Our church truly believes that the grave has no victory—not over our bodies, not over our bonds of love. We want to teach you and your family about the priesthood that God has restored in these latter days—how that priesthood can seal things on earth as in heaven, and how you can have these blessings in your own life. May we teach you this, Cristiano? Tiago?"

Passos's little brother lifted up his face at him, a mix of fear and implicit trust. Passos looked at his brother, then back at the missionaries, and felt the emotion building in him again, a thousand tiny fists behind his eyes. He fought them back by dint of a violent furrowing expression; a wave of minor panic crossed the elders' faces. His little brother's expression wavered too. Passos felt himself slipping, going under, but before it could happen, before it happened again, he said, "Yes. Yes."

Four years later Elder Passos told the story very differently. He left out the crying, for one. The surges of sickness. He left out most of the emotion, the *feeling*; he couldn't bear to see it dull. Already he had taken some of the deepest pain of his life and blunted it through overexposure, the story of his conversion like a river stone shorn of its edges from years of turning over. He'd told an abbreviated version of it to all his companions, including to McLeod, and even to a few investigators: how the missionaries came at a bad, bad time, or rather in the very nick of time. Passos knew the language of the story as well as the language of the missionary lessons—it was rote by now, automatic. How he'd been taught in charismatic Catholicism that his love for his mother was a lesser love, that in heaven he would have God and His angels for family. It just didn't seem right to Passos. He wanted more—he *needed* more—and the

Mormons promised it ardently. A gospel that could seal his family for eternity, steel it against the terrors of the grave.

And here Elder Passos left off his recitation. Here or a little earlier. Never later. He never included the baptism itself: the feeling of coming out of the water into an embrace. He'd only ever mentioned this part to his brothers, and only once, a week after the baptism. They each confided the same experience. Nana had been at the service too, though only to watch. She couldn't have understood. The feeling belonged to experience only, not to language.

Then again, Elder Passos thought, so did most religious feeling; so did God, ultimately. The task of a missionary was to distill the infinite into the finite, the inexpressible into the expressible. Something always got lost in translation, but the effort still justified itself. It must. Only in his dark moods did Passos doubt this, only in his sloughs did he fret about roteness. Truth did not get less true by repeating it—it only seemed that way in the face of Opposition. Elder Passos felt it now, he realized, hunched over in the crook of his arms, on his desk, by himself. He felt an Opposer shudder down his back, and he immediately straightened in his desk chair. Head lifted, eyes wide, he focused on the two framed pictures on his desk: his grandmother and brothers standing in front of their house, and his mother sitting cross-legged in front of a dark green Christmas tree, holding up a snow-white sweater, and smiling into the future. Passos's balance returned.

Why *shouldn't* he think about the future? Why shouldn't he pursue his righteous ambitions? President Mason himself had said that the Brazilians should practice English with their American companions—"to lay up in store, intellectually and professionally."

Those were the mission president's very words at the last zone leaders' conference. Why would he say them if he didn't mean them? And why, for that matter, would assistants to the mission president be eligible for scholarships to Brigham Young University if temporal welfare didn't matter? He needed to lay up in store. To build a house on the rock, both spiritually and professionally. On the rock of salvation, and on a sure earthly foundation. Like Elder Dos Santos.

João. He tried to get used to it. João had traveled to America after his mission to stay with Elder James (or Tyler) for a week, which turned into a few weeks, which turned into a few months, which led to his being admitted to BYU. He was finishing up school now, married and with a child, and with a good job already waiting in São Paulo on account of his language skills and his American degree.

Elder Passos reached into his desk drawer—he felt a quick shot of fear, remembering the drawer's contents—and carefully retrieved the photograph that had accompanied Dos Santos's latest letter. It showed Dos Santos and his wife in front of the Salt Lake Temple, each of them cupping a hand under their one-year-old's sweat-suited thigh. The chubby baby wore a blue pom-pom cap on his head, levitating between his parents. He reminded Passos of a smiling baby Buddha. Dos Santos and his wife (Renata—another expatriate) smiled too, *beamed,* their teeth as white as the snow in the background. "It's winter here!" Dos Santos had penned in the bottom margin. The photograph reminded Passos of what he so liked in Dos Santos: his openness, his generosity, big enough to turn visible even in pictures. On the mission Dos Santos had been a young zone leader, just like Passos, only Dos Santos had been universally loved, all the members of the ward and all the other missionaries bustling to be near him. Why couldn't Passos be more like that? If he were more open, more sociable, he might become the type of missionary to be liked, not merely respected.

He looked up, craning around at the sound of bedsprings squeaking from the bedroom, a quick chorus of them. He heard bare feet slapping linoleum. A second later McLeod leaned his upper body into the yellow-green light of the hallway, looking surprised. "I thought for sure you'd have your head buried in a letter or something." He gave a sideways grin. "Perhaps I should press my advantage."

McLeod crossed the room with a large thin book in his hand. He took a seat in his desk chair, facing it toward Passos. He dropped the book on Passos's desk. On the cover a cartoon boy balanced atop a skinny plateau-like structure of broad colored stripes: it looked like a giant sombrero.

"What's this?"

"It's yours if you want it," McLeod said. "It was a farewell present from my mom, but I thought you could use it to practice English with. I'm sure it's more interesting than that old grammar book you use. I'm pretty sure it's mission-appropriate, too. It's a children's book."

"*Oh, the Places You'll Go*?"

"That's it."

"Am I pronouncing it right?" Passos asked.

"Perfect," McLeod said.

Passos flipped through the first few pages: landscapes the color of ice cream, the little boy traipsing through them in what looked like pajamas, and on each page a paragraph of clear, colloquial prose. He looked up at McLeod. "You're giving this to me?"

"I figure you'll make better use of it," McLeod said, adding in English, "Good luck!"

Elder Passos felt something dislodge inside him, and spread. "Thank you, Elder. Really."

"Oh don't thank me yet," McLeod said. "You see, I was sitting in the bedroom a few minutes ago, reading some old letters, and all of a sudden I got bored with that and started thinking about your letter instead. You never told me what it was about, did you? I hadn't forgotten. I've decided to be nosy, you see."

Passos smiled. "I didn't think you had forgotten."

"Well?"

He relented, though only for an abbreviated version: his grand-mother, her ankle, his worries about her health. Nothing about his brothers, their truancy, their futures. Nothing much bigger than a few sentences could hold.

"I'm sorry to hear that," his companion said. He looked serious, genuinely concerned. "If there's anything I can do, I hope you'll feel comfortable asking."

"Thank you, Elder. Now your turn, right? What did you call it—your 'reciprocal vulnerability'?"

" 'Collateral,' I believe, but 'reciprocal' is pretty nerdy too." McLeod smiled. "But no, I mean, it's basically just—well, father problems. You know."

"I don't, actually."

"Oh, that's right. Sorry. I didn't mean it like—"

"I know you didn't. What kind of problems?"

"Well, for example, I was reading some of his letters in there. He doesn't write often, but when he does it's like, 'Hi, how are you? How come you don't bear your testimony in your letters home?' My dad's the bishop of the ward—I'm not sure if I told you that?—but it's like he's always wearing that hat when he writes. He wants me to come home like some Paul, some Peter—the kind of testimony that could send you to your martyrdom smiling. It's never come as easy for me, though. But I love him. I don't want to disappoint him . . . I don't know." After a long silence McLeod added, "That's the abbreviated version anyway. More later maybe."

Elder Passos nodded. "Me too."

One morning in late January, Passos asked McLeod to come over to his desk, where he pointed to a green-furred Seuss character holding a black, cone-shaped object, and said, "How do you say that?"

Passos asked the question in English, and McLeod once again felt a small jolt of surprise. "Your pronunciation," he said, also in English. "I swear it's getting better by the day."

"'I swear'?" Passos repeated, tilting his head, and smiling from the compliment.

McLeod translated the phrase.

"Ah, I see." Passos nodded his thanks. Then he tapped at the strange object on the page again.

"It sort of looks like an umbrella," McLeod said.

"How is it?"

"Umbrella." Then slowly: "Um-brel-la."

Passos repeated it even more slowly, weighing each syllable, seeming to taste the word. "Um-brel-la. Umbrella. Umbrella. Wow. What a beautiful word. It is too beautiful for English."

"Careful now," McLeod said, mock-stern.

The elders ate breakfast together after personal study, continuing their English practice over a meal of day-old cheese bread from the *padaría* down the street and gamy sinewy mango windfallen from the tree behind the *padaría*. Mangos often figured in the meals Elder McLeod prepared for himself at the apartment, especially toward the end of the month as his stipend waned. The mango trees and cherry trees particularly preened themselves as sources of caloric supplement to his diet of Nutella sandwiches and Guaraná. McLeod could have written his parents for extra money, as he knew some of the other Americans did on the sly, but besides the fact that President Mason had proscribed that very practice, McLeod wanted to limit himself to the closed economy of the mission. How easy it would be for him to step outside it—write home for a get-out-of-jail-free pass after a pricey dinner, say, like the one he and Passos had had at the *rodízio* a few weeks ago—but how galling it would be for others, and how insidious. McLeod knew Passos, for one, came from poverty. Two P-Days ago he'd observed him, quite by accident, folding a stack of *reais* into his letter home. And he'd seen the tiny house too, the hut his family lived in; it formed the backdrop to the picture Passos kept on his desk: two spiky-haired teens and a much shorter, older woman, and behind them a self-built brick box of the kind McLeod had seen in Zé's hilltop neighborhood.

The elders switched back to Portuguese for companionship study, dividing up the crucial lesson they would teach that night to Josefina and Leandro. Lesson six. It called for a discussion of the temple, the restored priesthood, the doctrine of eternal families, then the challenge to be baptized in the true church of Christ. Passos said he wanted them to stick largely to the script, including and especially the baptismal challenge ("You ever done one?" he asked McLeod. "No? Then tonight's your night, companion"). And this notwithstanding the fact that Leandro had weathered the last two difficult discussions with far less aplomb than Josefina. Leandro's eyes, if not quite his mouth, had balked at the Word of Wisdom in lesson four—no coffee, tea, tobacco, alcohol—and again at the law of tithing in lesson five, the law of fasting, the law of chastity . . . Where Josefina now accepted these tenets with a redoubled, almost unquestioning zeal ("I don't like coffee anyway . . ." "I'm *excited* to pay tithing . . ."), Leandro looked on with a wavering smile, the way a bettor might watch his horse's lead start to shrink. He remained nothing if not polite—always attentive, always smiling, nodding—but a certain distance intervened now, a holding back. Sometimes he turned to his wife during the lessons and his eyes communicated a sort of pleading, or so Elder McLeod interpreted it. *What was wrong with how things were? What was wrong with Catholicism? You want to go to Mass more often? We'll go more often. But this? What are we doing, Josefina?* During one of the elders' last visits, a routine follow-up, Leandro had excused himself to use the bathroom. "Go on without me," hc'd said. They waited. But then whole minutes passed as the three of them chatted, lapsing into occasional silences, chatting some more, until Josefina suddenly raised a finger to shush them. The burble of a TV wafted in from the back room. She called out to her husband. "Honey? You're not watching postgame, are you?" A minute later Leandro returned, eyes downcast. "Sorry about that. I was in the bathroom."

At the end of companionship study Elder McLeod and Elder Passos moved to the blue chairs near the front door. They put on their dusty battered shoes and knelt for companionship prayer, which Passos offered, praying for Leandro particularly. Then they stood up and moved to the door. Passos opened it, paused. He turned to McLeod, holding out his hand to shake. McLeod took his companion's hand uncertainly.

"I want to start doing something my first companion used to do with me," Passos said, looking McLeod straight in the eye. "We'd grip hands every morning before we left and bear testimony to each other, remind each other why we were doing what we were doing. I'll start. I know this is the true church of Christ, Elder McLeod. That this is the Lord's work we're engaged in, and that we are His duly ordained ministers on this earth. In the name of Jesus Christ, amen."

"Amen," McLeod said. He hesitated. "I know that too, Elder Passos. I know that . . ."

McLeod waited for alighting hands, something, and for a moment he thought he might have felt it, or maybe not. The confirmation of the Spirit. Saint John's litmus test. Was he imagining it? Did he want it too badly? His senior companion drew his attention back to him, dipping his head.

McLeod said, "And . . . that's all. For today anyway. In the name of Jesus Christ, amen."

Was he imagining it?

McLeod paced through the morning and afternoon, knocking as needed, smiling as needed, but almost nobody answered, not even the members' houses they knocked, and soon he fell into a sort of trance as he followed his senior companion through the stages of another day: doors, street contacts, a *padaría* for lunch, more doors.

He was trying again, like Sweeney and Kimball wanted, like his father wanted, but what did that actually mean? What did it mean to *will* belief? He wanted faith to be effortless; he wanted

God to compel it in him. He wanted the doctrinal earth to feel solid underfoot, but it didn't, and maybe it never would. He recalled his father's words: *You'll feel like you're falling, because you are.* One Sunday in the winter of his senior year he went to church for the sole purpose of seeing Jen, who had stopped answering his calls, his e-mails. The week before had been the fight in his idling Cavalier: the panic in her voice, his shouted words . . . That Sunday at church she managed to avoid him by traveling in a protective detail of friends, male and female, and all of them glaring or shaking their heads at him. After services let out McLeod headed for the parking lot, but one of his father's counselors in the bishopric, a thin bespectacled man who smiled too much, caught up with him a few yards shy of his car. "Seth, sorry, but your father wanted to see you."

"Tell him I'll see him at home."

"No, he said—he wanted to see you in his office. The bishop's office."

McLeod furrowed instantly. "Why?"

The counselor shrugged his shoulders, gave a quick grimace-grin.

Inside the church, McLeod navigated the still-crowded hallways at a pace that betrayed his resentment and attempted to quell his rising fear, as if he could wind-sweep it away, outpace it. He came to the windowless, nondescript wooden door and knocked after only a brief hesitation. His father opened the door a moment later. "Come on in, Seth."

"What do you want, Dad? Why can't we do this at home? I want to get out of here."

"Please come in, Seth. It won't take long."

McLeod followed his father into the tiny office and sat down across from him in front of a small brown desk that filled out most of the room: a few folding chairs lined the walls, a safe in the corner, a filing cabinet, a picture of the risen Christ on the wall.

"I'd like to begin with a prayer, Seth, if that's all right. May I offer it?"

"Why yes, Bishop McLeod, please do, please do," he said in his coldest voice, but even that betrayed a tremor.

His father sighed as he bowed his head. He asked the Lord to open their hearts as they discussed spiritual goals. He gave thanks for repentance, and for the atonement of Christ that made repentance possible.

"Repentance, eh?" McLeod said after the prayer. "Spiritual goals? What's this all about, Bishop McLeod?"

His father sighed again. "I know this is awkward for you, Seth, but it's not complicated. I wanted to meet with you in my office here at church because I'm acting now in my capacity as your bishop. Jen Tanner came to see me this morning."

McLeod went meek for a moment, thrown back. "She did?" Then his breath returned to him, and his anger. "Of course she did. What did she say about me? What grand conclusions did the two of you draw about the state of my soul?"

"We didn't talk about you, Seth. We talked about her. She felt she needed to tell me some things that had happened, for the sake of *her* repentance, not yours. But do *you* want to tell me anything? I'm not here to judge; I'm here to help."

McLeod sat in rigid, determined silence. He fixed his father with as blank a stare as he could manage.

"Well, I'm not here to pry a confession out of you, but I do think—and I suppose I'm talking as your father now—I think you owe Jen an apology. That's your first assignment. You owe her a real apology. Not because you're a member of the church but because you're a decent person, do you understand? I know you have doubts, Seth, and I know . . ." His father's eye caught on the slim black volume that McLeod had brought to church in place of his scriptures; he picked it up from the corner of the desk, inspecting it. "*A Dictionary of Mormon Arcana*, huh? You really think you're going to find the answers in here? And the fact that you'd bring this garbage to church, Seth . . . I don't understand it."

"That 'garbage' is written by a Mormon historian," McLeod said, grabbing back the book.

"Mormon in name only, I'm sure," his father said. "Seth, there's nothing special in doubting. Some of my colleagues at the office are devout atheists, and when we do talk about religion—it's rare, but when we do—they go on and on about the 'courage to question.' But do you know what I think? I think the real courage is in trying to believe. Doubt comes easy for a lot of people. It comes easy for people like you and me, Seth. But do you know what doesn't come easy? Faith. Faithfulness. Obedience. Humility. Self-denial. Self-sacrifice. There's your courage. It's not easy to conform your life to a worldview that makes demands, that is *not* morally relative. You can't cheat on your wife with impunity here, you can't pursue your every whim. You need to love your neighbor as yourself, and even your enemies. *There's* your courage.

"Now, I've got another assignment for you, Seth. I've got an experiment for you to carry out. I want you to conduct an 'experiment on the word,' as Alma calls it. Read the scriptures—forget your so-called arcana, forget that garbage. Read the scriptures. I know you've read them before, but I want you to really *read* them this time, that is to say *act* on them, live them. You won't find what you're looking for in your head, or even in your heart—not at first—but in your arms and legs and mouth. 'Faith is a principle of action.' That's the prophet Joseph Smith. Or the Lord Himself: 'If any man will *do* God's will, he shall know of the doctrine, whether it be of God, or whether I speak of myself.' What are you writing? Are you writing these down?"

"I'm not opposed to this stuff," McLeod said. "I'm not afraid of it. But I'm not afraid of the arcana either. I'm not afraid of any knowledge."

"Good," his father said. "That last one was John, seven seventeen, one of my favorites. Saint John's litmus test, I call it. Action precedes testimony—action *produces* it. You're eighteen years old, Seth. You'll be nineteen in a little over six months. And I feel obligated to tell you, as both your father *and* your bishop, that the Lord expects all worthy young men to serve a mission. You've done nothing to permanently disqualify you from that worthiness. And your doubts certainly don't disqualify you. But what you need to do is apologize to Jen, as many times as it takes, and to experiment on the word. Those are your assignments. Your testimony will come—I promise you it'll come—but when it does, it won't come as a lightning bolt. It doesn't work like that—at least not for me, and I doubt it will for you either. It'll be a feeling of abandon. It'll be a feeling of *dis*comfort. You'll feel like you're falling, because you are. That's the *leap*, Seth."

———

The day had moved at a glacial pace, but still: by the time he and Passos arrived at Josefina's for the lesson that night, the baptismal lesson, Elder McLeod felt he needed more time.

"You've got this," Passos said to him, a low reassurance as they waited for Josefina to answer the door.

Let me leap, McLeod thought. Let me leap. But then Leandro, and not Josefina, came to the door. He wore a red tank top that made his arms look longer, more segmented than usual, like a marionette's, and he smelled of cigarettes, a diffuse but unmistakable odor. He'd grown a dark goatee since the elders had last seen him.

Leandro gave a curt brief smile, said, "Come in, Elders," and led them toward the house. In the front room they took their regular places and started asking Leandro about his work, about the championships, how Brazil was doing in the tournament, and so on, with Elder McLeod wondering all the while where Josefina was.

"So we're into the quarters?" Passos was saying.

Then she emerged from the kitchen and McLeod felt a smile stretch and stretch across his face. He almost sighed with relief. Josefina carried a glass of pulpy red juice in either hand, balanced a plate of *biscoitos* in the crook of her left arm, and with her teeth she clenched the top of a bag of corn chips. She gestured at the plate with her head for him and Passos to take a cookie, which they did. Then McLeod lifted the plate from her arm as she stooped to put down the glasses on the table and release the bag, catlike, from her mouth. In the process her blouse dipped open, revealing brown, secret skin. McLeod tried, failed to angle his eyes away.

Josefina straightened up again, laughing. "Phew."

"Quite a feast," Passos said. "What's the occasion?"

"What do you mean what's the occasion?" Josefina backed into her seat next to Leandro, gesturing at the food with her hands. "Go ahead—eat!"

They all traded words between crunching bites of chips, cookies, sips of cherry juice mixed with something sour, then more chips, more cookies. She told them about a chapter in the Book of Mormon she'd particularly liked, smiling as she talked, gesticulating, filling her entryway/living room with a sort of osmosed vibrancy. And this really was her room. *Her* house. Ownership belonged to the more enthusiastic, the more zealous, and McLeod now knew that Josefina's zeal was genuine. She ate very little herself, mostly talking, watching the elders eat, smiling. At one point her husband half stood and leaned forward for another cookie. "Uh-uh," she said. Leandro glared at her. Passos picked up the cookie plate and held it for Leandro—"There's too much for us. Here"—and Leandro took a handful. He sat back down, leaning away from his wife, furrowing as he took quick squirrel-like bites down the length of the white rectangular wafers.

Soon enough the eating slowed, then stopped, and the missionaries set to the business at hand. At the very first words of the lesson ("Our Father's plan for us," Passos said, "is an eternal plan"), Elder McLeod felt his stomach muscles tighten. He felt the definite discomfort his father had promised, and managed to find a certain reassurance in this. Less so in the feeling of nervousness like nausea, the feeling that only got stronger as the lesson progressed, drawing all clarity of thought and speech into a merciless orbit around it. The stress of caring. Elder McLeod had not anticipated it. He recited his sections of the lesson in a kind of automated haze, moving quickly through the concepts, asking closed-ended questions of Josefina and Leandro, especially Leandro. McLeod couldn't stop looking at him, and in the wrong way, watching his eyes, dark and expressionless as a doll's. In the second-to-last section Elder Passos drew up to the lesson's emotional crescendo—"It is the power to seal families for time and all eternity, steel them against the terrors of the grave, worlds without end"—but even then Leandro's eyes remained lusterless, unmoved.

"I testify of this power," Passos concluded. "I know it is real indeed, very real. It is the doctrinal capstone of the restored gospel of Jesus Christ, the key to our salvation in the presence of God, with our families. Our *eternal* families."

A trace of Passos's charism heat was in the air after he finished, sliding about the room. But McLeod didn't feel it, didn't pay attention. He couldn't. He felt Passos's hand on his knee, and that barely. Then he saw the grave look on his companion's face—his eyebrows halfway to the V and his slow, deep nod.

McLeod turned to his audience. He cleared his throat and began, "Josefina and Leandro, we believe—rather, we know—that this message is true and saving. We know that all the messages we've shared with you are true. The restored gospel of Jesus Christ will bring us peace and security in this life and in the next, if we but follow it. But we must follow it. It is not an idle gospel. It is a gospel of action. We want to invite you, Josefina and Leandro, to take the important *action* of being baptized in the Church of Jesus Christ of Latter-day Saints." Elder McLeod half opened his mouth to add something more, then he stopped.

Josefina raised her eyebrows. "Were you finished?"

"Yes," he said.

Josefina nodded, made a low sublingual sound; it might have

been "Hmmm, hmmm." She closed her eyes, nodding again, as if she'd expected everything McLeod had just said. She kept her lids shut in meditation. A long, silent minute passed. Then Josefina opened her eyes and turned to her husband, sunk down in the threadbare sofa like an emaciate. He looked limp, boneless. He didn't return his wife's gaze.

Josefina said, "Elders, I think we need more time. I want to be baptized in this church—it's real for me now—but I want to take that step alongside my husband."

McLeod reacted to the note of apology in Josefina's voice. "Oh of course, of course. That's only natural. We—"

"It's more than natural," Passos cut in. "It's ordained of God. We *encourage* couples to wait until both parties are ready. The church believes in family unity, as I said. It is *built* on that. The very kingdom of heaven, as I just said, is *built* on that." All hints of warmth had left Passos's voice, and even McLeod could hear that. Now it was Passos who vibrated with a nervous, nerve-racking energy, as if each of his words had a fuse attached to it. "You say you need more time? Leandro? Is that right? If you do, that's fine. You need more time, Leandro? Is that right?"

Leandro lifted his gaze without lifting his head. He took in Passos for a brief second, then McLeod for a longer one, his eyes false-sad like a basset hound's. He nodded.

The next day was Wednesday. Another P-Day. McLeod and Passos cleaned the apartment, did laundry, shopped for what groceries they could afford, and did all of it largely in silence. In the late morning the mail came. A letter from McLeod's mother. They'd finished redoing the basement, she said. Were certainly open to the idea of renting it out—either that or turning it into a guest room. Dad was well. Karen too. Already dating seriously at BYU. Something in the water there. Was he eating well? And so on.

McLeod went into the entryway/living room; its corners were in shadow, darkness at midday. The clouds through the window looked low and leaden, almost purplish at patches. Passos sat at his desk. He leaned over a sheet of paper, frowning with concentration. He hadn't received any letters that day.

"Who are you writing?" McLeod asked him.

"Brother," Passos said.

"Oh. Cool."

McLeod sat down at his desk and composed a brief letter to his family. Things were good. They were still teaching Josefina and Leandro. Leandro was coming along a little slower than Josefina, but then again Josefina was really coming along. And so on. McLeod thought about bearing some kind of testimony to close the letter, mostly for his father's sake, but he couldn't muster the energy. He still felt drained from last night. He put the finished letter in an envelope, addressed it, took out a stamp from his desk drawer. Out of the corner of his eye he saw Passos still writing, his concentration unbroken. McLeod tidied the mugful of pens on his desk—highlighters, scripture markers, all recent additions. He pushed flush the spines of the Missionary Classics Paperback Library that he had pulled from the recesses of his suitcase. McLeod took out *Jesus the Christ,* which he'd started rereading. He made it through several pages about Christ's pre-mortal calling.

"Who are you writing now?" he asked Passos.

"Other brother."

"Oh."

He wandered into the bedroom, organized his closet. He had promised Sweeney he'd make it to his apartment today for a little powwow, as in their MTC days. Kimball would be there too, at noon, and Sweeney's and Kimball's companions, friends by now, would probably head out to do whatever it was they did. They could take Passos along too; he might enjoy himself.

A few minutes later Elder McLeod leaned his head out of the bedroom and asked his companion, still bowed over his writing, if he thought he'd be much longer. Passos said, "Might be." McLeod explained the situation. Did he think maybe he could finish the letters tonight?

Passos put down his pen—an audible clack on the wooden desk—and craned his neck to see the sky through the window. "It's going to open up out there," he said, and returned to his writing.

"It might not. We'll take umbrellas." McLeod repeated the word in English: "Umbrellas."

Passos stopped writing. His shoulders softened a bit. "We'll take the umbrellas," he said quietly, practicing.

The elders arrived at Sweeney's apartment, unrained-on, at a quarter to one, just as Sweeney's and Kimball's greenies, Nunes and Batista, made ready to leave. In shorts and T-shirts, they stuffed their shoulder bags with water, a stack of small orange cones, a soccer ball, and their ponchos, though Nunes said he doubted the sky would make good on its threat. He asked Passos if he wanted to come along. Passos begged off on account of letters he needed to write. Elder Nunes set Passos up at his desk and mumbled something in Portuguese, a quick burst of slang that McLeod didn't catch.

Passos chuckled. "I'll be fine."

Nunes nodded at McLeod and at the bedroom door in turn. "They're in there."

"Thanks," McLeod said.

He left his companion in the living room and let himself into the bedroom. Elders Kimball and Sweeney sat on opposite beds in jeans and T-shirts, Sweeney leaning forward in the position of holding forth, Kimball slumped back against the wall, hands joined behind his neck, elbows crooked out, smiling.

"Ask McLeod," Kimball said in English, pointing his chin at him. "He'll tell you the very same."

Sweeney turned to him with urgency in his face and said, "McLeod, back me up here—" He stopped short, cocking his head.

Elder McLeod pinched his dress shirt and let it go; he palmed his tie. "You're wondering about the proselytizing clothes? Is that it? I'm a rule abider now. Like you guys wanted."

"It's P-Day," Sweeney said.

"I had to travel to get here."

Sweeney's face was still a question mark.

"I can show it to you in the Missionary Handbook," McLeod said, reaching for the thin white booklet he'd taken to carrying in his breast pocket again.

"Whatever, whatever," Sweeney said. "Sit."

Kimball smacked the bed beside him and McLeod plopped down, noticing Kimball's T-shirt. It looked silk-screened, with a quote on the front of it attributed to Nietzsche ("God is dead") and below it another quote attributed to God ("Nietzsche is dead") and below that, inexplicably, a guitar in silhouette. Elder McLeod never quite got used to seeing his friends, or any fellow missionaries, in street clothes. Neither did he get used to the ungelled undifferentiated mass of brown hair, like one of those Russian fur hats, that Kimball wore on P-Days.

"The question is simple," Sweeney said. He held his hands out in the air as if to bracket McLeod's attention. "Does the church keep tabs on your sex life after you're married? To wit: Can you go down on your wife?"

"The church stays out of the bedroom," McLeod said.

"That's exactly what I said! Is that not exactly what I said, Kimball, you prude?"

"I'm not the prude. They're not my rules. I'm just saying. My brother's bishop told him when he got married—and this was BYU, mind you, this was officialdom—he told him oral sex was a no-no. Both the his and her variety. Off-limits."

"Your brother's bishop didn't know shit," Sweeney said.

"Whoa, hey now!" Kimball said, laughing. "Keep it Bible, dude. You know the rules."

"And keep it down too," McLeod said. "If you're going to be insane, Sweeney . . ." He spread his hands, palms down. "Right? My companion's out there."

"He didn't go out with his countrymen?" Kimball said.

"Your brother's bishop didn't know shit!" Sweeney said, rising to his feet.

"Bible, Bible!"

"Well I'm sorry, but I get worked up over this! If you think for one second—"

"Guys, seriously," McLeod said. "My companion."

And as if on cue, Passos opened the door. He leaned his head into the room, saying in Portuguese, "Could you guys please keep it down a little?"

"I was almost finished," Sweeney said, still in English.

"He can hear you," McLeod said. "I mean he understands English."

"I don't care who hears me! I'll tell it on the mountain! If you think for one second that Tiff and I aren't going to get a little *alternative*? You know, a little of this—" Sweeney put his hand on an invisible head in front of his crotch. "A little of this—" He adjusted his hands to an invisible pair of hips and pumped. "If you think we're not going to do that and more, you're crazy!" He turned to Passos. "You hear that, Your Highness? I've been a good little boy for twenty-one very long years and now the Man's going to tell me what I can and can't do in my conjugal bed? It's bullshit! You hear *that*, Your Highness? To hell with the Man! I'm five months to homecoming, which means I'm six months to the wedding, which means I'm six months and a few hours from me and my wife, my *female* companion, doing *this, this, this, this!* You think about that when you're still on the mission, Passos, when you're kneeling down for companionship prayer, all right? You think about that."

Elder Sweeney dropped back down onto his bed, mock panting. After a silence he said, "I yield the floor."

Kimball still chuckled. "Keep it Bible, man. That's all I'm saying."

McLeod shook his head, hand to face, a gesture he calculated for Sweeney and Kimball, but also for Passos, who stood several feet inside the door now. McLeod felt painfully conscious of his senior companion; he peeked at him through his fingers: the long thin face an utter blank, a floating mirror on top of the tall dresser of his body. Passos held his non-look for an agonizing minute more, then he smiled. There, then gone. A darting minnow. Elder McLeod wasn't sure he'd even seen it right until Passos showed another smile, a longer one—an effort at one, anyway—a tight if ingratiating upturn at the corners of his mouth and eyes. He crossed the room and gestured to the spot beside Sweeney. Sweeney squinted a bit, nodded.

Passos sat, laid a friendly hand on Sweeney's knee. Sweeney frowned at the hand; Passos retracted it.

"You know," Passos said in English, "I don't think I will think about that. But can I ask?"

A curious smile spread across Elder Sweeney's face. "Shoot."

"'Shoot'?"

"Ask your question," Sweeney said.

"What does it mean to say 'keep it Bible'?"

"Oh," Sweeney said, and he laughed a little. "That. I guess it means we don't use any bad words unless they're in the Bible. Or something like that." He laughed again. "It sounds pretty stupid when you explain it."

Elder McLeod watched his companion out of the corner of his eye, feeling something at the edge of amazement. The conversation moved on to other topics, safer topics. Though maybe even that was unfair—*safer topics*. Maybe he'd been inventing Passos all along, or allowing others to invent him for him. *For now we see through a glass, darkly* . . . The line flashed in McLeod's mind, shot through it like a tracer, and on its heels came the thought of his father. Paul's words were some of McLeod's favorite in all of scripture, but they were still only words to him. He needed to convert them into actions.

They traveled home that evening under big heavy clouds edged in gold, burnished by the sun sunk beneath them. It hadn't rained a drop the entire day, and it didn't start until McLeod and Passos had descended from the bus and turned onto their street, the late sunlight breaking along the bottle shards on property walls in multicolored beams. *The low sun makes the color* . . . Then the first small drops hit the pavement, growing larger by the second, pinging the broken bottles, the antennae on top of houses, making a bright ephemeral aural ring that then receded under the thousand drumming fingers of the rain. Passos yelped, and McLeod too, like coon hunters, and instead of opening their umbrellas they took off running, downing the street at a sprint, laughing the whole way.

They burst through the outer door and yanked from the clothesline the first of their soaked shirts pants socks garments until Passos shouted, "Leave them—who cares?" and they ran inside.

Later that night. Each elder at his desk. The rain still coming unabated, loud as an automatic car wash on the roof. Louder
through the windows, still open. The rain pounding in a coat of
water in the courtyard. The elders had to raise their voices almost
to a shout to be heard.

"You were right about it opening up," McLeod said.

"Well, we were both right," Passos said. "It held out. Sort of."

"Yeah, seriously."

"What?"

"Seriously!"

"One more time?"

Elder McLeod stood up and closed the metal blinds. The sound
of the rain dropped, though not by much. He looked down at the
materials spread out on Passos's desk. "Who are you writing now?"

"My grandmother."

"You are diligent."

"That's my name. His Royal Highness, Diligent Passos."

"Don't listen to Sweeney. He doesn't know you. Besides, he
already likes you by the transitive property of friendship. A is
friends with B, B is friends with C, therefore A is also friends
with C."

Passos smiled, put pen to paper again, then stopped. "You're
different from Sweeney, though, aren't you?"

"What do you mean?"

"He makes dirty jokes, you blush. He doesn't blush."

"I blushed?"

"You looked like a tomato. Like right now, actually. You can't hide it, whitey. None of you can."

"Careful now. Only Maurilho calls me whitey, and he says it with love."

"So do I. Of course."

"Well good," McLeod said, "because if you don't like whiteys you shouldn't be planning on BYU."

"Excuse me?"

"The place is crawling with them. You should see the pictures my sister sends. I bet they'd make an exception for you, though."

"Who said I'm planning on BYU?"

"Your BYU catalog. Your TOEFL book there."

"I'm practicing my English. Like the president said."

"And all your questions about the States. All the stories about your missionary friend who goes to BYU."

"I'm not planning to go to the States, Elder McLeod."

"No?"

"Who said I was?"

"Well, okay. Never mind then."

"What?"

"Well, I mean, you're not interested, obviously, but I was going to say that my mom's just refinished our basement and is thinking about renting it out in the future. Say in seven months or so? I thought I might ask if she'd have room for a diligent Brazilian getting ready for the TOEFL. But never mind. You don't want to visit the States after all."

"That's not what I said."

"No?"

"All I said was I wasn't planning on it. I wasn't."

"Ah."

"What?"

"Nothing."

"What? What are you smiling at?"

"Nothing."

Then January disappeared into February, and the people of Carinha disappeared into their houses completely—this even as temporary aluminum grandstands went up in the center of town, even as yellow-and-green banners and flags started filling the spaces above intersections like a second atmosphere. Elder Passos liked to picture the streets refilling after the final next week in an explosive epic hurry, Brazil having won—again!—the Latin crown. The roil of jerseys, the booming fireworks, the car horns combining like the sound of a million bagpipes . . . The mere thought of it could quicken Passos's blood, make a sea-rushing sound in his ears. But after a few minutes the sound usually faded and the stark eerie quiet of late-stage-championships Brazil reasserted itself. The wind moving in the trees and the tick of each leaf. The *clop, clop, clop* of their own footsteps floating up behind them like the ghosts of footsteps.

On Monday morning the elders walked all the way from their apartment to the main square downtown and inspected the grandstands. The banked silver rows gleaming powerfully in the sun put Passos in mind of abandoned ancient monoliths. No bodies around, just the seats to sit them in. It was as if all the townspeople had been abducted in the middle of Carnival.

"Maybe everybody's too busy preparing for my birthday," McLeod said.

"I'm sure that's it," Passos said. "Celebrate the Ugly American during the last week of Latin Championships."

McLeod's eyes flared. "So now I'm ugly?"

"It's the title of a book," Passos said. "I was just kidding."

"So was I," McLeod said, smiling. "I've read it too. It wasn't bad."

Mondays, lately, had been the hardest days for Passos. He dreaded going back to the barren streets and lifeless doors after the relative reprieve of Sunday, which in a sense had become more rejuvenating than P-Day, especially when McLeod got it into his head to cross the city for a "powwow," as he called it, with his friends. Last Wednesday Passos had managed to persuade McLeod to cancel his planned visit to Sweeney's. It would have taken up most of their day off, and besides, neither he nor McLeod could afford the uncleanness that Sweeney and Kimball represented. They needed to be pure vessels, meet for the Work, meet for their principal task of guiding Leandro to baptism.

Really, it was their only task. Traditional contacting had become a fool's errand: nobody, nobody answered their doors during the day, and only Josefina and Leandro did at night. For most of the sunlit hours, then, the elders wandered the streets like vagabonds, calling out novel church signs to pass the time. On the way out of the main square, Elder Passos called a little storefront Baptist church set back in an orange-brick alleyway: " 'The Great God Church.' I'm up six to five."

"I called that church the other day," McLeod said.

"Good for you, whitey. I called it today."

"You can't do that. That's against the rules."

"I'm your senior companion, Elder. I *am* the rules."

"Kidding again, I hope. Elder."

Passos heard something small but hard-edged in his junior companion's voice. For a second it unnerved him.

"Fine." Passos jutted his chin at another church sign up ahead. " 'God's Rainbow.' That one's new. I'm up six to five again."

At last it was lunchtime, and time for the church-names game, as the elders called it, to suspend for an hour, maybe more. Passos *hoped* for more, anyway. The elders boarded a bus en route to Maurilho's, where their weekly lunch appointment never fell through. At times the family needed to keep to the allotted hour—Maurilho off to a job interview, or Rômulo back to class—but today Elder Passos felt luck at his back. They'd chanced into an outbound bus during a time of championships-induced bus drought. If that could happen, why not a two-hour lunch?

Passos watched the sights of the city, familiar to him now, pass by like the frames of a silent film. The glass storefronts of downtown with the sun tracking in them, a slow, mute meteor. The public green, the Assembly of God megachurch, its gray steeples like turrets. Then under the overpass and left toward home, past the supermarket, the bank, past blocks of apartment buildings, past the drive-through—that stain on the neighborhood, on the whole city. In spite of himself Passos thought of what went on behind those walls. He thought of the magazine still hidden in his desk drawer. The sting of guilt, and now of hypocrisy. How could he make demands on McLeod about purity when he himself was impure? And his house on the rock, his thoughts of America—now more like prospects than thoughts, more like plans—how could he threaten all that? McLeod had heard back from his mother already. Apparently he'd suggested the idea of Passos coming to stay with them weeks ago, before his family's basement had even been finished. They'd be glad to make room for a friend of his, McLeod's mother had said. They'd actually been hoping for an LDS tenant, and they knew how important an immersion experience was for language learning. She said they'd even be willing to help with expenses on the understanding that Elder Passos would earn it back through work around the house or yard—maybe help with the new patio she'd been talking about for a year and a half? She never did lack for projects.

That was a week ago. Passos felt grateful for the offer, excited, but at times he felt another set of emotions underneath, more grayscale, more ambivalent. Something about the sudden solicitousness of it all. The heroic Americans rescuing the poor *favela* dweller. He didn't want to be an object of charity. And why did they assume he could only do yard work? He wondered how Dos Santos would balance these feelings—he wondered how he *did* balance them, or if he even needed to—and usually it was that thought, sanguine Dos Santos, savvy Dos Santos, that brought Passos back around to consider the great blessing, the great opportunity in front of him. For one foundation builds the other, he reminded himself. A spiritual house on the rock, and now a temporal one.

The bus let them out about a block short of the drive-through, a block and a half from Maurilho's. Elder Passos led his companion past the brothel's outer walls at a near run, Maurilho's blue-painted house jogging up above the property wall as the elders rounded the final corner. Inside the house he and McLeod heaved sighs to be finally off their feet. Maurilho updated them on the championships. It looked like Argentina would beat Chile easily that afternoon. That's what all the pregame was saying. If the bars stayed quiet that night, they could know that Argentina was into the finals. But it didn't matter: Brazil was good enough to beat them, them and all their money, their European airs. Brazil itself faced off against Venezuela tomorrow. Same thing: listen for the bars.

"Are you going to watch the game this afternoon? Or do you have another job interview?" Passos asked.

"Nope. Nothing's doing out there. Nothing at all."

"Dad's even letting me skip the rest of school," Rômulo said, shuffling into the living room in his Ronaldo jersey and a lopsided smile. He shook hands with the elders, sat down beside his father on the couch.

"It's not like they're getting in any teaching these days," Maurilho said.

"You don't have to tell *us* about not teaching," Passos said, but he smiled, and got more comfortable on the couch.

Maurilho cleared his throat, and his face changed. "Meanwhile and in other news—" He turned to McLeod. "It sounds like Bush really is thinking about a Mideast invasion. Just like his daddy. You'd better tell your president to take his finger off the trigger."

McLeod rolled his eyes—in jest, Passos thought, though he wasn't sure.

Rômulo said, "Okay, Pop, come on."

"What? America hasn't spilled enough blood already? Bush better be blowing smoke, whitey. You tell him."

"I'll be sure to do that," McLeod said. "I'll be sure to tell him that the next time we talk."

"Pop," Rômulo said, "remember the pamphlet? You want me to get it? I'll get it."

"Huh?" Maurilho said. "Oh yeah, yeah. Go get it."

Rômulo went into the back room and his father turned his attention back to McLeod. He raised a finger that looked ready to hold forth, or scold.

Passos said, "What's this pamphlet about?"

"Oh, it's just something my evangelical neighbor gave me. He thinks Mormons are going to hell."

Rômulo emerged from the back room with a small pamphlet, the paper unglossed, the graphics gray and pixilated as if they'd been printed from a home computer and photocopied. Rômulo unfolded the pamphlet and swept his free hand across it like a model on a TV shopping show. Then he handed it to his father. "Do one of your readings, Pop."

The big man cleared his throat and read the title, "What Mormons Really Believe," placing ominous stress on the *Really*, warming to his role. " 'Did you know Mormons,' " he quoted in a high mocking voice, " 'believe Jesus was sexually active?' "

"Oh brother," McLeod said. "One of these, huh?"

" 'Did you know Mormons believe that Jesus and Lucifer were brothers?' " Maurilho lowered the pamphlet and raised his eyebrows. "Whitey? You didn't know that, did you? That Jesus and the Devil shared a bunk bed in the preexistence? Hmm? Did you?"

"It's truly shocking."

"Passos? Hmmm?"

He played along, offered, "I hadn't heard about the bunk bed," and smiled a distracted, inward smile. Where had the first distortion come from? Jesus as sexually active? He hadn't heard that one before.

Elder Passos hated these conversations, common though they were around the mission. He found them not at all funny, not at all constructive. Rarely did the anti-Mormons much deviate from their limited scripts—Jesus and Lucifer as brothers, polygamy, cultish temple rites, Joseph Smith worship, man-Gods—but the propaganda still set him on edge, and not because he couldn't dismiss it out of hand. It made him edgy by virtue of the fact that it reminded him, almost inevitably, of edgier times: the first months after his and his brothers' baptisms and the barrage of "concern" from his grandmother and her devout friends: the pamphlets Nana brought home with her from Mass ("If I'd known what those young men were teaching you I'd have never allowed it"), and the scraps of paper inserted as bookmarks into his Bible, bearing Nana's unmistakable scrawl: *Read the Lord's words about false prophets in the last days,* or *Read what Paul says about an angel descending and preaching a different gospel. "Let them be anathema!" Read the Word, the true Word, and pray about it, my little son. That's all I ask of you. I love you.* He remembered one Sunday afternoon in particular. He and his brothers had just returned from church when Nana and one of her friends from the parish marched into the house, their Bibles under their arms, and sat down across from them as the missionaries had done just a few months earlier.

"Sister Renilde understands the Word even better than I do," Nana said by way of explanation.

The old woman gave a thin smile. "We've missed you at the parish, boys." Her voice was dry, perfunctory. Passos recognized this woman from the many years he and his mother and brothers attended church with her, though they had never much spoken. She kept to herself, sitting in a pew apart and rocking her upper body over the open pages of her Bible, moaning. Even in a church as Spirit-haunted as the one Passos grew up in, she was an unusually spectral figure.

"So serious, that woman," his mother once remarked to him, "so very, very serious. Only your grandmother has the courage to even talk to her. Bless Nana's Christian heart."

And now his grandmother sat beside the woman in their living room, turning pages in her Bible, following Sister Renilde's lead. Nana glanced up at one point, said, "Boys, do you have your Bibles nearby? Would you go get them please?"

Tiago, on Passos's left, and even Felipe on his right, looked to him, their faces uncertain. Passos stretched out a hand to either side.

"No. We'd rather not do that," Passos said. He had just turned seventeen.

"Your grandmother is only trying to help you," the woman said, not looking up from her Bible. She found the page she sought, then she slew her eyes over to Passos alone. "Have you read any of the passages your grandmother marked? Did you ask the good Lord to guide you?"

"We're not children anymore," Passos said. "We can make our own—"

"Luke, chapter twenty-one, verse eight." The woman read: " 'And Jesus said, Beware that you are not deceived, for many will come in my name, saying, I am Christ; and the time is near; therefore do not go after them.' "

She turned her face up and encased them, each of them, in a long stare. "The word of the Lord. Thanks be to the Lord. May He lead us and guide us in the true path."

"I am grateful to the Lord," Passos said, "and I do believe—*we* do believe—that He is guiding us along the true path."

"But who are these young men who come to visit you? What can they know about the Lord's Word? They are no older than you."

"They know more than you do," Felipe said suddenly. "What do *you* know?"

Passos put a hand to his brother's knee. He felt a rigidness in Felipe's body, an anger that surprised him, though he felt it in himself too.

Sister Renilde flipped to another passage. "Galatians, chapter one, verse eight. 'But even if we or an angel from heaven should preach a gospel other than the one we preached to you, let them be anathema!'" She slid her eyes up again. "The Word is speaking to you directly. An angel from heaven, like your Angel of Mormon who brought the Book of Mormon, which is not the Lord's gospel but the Devil's. The very Word of the Lord is telling you that. Thanks be to the Lord."

Passos stared at the woman with something close to hatred. "Are you finished? Because I have a question for *you* now."

She kept her head down, flipping to another passage.

"Where's my mother?" Passos said.

Sister Renilde stopped. Nana looked up, an expression of pained surprise. Passos kept his eyes fixed on the old woman, her gray, still head. She didn't look up. "Where is our mother right now?" he said. "Can you tell me that? *Who* is she now? When will we see her again? What does your Word have to say about that?"

"Oh my little son," Nana said, but Sister Renilde held up a hand. Then, slowly, she lowered it to the pages of her Bible and began flipping, flipping. She stopped. "Matthew, chapter twenty-two, verses twenty-nine through thirty. 'And Jesus said, You are in error because you do not know the Scriptures or the power of God. At the resurrection people will neither marry nor be given in marriage; they will be like the angels in heaven.' "

The woman lifted her head altogether now. She tempered the look of cold righteousness in her eyes, or she tried to, and this only angered Passos more. He felt the sickness building in him again, the first signs of an emotion so much bigger than him, so much bigger than all of them, a shadow overspreading the world, that Passos knew it must come from God. But still he resisted it.

"In heaven we will have God and His angels for family," Sister Renilde said. "This is the Word of the—"

"No!" Passos shouted. "It's not good enough! It's not—" He broke off, gritting his teeth to keep from crying. He felt the muscles tightening, burning in his jaw, and the rigidness in the body of his brother at his right, and now, on his left, the first shivering convulsions in little Tiago.

"Not 'good enough'?" Sister Renilde repeated. "It is not for *us* to judge the Word. The Word judges us. God's ways are higher than our ways."

"No," Passos said, his voice quiet, fallen back. "You're wrong. I know what I know. All three of us. We know what we know."

———————

The sound of tearing brought Elder Passos out from under his memories.

"It goes on like that for three pages," Maurilho said. He tore the pamphlet crosswise now, slowly, ceremoniously, as if he'd been waiting to do it. "Half-truths and exaggerations. Everything out of context."

"Was that the nonsense from the neighbor?" Rose said, appearing in the living-room doorway for the first time. They all exchanged nods and smiles.

"Maurilho was reading us selections," McLeod said. "Most entertainment we've had all week."

They filed into the kitchen/dining room where the rectangular wooden table was set more elaborately than usual: matching white porcelain dishes and plates, steaming bowls of rice and beans, a side of *farofa*, dishes of carrots, chicken, potato salad. A glass pitcher of *maracujá* sat beading in the center of the table, and at his companion's place a can of Guaraná sweated too. Passos spied a very American-looking chocolate cake on the kitchen counter behind McLeod.

Maurilho settled into his seat at the head of the table, beaming. "Ah, Elders. I *love* Mondays. Best food of the week, hands down."

"Only when it's warm," Rose said.

Maurilho took the hint. "Elder Passos, would you offer the blessing?"

Elder Passos gave thanks for the food and the hands that had prepared it, for all their many blessings, and as he opened his eyes after the prayer a familiar warmth washed over him—that sense of peace, an almost sedated feeling, like relaxing under your covers at night. No matter how rote the prayer, he thought, *prayer worked. The gospel worked. I know what I know.* If only for a moment, then, Elder Passos felt at utter peace with his life and what he was doing with it for these two years. He was thousands of kilometers from his family, true, but he had reason to hope—he had reason to *expect*—that their hardest days lay behind them. He felt at peace with the righteous ambition inside him. He felt at peace with his sins even, for he knew he would abandon them. He and McLeod would both be meet for the message, would work harder than ever to make Leandro soften, and if the Lord willed it, Passos knew Leandro *would* soften.

Just then McLeod's hand reached into Passos's line of sight and ladled spoonfuls of rice onto his plate, then beans—not on top of the rice, but beside it, just as he liked. Passos looked into his junior companion's face, stout and pink, like an under-ripe strawberry, and he smiled. He felt at peace with his companion too. McLeod might be irreverent at times, and too timid in teaching, but he was good and kind and generous.

"Thank you, Elder," Passos said, "but shouldn't I be serving you? You're the birthday boy."

"Your birthday's today?" Rose said. "I thought it was Thursday."

"It's actually tomorrow," McLeod said, "but Thursday's the party. Are you guys still coming?"

Maurilho looked up from his food. "You mean the party at Josefina's and—oh, I should know this by now—"

"Leandro," Passos said. "McLeod just mentioned his birthday in passing and they insisted on hosting a party. Those people are just amazing. Golden."

"Is Leandro still . . . ?" Maurilho said, and mimed smoking a cigarette, sucking and blowing.

McLeod nodded his head in response, letting it sink with each nod. "It's getting worse, actually. We come in the house now and you can smell it on him. I'm sure Josefina's working with him— she really *is* golden—I'm just not sure Leandro's as interested."

"Well," Maurilho said, hovering a forkful of rice halfway to his mouth. He shook his head and mumbled, "Yeah, that's tough," and took a bite. McLeod nodded again and took a bite of his own food. The whole table nodded, a brief wave of sympathy, then continued on with their meal, as if his companion's pessimism were sure prophecy, as if everyone had already given up Leandro for lost. Passos looked around for a face to share in his sense of wrong, and finding none, he turned to his companion. Look at him: chewing, staring off like a cow, as if nothing had happened, as if he were just a bystander.

"Elder McLeod," Passos said, and stopped. The virulence in his voice surprised even him. The table froze. His companion turned, wide-eyed.

"We don't know that Leandro smokes," Passos said.

McLeod paused. "Well, I think . . . I think it's a pretty safe assumption. I'm just trying to be realistic."

"*Realistic*," Passos said—spat, really. Again he surprised himself. The silence wound around them all like something living, snakelike. The sounds of chewing magnified.

After a long time Rose said, "Do you like the food, Elders?"

The next morning during companionship study Elder Passos apologized for his outburst, as he called it. He knew the word was an overstatement, but he wanted to hedge on the side of penitence, especially in his role as the senior companion and zone leader, in his role as the exemplar.

McLeod raised a quick clement hand, which bothered Passos. He decided to go a step further. "On a different note, I've been meaning to ask you about something from Maurilho's pamphlet yesterday."

He would let McLeod play teacher to his senior companion, something juniors, and Americans in general, seemed to relish. McLeod especially seemed to pride himself on his knowledge of the gospel, if not his testimony of it. *Learning, always learning,* as Paul said, *but never coming to a knowledge of the truth.* More than once during companionship study McLeod had sought to settle a debate by recursing to his Bible Dictionary, a feature available only in the English version of the quad, or to one of the missionary classics, so-called, also available only in English. Sometimes the debates concerned doctrine—usually obscure, inessential doctrine—and sometimes church history, which Passos considered inessential by definition. For how could the temporal chronology of the church at all rival in importance the gospel contained within the church? The gospel was bigger than any nation or tongue, bigger than any localized history. Not that Elder Passos didn't take a certain interest. He'd learned all about polygamy, when and why it ended, all about the ban on blacks in the priesthood, when and why *it* ended. If only to arm himself against his grandmother and her friends, Passos had taken the church's several skeletons out of the closet, one by one, and turned them around in the light.

McLeod prompted him. "What do you want to know?"

Passos ignored the hubris in the question. "What I wanted to ask was where the anti-Mormons got the Jesus-as-sexually-active lie. That one was new. I hadn't heard that one before. What sources did they wrench? What quotes did they twist?"

"They didn't wrench or twist anything," McLeod said. "That's what the church believes. Brigham Young said it. Others have said it."

"That Jesus was sexually active?"

"That he was married, yes."

Elder Passos felt his face go hot and compressed. His companion said, "Uh-oh, the eyebrows."

"Where is that written?" Passos said. "Show it to me."

"I can if you want me to. You really want me to?"

"Show me in the scriptures where it says that Jesus was married, that he was sexually active."

McLeod leaned away, said, "Calm down, calm down," which of course had the opposite effect on Elder Passos. He said he wanted McLeod to *show* him, right now, chapter and verse.

"Well, look," McLeod said, "it's not that simple. It's not in the scriptures, or it's not obvious anyway. I could show you—I will, right now— but you have to take off your senior-companion hat, your zone-leader hat, for just a minute. I only brought one piece of contraband from home, and it's nothing bad, but I need a guarantee all the same. Do I have one?"

"Just show me what you've got," Passos said.

"I'll take that as a yes?"

"Just show me already."

"That's a yes, then," McLeod said, and he reached his hand deep into his desk drawer and pulled out a small, black paperback volume called *From Adam-ondi-Ahman to Zion's Camp: A Dictionary of Mormon Arcana.* Before Passos could even lay hands on it his companion had launched into an explanation, starting with the title: how Adam-ondi-Ahman was what Joseph Smith called the Garden of Eden, how Zion's Camp was a ragtag military expedition charged with taking back land the church had lost to—

"I already knew all that," Elder Passos said, though he hadn't known any of it. "Get to the point."

McLeod nodded for Passos to bring his chair closer to his desk as he flipped to the index, scanning aloud until he found "Jesus Christ, marriage of." He turned to the first of several page numbers, then pressed the book flat with his hand so that Passos could check his translation, he said.

"Just go," Passos said.

" 'The church does not have an official position on the question of Jesus's marriage,' " McLeod began, " 'though many early church leaders suggested from the pulpit that the marriage at Cana, as recorded in the New Testament, was Jesus's own marriage to Mary and Martha. Some leaders further believed that Jesus bore children. To quote Brigham Young: "The Scripture says that He, the Lord, came walking in the Temple, with His train. I do not know who *they* were, unless His wives and children." ' "

McLeod broke off. "That's sourced from the *Journal of Discourses,* which is a collection of—"

"I know about the *Journal of Discourses,* Elder!"

"Okay, sorry, sorry." McLeod continued. " 'Orson Hyde, one of Young's fellow apostles, went even further, speaking on the nascent church's behalf: "We say it was Jesus Christ who was married, to be brought into the relation whereby He could see His seed before He was crucified." Hyde's literal reading of Isaiah 53:10 was not uncommon among the early brethren. In July of 1899, in a solemn assembly in the Salt Lake City Temple, Apostle George Q. Cannon proclaimed: "There are those in this audience who are descendants of the Lord's Twelve Apostles—and, shall I say it?—yes, descendants of the Savior Himself. His seed is represented in the body of these men."'"

McLeod looked up from the page and said, "You want me to keep going? There's more."

"Let me see that." Elder Passos pulled the book closer and read the entry again, understanding most of the words, and all of the operative ones. He turned to the copyright page: the book was published by a press called the Zion Underground. "This isn't even published by the church. I've never heard of this publisher. And the entry says it isn't even the church's position."

"Not officially," McLeod said.

"You're not even supposed to have this, you know."

"Passos," McLeod said, his voice low with warning.

"I know, I know. I won't report this . . . this *garbage*—though I probably should." He held the book out over McLeod's desk with his thumb and forefinger, as if to show what a reeking thing it was. Then he dropped it. "I don't know why you read that crap anyway. I guess if you're not *talking* filth with Sweeney and Kimball, then you're reading it, is that right?"

"Me and Brigham Young," McLeod said. "Filth peddlers."

"I'm serious," Passos said.

"I know you are."

"Good."

For the rest of companionship study the elders ran through the lesson they had designed for Josefina and Leandro for that night.

Their discussions now centered around specific gospel topics that the missionaries felt, after prayer and pondering, might suit the couple's needs. Tonight's lesson took up obedience and sacrifice, and enduring to the end. The essentials, Passos thought. At one point during the run-through, Elder Passos looked up a supporting passage in the Book of Mormon and readied himself to read it aloud. "The *real* gospel," he muttered into the page.

By the time the elders arrived that night at Josefina's, Brazil had already beaten Venezuela and most of the attendant postgame revelry had quieted or moved indoors. Josefina came to her door in a white flowing blouse and black pants, both modest, her hair done up in a bun. Her look fell closer to the formality of her Sunday dress than the casualness of her usual attire. Why the change? McLeod wondered—worried. Has she seen me . . . seeing? Is that the reason for her modesty?

"Elders," Josefina said. "You're early."

"Do you need us to come back? We can come back," McLeod said.

"No, no. Nonsense, nonsense. No, it's fine, it's fine, it's fine." She led them quickly into the house, where Maurilho and Rômulo, to McLeod's surprise, sat on the love seat in the entryway/living room. He watched Josefina disappear into the kitchen, noticed Rose at the kitchen counter, facing away from them, her hands fast and furtive. Rose came into the front room a moment later and squeezed down beside her husband.

"Well, hello," McLeod finally said to the group, his voice questioning.

Maurilho and Rômulo and Rose looked up as Josefina reemerged from the back room carrying what looked like a camping chair. She forced a tight smile. "Please, Elders, please have a seat.

Rose and her family were kind enough to accompany our lesson tonight."

The three of them smiled for the elders as if they'd been waiting for Josefina's permission. McLeod and Passos sat down in their usual spots on the couch as Josefina settled into the camping chair. Behind Josefina the bookshelf had filled out—a new volume of the *World Book Encyclopedia*, *A–B*, caught McLeod's eye among the other books, the faded gold lettering on the spine like light off the river—and in front of Josefina the coffee table featured a new centerpiece, a bowl of polished stones. Fanned out around the bowl were the several preview pamphlets that the elders had left after their first lesson, and also Josefina's well-read copy of the Book of Mormon. Leandro's copy too, Elder McLeod thought, though the thought felt dutiful.

Passos looked to the kitchen doorway with expectation on his face.

"He isn't here," Josefina said. "Leandro's not coming tonight."

"Oh," Passos said.

McLeod spoke up after a long silence. "We heard people going crazy earlier. Sounds like Brazil won today."

"Four to one," Maurilho said softly. "Final's on Sunday. Against Argentina."

"He's out celebrating with friends," Josefina said.

"At the bar?" Passos said.

Josefina turned her face aside at the question, her cheeks gathered into a pained, apologetic wince. The look seemed well-worn to McLeod, slipping easily, too easily, into the ruts of her features. He wondered how much occasion Leandro had given Josefina for such a pained expression. And why their gospel hadn't changed that.

"Oh," Passos said.

"You know what?" McLeod said, after another silence. "You can't control him, right? You can't be responsible for him. He has his own agency, his own mind."

"Right. *Right*," Josefina said, lighting up the word. She straightened in her chair, seemed to take courage. "I was going to say that, Elder. Just that. I prayed about it, and I felt the Lord give me that answer. If Leandro doesn't want it, I can't force him, right? If he doesn't want to quit smoking, if he doesn't want to quit drinking—"

"He said he had quit drinking," Passos said.

Josefina flushed red. Her eyes watered, brimmed over. "That's what I mean. That's what I mean. If he's going to sit here and lie to you . . . Oh Elders, I hate it so much when he lies to you. You're dedicating two years of your lives to God and the least you deserve . . . the least is honesty. And Elder McLeod, it's your birthday, and Leandro promised he'd bring the cake. Tonight was going to be a surprise and—" She lost her next words in a choking, almost animal sound, something dredged from the bottom of her chest, a low, pitiful, scraped-out moan. It made McLeod's own chest hurt, made his own eyes sting. Josefina put her hand to her sternum as if to restart the airflow. The stinging in Elder McLeod's eyes turned to burning and he rushed to the kitchen. A bowl of nachos sat on the kitchen table. A few balloons bobbed slowly under the low-hung ceiling. He found a stack of napkins on the counter and ran one across his face—hard. He went back into the front room and handed a napkin to Josefina. She took it and dabbed her eyes. She tried to laugh. "You guys must think I'm crazy, huh? The thing is, though, I'm not even sad anymore. We were going to be baptized on Sunday, both of us—that was going to be another surprise. Then late last night he comes home drunk as ever and this morning he leaves for the bar without a word, and all this when I'm . . . when we're . . ." She looked down at what McLeod first thought was her lap, but then her hands formed around her stomach, delicately, and he understood. Tears slid down her cheeks in silence, and Rose reached over from the love seat and laid a hand on her forearm, like she'd known about it beforehand. Josefina smiled at Rose. "You're not supposed to tell people until you're sure it's safe. Not for three months, they say. Another ruined surprise."

"It's safe," Rose whispered. "It's safe."

McLeod studied Josefina's stomach, irresistibly, and he couldn't tell. She was in a flowing blouse, but even still: he felt he should be able to tell, and he couldn't.

He was on the verge of saying something. He felt he should say something. He began to form *congratulations*, but Josefina faced the elders again with sudden, startling purpose. Her face was gleaming, her voice soft yet resolute. "I want to be baptized, Elders. I prayed to the Lord, like you taught me, and He told me what to do. He wants me to join His church as soon as possible. Then maybe Leandro will follow my example, right? Maybe he'll want to follow me into the waters?" Her eyes sought approval from the elders, confirmation—mostly they sought it from McLeod. Maurilho and Rose and Rômulo studied the floor at the exact same angle, an inert choreography. McLeod felt lifeless—his face felt lifeless—empty of movement, empty of all expression. Josefina's lips flattened into a determined line. "Anyway, I prayed about it. The Lord told me what to do. I'm going to be baptized this Sunday."

Passos stirred in his seat. "Listen, Josefina . . ." He paused. "I know you're trying to—"

"I remember what you said. You prefer to wait until the spouse is ready. But I prayed about it, Elder. The Lord told me."

Passos opened his mouth to speak again, then stopped.

"Maybe what my companion is trying to say," McLeod came in, "is that there's some paperwork we'll need to put in process. There's a baptismal interview, a few other things, and it might take longer than a few days."

"As soon as possible then," Josefina said. "As soon as possible."

———

Early the next morning, in bed. The red numbers on McLeod's bedside clock resolving unsteadily into 5:58, and in the time it took to blink, 5:59. More than half an hour before he needed to be up. He felt an unfamiliar heaviness in his body—the leaden feeling not of too little sleep but of too much, though he knew he hadn't rested well. He remembered rousing hours earlier, around one o'clock, and then again at three thirty. Turning over each time, squinting, trying to make the red numbers come clear of their blur. He blinked again now, wiped the sleep from his eyes, and the numbers resolved for good: 6:00.

The rest of the world came clear on its own time, and no amount of squinting on McLeod's part could preempt it, or delay it, or change it at all, really. Josefina believed; Leandro simply did not. Perhaps in some offset time and space it had always been this way. Perhaps the ranks of believers and doubters had already been determined, split along an eternal binary. The heart swells with belief, like a child inside you—or it doesn't. The ground is fertile, or it isn't.

McLeod's eyes had adjusted to the light in the room—blue-green, shading clearer—and now they moved from the pale rectangle of light in the middle of the floor to the foot of Passos's bed. Only then did he see that the bed was empty, the faint-glowing sheets cast loosely over the mattress.

McLeod padded out into the entryway/living room, shielding his eyes from the bare bulb overhead. Through his squinting he thought he saw—then he knew he did, rubbing his eyes again—his senior companion, in full missionary dress, sitting at his, McLeod's, desk. Elder Passos half turned at the sound of his approach. McLeod noticed his book, *A Dictionary of Mormon Arcana*, balancing facedown on the desk like a lean-to, and beside it, an open book of scripture.

"What's going on?" McLeod said.

Passos pulled the chair from his own desk over to where he sat. "I want to show you something, Elder. Have a seat."

"What are you doing?"

"Sit down and I'll show you."

McLeod went to the bathroom and came back and stood behind the chair, his hands gripping the back of it like a high railing.

"Will you please sit down?" Passos said.

"If I do, are you going to tell me how you possibly thought going through my private things was okay?" He pulled the chair away from Passos and dropped down into the seat.

"Elder, I have been pondering," Passos said. McLeod noticed

the cadence in his voice already. "I have been reasoning with the Lord."

"And how was *rea*-son-ing with the *Lord*?" McLeod said.

Passos's eyebrows did their familiar knitting—the dark *V,* the face's instinctual flinch. After a moment the hard line softened, relaxed, and Passos said, "Don't you see, Elder? That right there is part of the problem."

Elder Passos reached for the slim paperback and flipped it over and flattened the pages against the desk. He pointed to an entry that said "Jesus Christ as polygamist, early Mormon speculations about."

"Let me guess," McLeod said. "You've come around to the idea."

The hand pointing to the page made a fist, suddenly, and pounded the book against the desk. McLeod flinched at the *crack* of the volume's binding on the wood. "Don't you see, Elder McLeod? This sarcasm, and this—" He waved the book in the air, nailed it to the desk again. "*This* is part of the problem!"

Elder McLeod met his senior companion's stare, dead-on, for a long, still moment, silent but for the sounds of their quickened breathing, still but for the tiny flarings of their nostrils. He met the stare long enough to show he wasn't afraid to meet it. Senior companion, district leader, zone leader, assistant to the president—none of it mattered. All the titles in the world didn't matter to McLeod.

"Elder McLeod," Passos said, and now his voice had changed, his eyes too. They beseeched. "I've been pondering about last night, pondering and praying about what we can do, what we *need* to do, to help Leandro. I woke up very early this morning. I arose in the Lord. I arose in His grace and His Spirit, Elder McLeod, and I asked Him what to do, and He told me."

Passos turned the open book of scripture to him. "Will you read verse nine, Elder? Aloud?" He preempted the look that McLeod could feel half twisting the corners of his mouth. "*Please*, companion. Please."

McLeod cleared his throat and read quickly. " 'My brethren, all you that have assembled yourselves together, you that can hear my words which I shall speak unto you this day; for I have not commanded you to come up hither to trifle with the words which I shall speak, but that you should hearken unto me, and open your eyes that ye may hear, and your hearts that ye may understand, and your minds that the mysteries of God may be unfolded to your view.' "

He looked up from the verse to see Passos's face trembling with soberness—big, funereal eyes. "Our sin," he said, "has been to *trifle* with the words of God. We show up to Josefina and Leandro's and what do we talk about? Football. Or work. Or how hot it is outside, how tasty the cookies are. We do too much chitchatting, too much joking around."

"People like it," McLeod said. "It's friendly."

Passos pursed his lips. "Elder McLeod, last night we had a birthday party, a ruined birthday party, instead of a missionary lesson. When we found out Leandro wasn't coming to the discussion, isn't living the truths we've taught him, doesn't want to be baptized with his wife—the woman he's about to start a family with, the woman he's *supposed* to be with in the eternities—you take it all in stride. It doesn't even faze you. Either of us! We're too busy eating chips and cookies—it'd be a shame to let them go to waste, right? Eating and drinking and making merry. That's all we do lately! We play that stupid church-names game all day, and on P-Days we listen to that filth from your friends. Then we come home and we read *this* filth!" Passos picked up the slim volume. "How Jesus was married! Jesus was a polygamist! Jesus and all the rest of us will be polygamists in the afterlife!"

"Passos, *I* didn't say those things—"

"I don't care who said them! This is not my religion! It's more trifling, is what it is!" He pounded the book again, rattling the desk, then leveled his finger at Elder McLeod. "That book is a bunch of trifling *garbage*, and it offends the Spirit. It's holding us back. We're going to burn it, Elder. We're going to burn it right now."

"Excuse me?" McLeod laughed a breathy, incredulous laugh. He crossed his arms over his chest. "And who's 'we'? You and I, you mean? Or you and the Lord? Is this what he told you to do? To burn books?"

Elder Passos scraped back his chair and stood abruptly. He crossed over to his own desk and opened the drawer and bent forward to get his arm in deep, as if to birth a calf. At last he pulled out a bright, glossy magazine. He rolled it up, closed the drawer. He came back to McLeod's desk and stood above it. The rolled-up magazine shook in his hand.

"What is it?" McLeod said, though by now he had an idea.

Passos dropped the magazine on his desk; it bounced once and unrolled. A naked woman on the cover. Her legs just parted, reclining on a bed. How long had it been since he'd seen something like this, and not just the peripheral blur of it at newsstands? McLeod stared helplessly. "Elder," Passos chided, and turned the magazine over. On the back cover a woman kneeled on all fours, her breasts hanging down like strange fruit. "Elder!" Passos said. He took the magazine and rolled it up and put it behind his back. "Is this something you struggle with too?"

"Not lately," McLeod said. He thought of the pictures wreathing the bathroom mirror, Passos's guard against temptation, he realized: Jesus in Gethsemane, Jesus on the cross, Jesus with the little children, Jesus in the clouds of glory.

"Okay, then," Passos said. He nodded at the black paperback volume on the desk, not meeting McLeod's eye. "We'll repent of our sins together."

Passos took McLeod's book from the desk and moved to the front door. McLeod followed without protest, the women spinning past the backs of his eyes like the images in a slot machine. Part of him tried to fix on the images. He felt he might need them later on.

Outside, Passos knelt in the little concrete courtyard. He tore a few pages from the magazine for kindling, the scraps lurid with browns and beiges. He produced a book of matches from his pocket and lit and dropped the matches one by one, holding back his tie. The fire bloomed. Elder McLeod saw a shapely leg curling up and turning charcoal black. He saw a bare stomach singe and disappear. His companion fed the rest of the magazine into the fire and then, with a toss of his wrist, added the dictionary of Mormon arcana. The fire inhaled, then slowly exhaled. McLeod wondered aloud, half ironically, if his father would be proud of him at a moment like this.

Passos said, "He's proud of you. He is."

The fire swallowed up the book, burning away the pages like

so much dross. In the clear morning light the flames were pale, unglowing, almost unnoticeable. You saw the fire mostly by its effects, the pages shrinking darkly, glowing a brief lantern-orange, then dimming to colorless ash.

It was morning again, and again McLeod noticed his companion's absence from the darkened room. The bare pillow, the collapsed luminescent sheets. He thought, too, he smelled something faintly burnt on the air. McLeod hazarded out into the light of the hallway, half bracing himself for another confrontation, half expecting to see Elder Passos at his desk, rifling through his drawer for contraband that wasn't there. What little he'd had still lay in a pile of ashes in the courtyard. Passos is fallen too, McLeod remembered. Josefina is pregnant. The world is not what it seems.

"Good morning, birthday boy! Well, slightly belated birthday boy."

The voice called out from the kitchen. McLeod craned his head to see down the hallway into the cramped little light-poor room: Passos stood in the center of it, fully dressed, and aproned. "I was just about to wake you up. Are you hungry?" He made a face, mocking his own question. "Let me put it this way: Could you be made to eat?"

McLeod nodded.

"Good," Passos said. "Do what you need to do and come join me in the kitchen. I've got something for you."

A minute later McLeod left the lighted bathroom, the pictures on the mirror like sentinels now, and stepped into the redoubled darkness of the apartment. The hall and kitchen lights had been extinguished.

"McLeod?" Passos called. "Follow my voice, okay? Trust me— it's for effect."

McLeod palmed his way along the cool hallway wall toward the kitchen, following Passos's "I'm here, I'm here," and the rising smell of flour and sugar, somehow sharp. In the kitchen proper McLeod came to a stop. Passos said, as if answering the smell, "I'm not much of a baker, I guess. Or I'm a whole lot better at cheese bread than birthday cake. But—" The meager lightbulb came on and revealed a single-layer chocolate cake resting, rather sunken, in the middle of a plate in the middle of the kitchen table. The rounded slab looked something like a porcupine, covered in quills that on closer inspection—McLeod bending forward, peering, chuckling—turned out to be matches, twenty-one of them, stuck heads-up in the cake.

"You made this for me?" McLeod said, still chuckling. He didn't know how else to react.

"I used some of your Nutella," Passos said. "I hope that's okay." Then he said, "What? Why are you laughing?"

"Was this your plan all along?" McLeod said. "To burn my book one morning, then make me a cake the next?"

"Not just your book—"

"I know, I know. It's just . . . How early did you get up?"

"Early." Then again: "Why are you laughing?"

"You're insane, Passos."

"Why am I insane? Why would you say that?" His companion's brows knitted halfway to the V.

"It's just a joke," McLeod said. "I'm just saying—we burned

the books, and now this cake here, which looks ready to blaze too, by the way."

"So you'd make that joke to Sweeney? You'd say that to a friend?"

"You *are* my friend, Passos. And of course I'd say that to Sweeney—I do. He's certifiable."

Elder Passos considered this for a moment. He wore a look of distracted concentration, as if he might be doing a math problem in his head. Then his stern face broke; he smiled at the cake. "It does look dangerous, doesn't it?"

"Who needs candles?" McLeod said.

"Oh and here," Passos said, retrieving from the chair beside him a small package wrapped in teaching pamphlets.

McLeod felt surprised, and a little exposed. He tore the wrapping away quickly to not make too much of the moment: it was a blue hardback book, *Vocabulário e gramática avançada*, and it really was advanced, Passos was saying, sounding rushed and exposed as well, which endeared him to McLeod. He didn't want to suggest that McLeod needed the practice, Passos was saying. He spoke so well already and so this book was more geared toward difficult reading—it had example passages from some of Brazil's greatest writers; Passos himself had used a book just like it in his secondary school—and he figured it might be a nice introduction to Brazilian literature that was still within the mission rules. He knew that McLeod liked literature.

Passos said, "So that's that," and took a matchbook out of his pocket.

"Hey." McLeod waited for Passos to look up at him. "I really like it, companion. Thank you."

"Well, good," Passos said, and he smiled. He hit the light and struck a match in the darkness, touching it to a match head in the very center of the cake. The elders watched the little bloom of fire spread to the match head beside it and the one beside it, moving out and out, until the cake looked constellatory.

Late Sunday morning they started for church on foot, through bright and bus-less streets, unpeopled but for the occasional aproned bartender setting up folding chairs at the edge of a dark-mouthed *barzinho*. Elder Passos could see the hunched forms of men inside—solider darknesses in the darkness. In t minus an hour the final would begin. In t minus two hours church would begin. This meant that sacrament meeting would overlap the game's second half almost exactly, and Passos himself had been asked to speak. A personal visit from the bishop late last night. The concluding speaker had come down with something.

The elders passed another assembling *barzinho* and Passos muttered, "I wish *I* could come down with something." He sensed McLeod's eyes on him. "I'm not complaining, I'm just saying. On a day like today who *wouldn't* come down with something?"

" 'To whom much is given,' right?" McLeod said. He chuckled.

Passos didn't see humor in the situation, and he said as much. Only an outsider could insist on holding church services at the same time as the finals, as President Mason had done. Passos wasn't sure a mission president even had that authority. Wouldn't the authority reside with the local bishop? In any case, the president had made it known he'd be in attendance at the ward that afternoon, as if to intimidate it into obedience. And again, Passos wasn't complaining—

"You're just saying," McLeod said.

"Well, it's true, Elder. Do you doubt it?"

"I don't, actually. I'm just not used to you bad-mouthing the mission president. You of all people."

"I'm not bad-mouthing the mission president. And what does that mean—'you of all people'?"

"Nothing," McLeod said. "I didn't mean to offend."

"I'm not offended. I just don't know what you mean."

"I misspoke."

A few minutes later Elder Passos banked left at the approach of the drive-through, detouring through the streets behind it. McLeod looked confused. "Why the scenic route?"

"Use your imagination," Passos said.

His companion squinted in concentration.

"Not literally," Passos said. "You know what I mean. You're a real comedian this morning, aren't you?"

"What?"

The elders passed the supermarket, the bank, the shops along the main street, all the windows mirrorlike in their darkness. The yellow-green banners spanning the intersections reminded Passos of the crossbeams over the Israelites' doors. The Lord's Passover. Obedience. Sacrifice. Elder Passos had fished the theme for his talk out of the preoccupations already swimming in his mind. Last night and this morning he'd made as many notes as time allowed, getting down the few complete sentences as they came to him. He intended his words for the whole congregation, of course, but specifically for Josefina. He felt certain she'd be there today. He felt certain Leandro would not be. Or maybe it wasn't quite certainty; maybe it was fear. Creeping doubt. Something to be guarded against, combated. He couldn't lose hope.

Passos and McLeod had agreed to continue working so that Leandro might change his heart, and soon, that he and his wife might be baptized together. The Lord intended for a family to be joined for time and all eternity, but only members of the church could undergo the sealing ordinances. Baptizing Josefina without Leandro risked alienating Leandro completely, and cutting him off, everlastingly, from his wife and now his child. The point of the gospel, Passos meant to tell Josefina, was *eternal* family unity. He would tell her today. After sacrament meeting. After his talk on obedience and sacrifice. This is *your* sacrifice, Josefina. To wait just a little while longer. In the scheme of eternity, time is meaningless, and to have your family by your side is meaning itself.

By the time the elders finally got downtown the aluminum grandstands had filled. People milled about the square, everyone in yellow, a giant convocation of bees crowding the hive: above their heads, a corridor of complicated light that ran from a high projecting booth behind the grandstand to a giant screen hanging from the town hall façade, showing pregame. The footage alternated between shots of a panel of suited men and a series of highlights from previous games, the field onscreen like a vast swimming pool of green, the figures streaking across it like water bugs . . . For a second Passos lost himself and stopped walking, awash in beauty.

"Obedience and sacrifice?" McLeod said, looking back.

"Indeed," Passos sighed. "Indeed."

They funneled into an alleyway on their way out of the square, passing a group of young people the elders' age, and all of them in the uniform of the day. Passos half put his head down, expecting ridicule—*What, going to church? Today?*—but the faces looked right past him toward the giant screen. Passos realized he'd actually been hoping for a little ribbing. He would have preferred it, almost any abuse, to this: this sense of invisibility, this sense of foreignness in his own country.

They arrived well early at the church, just after the trumpetlike burst of air horns had announced kickoff. Elder Passos stopped in the chapel's doorway and watched the bars at either end of the street: how they writhed with a sort of frantic attention, the folding chairs all empty as the wall of latecomers strained at the mouth of each bar, more like fish than bees now, a yellow school of them, each member bristling for a better view. Passos felt another stab of dislocation, and he couldn't help thinking—the idea breached despite him—that he'd given up something of himself, something important, to be a member of what was still an American-controlled church, on an American-controlled mission, under an American mission president, a man who could look at an entire culture and see a game, merely, who could look at a countrywide communion and see a crowd.

———————

During sacrament meeting President Mason and Sister Mason, a plump, pale couple that could have been brother and sister as easily as husband and wife, sat in the otherwise empty front row, their pew upholstered, like all the pews, in a muted orange fabric that must have seemed fashionable or timeless at one point; it was neither now. From Elder Passos's vantage—he sat on a dais at the front of the chapel—the pew backs and seats looked uglier than usual. His view of the room let Passos see just how few the bodies were to cover up or distract from the upholstery. He did notice Maurilho and Rose (but not Rômulo) in their usual place in the middle pews. Several other members Passos knew by sight sat scattered around them, to the left and right.

Josefina sat in the very back pew, to Passos's great relief, and his companion sat beside her. McLeod leaned over several times during the opening hymn, then the sacrament hymn, whispering to Josefina. He couldn't know what McLeod was saying, of course, but the very fact of his whispering into her ear struck Passos as inappropriate no matter how didactic the look on his face.

Elder Passos felt eyes on him—President Mason's, small and blue—and he returned his attention to his hymnbook. After the sacrament hymn only three deacons stood up to distribute the broken bread and water, but they were more than adequate to the size of the congregation. Then the bishop, a balding, murmuring man, went to the pulpit at the front of the dais and introduced the speakers. José Melão, their youth speaker, went first, taking less than five minutes on the subject of faith. José's mother, Sister Melão, followed him, treating the same subject in more adult terms, though not, Passos was startled to realize, in much longer ones. She started into her talk-ending testimony ("I know these things are true . . .") after only ten minutes at the pulpit, which meant that Passos needed to fill—a wide-eyed stare at the wall clock, panicked calculation—some thirty-five minutes, or fifteen minutes in excess of the twenty he had only felt vaguely prepared to fill in the first place.

Sister Melão sat down after a sparse, unisonous "Amen," and Passos stood up, very slowly. He moved to the pulpit. It wasn't half past the hour. He told a joke he'd heard once, stalling for time. A high priest dies in the middle of a quorum meeting, all those nodding gray heads, and it takes the paramedics three tries to find the one who's really dead. Rose and Maurilho obliged with a laugh-groan; McLeod did too; even Sister Mason did. But the mission president himself sat straight-faced.

Passos felt chastened. "Only kidding, of course." He looked up at the clock but not long enough to make out the precise minutes. What did he have—thirty-two minutes left, thirty? He gripped the pulpit on either side and put his head down and started reading more or less verbatim from his notes. He used none of his evangelical cadence; he couldn't have conjured it if he'd wanted to. In a low, too-quick mumble he uttered sentences like, "Something else I wanted to say is, well, consider how long the Lord has required sacrifice of His people. Consider the Israelites . . ." or "Remember, too, that Moses's law—the Law of Moses—was merely a preparatory law, as we read in the Book of Mormon . . ." or "I wanted to read a scripture about this. I'll read the entire passage because I think . . . I think it just illustrates my point very well . . ."

Elder Passos looked up at the clock as he reached the last bullet point on his page of notes, a bare directive: *Close with the story about the Passover (Ex. 12:12–13)—the Lord's Atonement—a broken heart and a contrite spirit* . . . The clock showed twenty minutes remaining. He arranged in his head the story of the Passover while praying for a miracle of his own, a rescue of his own. And hadn't he earned one? He had made himself clean; he had rid himself of his sins. Of the most obvious sins, anyway.

Passos folded away his page of notes and looked up into the faces of the congregation: President's and Sister Mason's, Maurilho's, Rose's, his companion's, Josefina's. "You all know the story of Moses and the plagues, I'm sure, but I wanted to tell it again . . .

because it's a remarkable story, my brothers and sisters. It's a truly remarkable story. The Lord tells Pharaoh, through His prophet Moses, to free the Israelites from bondage, and what does Pharaoh do? He hardens his heart. The Lord sends plagues—of frogs, lice, flies—upon all the land of Egypt, and still Pharaoh refuses to let God's people go. The Lord destroys the Egyptians' cattle. He sends a plague of pestilence, and another of boils, and another of hail. He sends locusts. He sends a terrible plague of three days' darkness, and after all this, what does Pharaoh do? He hardens his heart even more. So what happens next? I want to read it to you, brothers and sisters. I'd be remiss to paraphrase the Lord's words here. In Exodus, chapter twelve, the Lord has instituted the Passover: each family is to sacrifice an unblemished lamb, and take the blood of that lamb and put it on their doorposts, then eat the lamb standing up, with their shoes on, eating it with bread that hasn't even risen, ready to flee at a moment's notice, and why? In verses twelve and thirteen of chapter twelve, the Lord tells us: 'For on this same night I will pass through Egypt and strike down every firstborn—both men and animals—and I will bring judgment on all the gods of Egypt. I am the Lord. The blood will be a sign for you on the houses where you are; and when I see the blood, I will pass over you, and the plague of destruction will not touch you when I strike the land of Egypt.'

"He is the Lord indeed, brothers and sisters. I testify of that. And I testify that in the meridian of time He came down to earth and gave Himself as a sacrifice for all of us—the unblemished Lamb of God—so that the destroying angel might pass over us, too, over our houses and over our hearts. Christ's blood is a memorial to us, and a sign. We eat bread and drink water each week during the sacrament in remembrance of Him and His atoning sacrifice. This is our weekly Passover.

"But what of our sacrifice? What is the sacrifice required of the people of Christ today? The Law of Moses has been fulfilled in Christ, remember; we are no longer required to offer up animals. So what must we give to the Lord to show Him that we are indeed His people?" Passos looked up at the clock again: more than fifteen minutes remaining. "I want to end with one more scripture, in the Book of Mormon, and I know I'm ending early, but—"

Elder Passos jerked away from the microphone as if stung by it, as if the sudden explosion of shouting from outside, the first of several warlike bangs, grew not out of sheerest pleasure and celebration but pain and surprise. The game. He had nearly forgotten. Passos smiled, and the smile grew wider as the noise built. His companion in the back caught his attention, mouthing *Goooooooaaalll*, and big Maurilho closed his eyes and nodded several times as if to acknowledge an answered prayer. An excited murmur pulsed through the whole congregation, but then the noise outside began to fall—the game must not have been over—and President Mason turned around, roving his head from side to side at the congregation, showing a pursed warning look, turning it on Passos, a straight line in the middle of a round face. Passos stepped back to the microphone and gripped the pulpit even harder now, as if to tame it. He raised his voice to charismatic volume. "In the third book of Nephi, chapter nine, verses nineteen and twenty, we read"—and here he closed the book, reciting the verses from memory, the heat filling him—"'And ye shall offer for a sacrifice unto me a broken heart and a contrite spirit. And whoso cometh unto me with a broken heart . . . him will I baptize with fire and with the Holy Ghost.' Brothers and sisters, I testify to you—"

Another explosion rocked the street, and this time the cheer sustained over the sounds of fireworks and firecrackers and air horns and car horns dragging their long Doppler tails behind them, just like he'd imagined, a million bagpipes. Passos smiled again, but only for a moment, because he still had a talk to finish and because the frown on President Mason's face was deepening as a loudspeaker outside blasted samba and a sound car motored by—"BRAZIL WINS ON GOAL IN THE EIGHTY-EIGHTH MINUTE! BRAZIL WINS ON GOAL IN THE EIGHTY-EIGHTH MINUTE! BRAZIL TAKES THE TITLE IN A MIRACLE!"—and as the very members of the congregation snuck miniature flags from their lapels, waving them in tight arcs, moving their shoulders to the bouncing music. Passos leaned into the microphone to testify as loud as he could that "the Lord requires of us obedience and sacrifice, these things, and out of the firstfruits of the heart we produce our offerings, in the bright light of a new day, indeed, brothers and sisters, a *better* day"—as all the people outside drowned him out, or maybe they seconded him with their own raucous chorus of *Amens*, and as Passos finished he outright yelled now—"in the name of Jesus Christ, amen!" and the congregation yelled back, in one accord, "Amen!"

———

The bishop hurried up to the pulpit after Passos sat down. He thanked all the speakers for their wonderful, wonderful talks, then he dismissed church a full two hours early.

"We'll resume our normal schedule next week," the bishop said in a voice as loud and resonant as any Passos had heard from him. The man smiled like a lighthouse—big, shining eyes. "Next week we'll be able to hear ourselves think. Until then, God bless you. And God bless Brazil!"

After the closing prayer Elder Passos descended the dais and passed President Mason going up it. The president shook Passos's hand, said, "Good job, good job," but he looked past him to the bishop, that same tight line in the middle of his face.

In the hallway Passos met up with Maurilho and Rose, and Josefina and McLeod too, all of them matching his smile inch for inch.

"Great talk, companion," McLeod said. "Especially the end."

"Could you hear it?"

"Nobody heard it," Maurilho said, "but it was the greatest talk I've ever not heard!"

"Is that the talk?" Josefina said. She pointed to the folded-up page in Passos's hand.

"Sort of, yeah," he said. "Did I hear it right that they scored in the eighty-eighth minute?"

Maurilho pulled a thin black bud-capped wire out of his collar, letting it droop down like a wilted flower stalk over his tie. He smiled. "Yes. I can confirm that."

Rose shook her head at her husband, though she smiled too. Elder McLeod threw his head back and laughed.

"The eighty-eighth minute," Passos said. "Man! Can you imagine if we hadn't come to church today?"

The group moved in loose concert down the hallway, walking toward the glass double doors that gave a view onto the river of yellow and green rushing by. It looked even better than it had in Passos's daydreams. He felt a wave of gratitude lifting him, then a hand on his shoulder.

"Elder?"

When he turned around he saw Josefina and a look of startling earnestness. "I wanted to hear the end of your talk," she said, "but then all *that* happened." She gestured to the scene beyond the doors. "I was wondering if you'd let me borrow what you wrote down—your notes?—so I could read them and study them. I could give them back to you tomorrow."

"Oh Josefina," Passos said, and for a moment it was all he could do not to hug her. "Josefina, you are golden, did you know that? Here, take it, keep it. Show it to Leandro. I want you to have it. In fact, I wanted to talk to you. Well, *we* wanted to talk to you . . ." He looked up at the hall as Maurilho and Rose and McLeod reached the front door. Maurilho made excited explanatory gestures as McLeod nodded, laughed a little, nodded again. The three went outside, the doors opening and shutting. An envelope of brighter louder air came rushing down the hall to Passos and Josefina; it passed just as quickly.

"About the date for my baptism?" Josefina said.

"That's what we wanted to talk to you about."

"What's wrong?"

"Nothing's wrong. We just wanted to talk to you. And Leandro. We wanted to talk to the both of you. Do you think there's any chance he'll be home later tonight?"

"Is it about my baptism?"

"Yes, among other things. Can we come by and talk more tonight? Say seven?"

"When am I going to be baptized, Elder Passos? The Lord told me. He answered my prayers. When is my baptism?"

"Soon," Passos said.

"You mean this week?"

Elder Passos looked for his companion through the door, couldn't see him. He looked around for anyone, but the corridor had emptied out like the last day of school.

Josefina hadn't taken her eyes off him. "It's going to be this week, then, right? You said the paperwork would take a few days. So this week?"

Passos said, "Okay."

"Really?"

"Yes. We'll talk about it more tonight."

The elders walked all the way home with Maurilho and Rose and Josefina. Rose had invited them all for a late, celebratory lunch. Passos demurred on account of another appointment, and at first Josefina demurred, too. When Rose insisted, Josefina lit up like a carnival game and said how thoughtful they were, how kind. She'd have gone back to an empty house, she was sure of it. Who knew where her husband was in all this chaos?

The streets still writhed with people, some of whom noticed them all in their Sunday best and shouted, "God is Brazilian! God is Brazilian!" At Rose and Maurilho's outer gate Rose asked Passos if they couldn't reschedule their appointment, or be a little late for it. Passos was afraid they couldn't. He said goodbye to Maurilho and Rose and told Josefina they'd see her at seven o'clock that night.

"So you're a liar now?" McLeod said after they left the group. "Excuse me?"

"Easy now, Eyebrows. I'm mostly kidding. But why did you say we had plans?"

"Oh, that," Passos said. "I figure it's better for Josefina if we're not around all the time. Let her make friends with the members independent of us."

"I guess you're right," McLeod said.

They went back to the apartment and ate and decided to stay in for the rest of the afternoon, since who could work in that generalized clamor anyway? Car horns swept the neighborhood. Odd firecrackers, shouting, and of course samba—pounding, ubiquitous samba. Elder Passos closed the bedroom window and lay down for a nap. McLeod tried to follow his lead, but after several minutes Passos heard him sigh with impatience. His companion cleared his throat, stage-whispering across the space between their narrow beds. "Passos? You asleep over there?"

"Almost."

"How can you sleep in this?"

"You get used to it," Passos said. He kept his eyes closed, but a slow smile spread across his face. "When you win this many titles . . ."

He held that smile into the evening, he and the rest of Brazil. At the first reddening of the sky the elders started for Josefina's, still on foot, and every face they saw in the street seemed caught up in the same private lovely thought. It almost made Elder Passos forget what he'd said. That they'd baptize Josefina this week. She'd backed him into it, and now what? He could tell her that the paperwork was taking longer than expected, or that the mission president was out of town, or something. But of course then McLeod would know, and Passos wasn't in the habit of lying. Maybe he should explain it to Josefina. Or maybe Leandro would actually be there. Maybe now that the championships were over he'd take more interest, he'd soften. It wasn't out of the realm of possibility. On a day like today almost anything was possible.

They passed *barzinhos* letting out a fairly steady stream of revelers. Car horns still pierced the air now and then. On the other side of the street Passos spotted a family of Pentecostals walking, he assumed, to Sunday-evening services, the father in a dark suit, a Bible under his arm, and his wife and two daughters following close behind him. They all walked bolt upright, like a phalanx of imperial soldiers, but even *they* appeared to be smiling. Passos watched them turn off the main street with something close to tenderness. He started whistling, unconsciously at first, but then he matched the words to the tune and it made sense. *We are all enlisted till the conflict is o'er. Happy are we, happy are we . . .*

Was that what he thought it was? Was that— He listened as the melody dropped down into the chorus, marching, marching, a martial line. It was. Elder McLeod hated the hymn, always had. His companion continued his quiet whistling, quiet yet clear, a sharp stream of air that cut through the reveling noise around them. Passos started into another verse and McLeod said, "Do me a favor?"

"What?"

"Knock that off. I can't stand that hymn."

" 'We Are All Enlisted'?"

"It sets my teeth on edge. Seriously."

"Ah, it's a great hymn, Elder. It's a great hymn."

Passos kept on with his whistling—down into the chorus, then up into yet another verse—as if McLeod hadn't said a word, as if he'd actually encouraged him. *More terrible-hymn whistling, please. Louder!* But in fact he'd meant what he said and he'd said what he meant—no sarcasm, no trifling. At the edge of the fourth verse Elder Passos stopped his whistling. McLeod muttered a thank-you, but his companion didn't acknowledge it. Passos had stopped his walking too. He stood in the middle of the sidewalk, straining his eyes at something ahead of them. "No," he whispered.

McLeod followed Passos's gaze to a huddle of men in front of a *barzinho* across the street, all of them nursing dark bottles, some nodding to the music. One man in particular, dark brown, lanky, cocked his head drunkenly back at them. He separated himself from the group, steps hitching, starting across the street. At the first sound of his voice—"Elders?" he shouted. "Is that you?"—he became Leandro. "Elders! Oh Elders! Wait for me!"

Passos had started walking again, and McLeod couldn't tell if he intended to hurry *to* Leandro or past him. He followed behind as Leandro veered onto the sidewalk ahead of them, and Passos abruptly stopped. Josefina's husband looked looser, shufflier in his walk, as if he'd been deboned in the legs and arms. He moved in ways that seemed to surprise even him.

"Oh Elders!" Leandro said. He closed the last yards between them holding a sad-looking brown bottle shorn of its label. McLeod could hear what was left in the bottle sloshing from Leandro's movements. He wore a faded yellow Brazil jersey, mesh shorts, rubber sandals. He looked even tanner than the last time they'd seen him, rangier, his goatee gone to seed. That he worked construction seemed suddenly fitting to McLeod: it looked as if a loose jumble of two-by-fours was sidling up to them, was smiling at them, laughing a loud stupid laugh.

"Oh Elders," he said, "you see the game?"

Leandro's breath shocked of foul *cachaça*. His pink eyes swam in their sockets.

Passos stepped forward and gestured his hand at McLeod as if to keep him back—something tender in this, McLeod felt, but also patronizing. His companion ducked his head, tracking Leandro's. "How much have you had to drink, Leandro?"

"I'm talking about the *game*," Leandro said. "The game! Did you see it?"

"Missionaries aren't allowed to watch TV," McLeod said. "Remember?"

Passos turned to him and shook his head—*I'll handle this.* He turned back around just as Leandro swung his left arm over Passos's shoulder. Leandro lifted his other arm, disjointed and exultant, waving the *cachaça* bottle like a flag. "We won!" he shouted. "Again! What joy to be Brazilian!"

Elder Passos slipped Leandro's beery embrace like a prizefighter, ducking under and out with such agility that Leandro lost his balance, listed left, then right, overcorrecting. The brown bottle sang as he threw out his arms for support. Passos took Leandro by the shoulders, steadied him. "Why don't you come home with us?" he said. "To *your* home. We're on our way there to visit your wife. Leandro? When's the last time you were home?"

"My wife! Of course! Hey guys," he shouted, wheeling around to address his huddle of friends across the street, which had since dispersed. "Guys, where are you? These are the kids I was telling you about. Guys?" He visored his forehead with his left hand and bent a little, straining his gaze in the direction of the bar. "Ah, fuck," he muttered. He turned back to the elders. "Of course you're going to visit my wife. You love my wife, don't you? Especially gringo here." He jerked a thumb past Passos to McLeod. "Don't you, Elder Gringo?"

McLeod thought he hadn't heard him, or understood him. But his face began to burn. Leandro swung his arm around Passos again and said out of the side of his mouth, "He comes to our country, eh Passos, and tries to steal our women, eh?"

Passos ducked out and under again. "You're drunk, Leandro. Go sleep it off."

"Go home," McLeod said. His voice sounded hoarse all of a sudden, obstructed.

And all of a sudden Leandro straightened, clamped his eyes on McLeod. "What are you doing with my wife?" He shouted, "Are you *fucking* my wife?" Leandro lunged and threw a loose, waving punch at McLeod, narrowly missing. His body pitched forward with his arm's momentum, landing him facedown in the street.

Adrenaline fired in every cell of McLeod's body. His heart thudded high up in his throat. Passos put a quick hand under McLeod's chin. "He didn't get you?"

Leandro tried to lift himself from the street, collapsed. He tried again and collapsed again. He writhed like a catch in its throes, struggling for something it no longer has the means of. Escape. Dignity.

"Help!" Leandro wailed into the pavement. "Help me up, for Christ's sake! Elders!"

Passos moved McLeod back another step, then bent down and rolled Leandro onto his back. The man blinked several times, his right cheek coated in dust. Passos held out his hand. "Come on."

Leandro took the hand and mocked, "Come on, come on. Let's go fuck Leandro's wife. That's what you do when I'm not there, right? Just like your Joseph Smith. The church of the wife-fuckers."

Passos wrenched his hand away and sent the jumble of a man back down to the dusty street. Leandro tried to prop himself up from his back now—his legs spread, crablike—but he fell back. Elder McLeod stepped forward and his companion said, "No. Leave him where he is." He took McLeod by the wrist and upper arm and rushed him off down the street as Leandro screamed after them, a torrent of imprecations that Passos covered with a low, rapid voice in McLeod's ear: "Leave him where he is, in the dirt, in the filth, just leave him, don't even look back . . ."

An hour later the scene still spun in McLeod's mind in a sort of horror-movie loop: Leandro's voice catching on the *f* of *Are you fff-fucking my wife,* McLeod literally flinching at the word, he and Passos both, the burn of *cachaça* in their nostrils, and again. It felt surreal at moments, or if not quite that, if not quite past reality, then past explanation, exempt from it. But no. McLeod arrived with his companion at the edge of Josefina's street and knew that a very real reckoning must come.

"Just . . ." McLeod said. "Just give me a minute."

In the near distance the river ran brownish pink and red. The sound of it promised calm. McLeod walked to it, his senior companion following after. They sat in silence on the corrugated guardrail that separated the road from the shallow bank beneath them, the occasional prods and nubs of drainage pipes sticking out of the dirt like uncovered limbs. The low sun making the color on the river. For the moment it looked blood-red.

McLeod spoke first. "Now what?"

"We baptize Josefina."

"You mean—"

"We baptize Josefina without Leandro. We don't even tell her that we'd changed our minds. She doesn't need to know that. We pick up where we left off Tuesday night."

A long silence soaked into the air around them. They heard no fireworks anymore, no car horns—only the runs and riffles below, a continuous sound but somehow dislocated, fragmented, like the glow on the water. McLeod asked about the time.

"We were supposed to be there half an hour ago," Passos said.

"Okay," McLeod said. "One more minute."

The elders knocked at Josefina's door and waited for what seemed to Elder McLeod like a very long time. She came to the door, smiling, still in her Sunday best. McLeod exhaled. Inside, the elders took their usual seats as Josefina started toward the kitchen. Passos called her back. "No need for snacks tonight, Josefina. But thank you. We won't be taking that much of your time."

Josefina hesitated in the kitchen doorway. "It's just water and some cookies—nothing heavy."

"We appreciate that," Passos said, "but please," and he motioned at the catty-corner love seat. At length Josefina sat down—on the side away from them, Elder McLeod noticed—smoothing her knee-length skirt, her legs tight together. Was she self-conscious in front of them? In front of me? Does she know? Did he tell her?

McLeod thought of Leandro with hatred. He kept his head down. For long minutes he fixed his eyes on the patch of pocked cement between his shoes. If he had to look up at Josefina, if she mentioned him by name, he looked her straight in the eyes, the pupils, those mute black dots like the points on a compass. He moved between those poles: the floor between his feet, the very center of her eyes. Elder McLeod wished he had run from Leandro, *sprinted*, no matter how rude or cowardly it might have seemed, for now he could think of little else but what Leandro had said, and how he'd said it—that initial *f*, the explosion past it—and how the very word had created something in him, a rank world, the images storming his mind now, spinning past the backs of his eyes like the women from Passos's magazine, all of it running together, and he couldn't stop it, he couldn't make it stop, the thought of her pregnancy couldn't even stop it. He blamed Leandro. He blamed Leandro for all of it. Leandro Leandro Leandro. Elder McLeod glared at the floor and considered the name with such vehemence, such hate, like a sort of crazed mantra—*Leandro Leandro Leandro*—that he couldn't be sure if he'd imagined the name or if he'd heard it come out of Josefina's mouth.

It had come out of Josefina's mouth. It hung in the air in front of McLeod, twisting, like a strung-up thing.

"Well?" Josefina said.

"Look," Passos said, "Josefina—"

"I asked Elder McLeod," Josefina said.

At the sound of his own name he started even more, looked up, and his untrained eyes caught the sheen of her knees. McLeod jerked his gaze up to Josefina's pupils and held to them like ropes over an abyss. "I'm sorry? What did you say?"

"When did he call?" Passos interrupted.

"Half an hour ago," Josefina said. "He said Elder McLeod pushed him to the ground and the two of you just left him like that. Is that true? Elder McLeod? Is it?"

Elder McLeod formed his lips around the word but no sound came. He held the *O* of his mouth like a suffocating fish. He, McLeod, the catch now, struggling, and Leandro streaming in the reel.

Passos said, "Wait. Wait, Josefina. What did he sound like on the phone? Did he sound like he'd been drinking? He was drunk, Josefina. He was angry. We tried to tell him to come home but he wouldn't. I asked when was the last time he'd been home and he got angry with us. He tried to hit my companion. Then he fell down and we tried to help him back up but he wouldn't accept our help. He just kept yelling at us. That's the truth, Josefina."

Josefina turned back to McLeod, her eyes fathom-dark. "Is that true, Elder McLeod? Because he said you pushed him. He said you pushed him down and left him there."

Elder McLeod shook his head. He managed, "No. I never pushed him."

She studied his face. "What was he yelling at you?"

"I don't want to repeat it."

Josefina's eyes held for a minute more, steadily, but then they cracked and broke like shells. "I am so embarrassed," she whispered. "Oh Elders, I'm so embarrassed."

"Don't be," Elder McLeod said.

"Don't be," Passos said.

"I'm so sorry. Please forgive me, Elders. I can't believe—" She broke off to push back sudden emotion, bracing her hand against her sternum. "Please, Elders, please let me get you some cookies, some water." She stood up and turned toward the kitchen as McLeod snapped his head down. Josefina might have noticed; his companion must have. But he couldn't afford to be subtle any longer. Josefina came back after several minutes bearing one tray of glasses and another of cookies, neither of which Elder McLeod actually saw until they touched down on the coffee table in front of him: an array of white wafers, three clear glasses, and Josefina's hand placing them there, like a still life. McLeod thanked Josefina without looking up. He ate and drank in silence. All three of them did.

After a long while Josefina said, "Really, Elders, I am sorry. Why I ever believed him over you . . . He's not dependable. He's not . . . I hope you can forgive me."

Passos put his hand up, an imperial gesture. He said, "That's not what we've come to talk about, Josefina. We've come to talk about your baptism. Do you still have the desire to be baptized in the Lord's church? That is to say: Will you be baptized, Josefina?"

"Of course I do. Yes. I want that very much."

Elder McLeod chewed his cookies like a chastened child. He felt disconnected from the moment, irrelevant to it: his companion taking out his planner, scheduling the baptism for next Sunday ("We'll do it right after church," Passos said), and tentatively scheduling the baptismal interview with the president ("We'll try for next Thursday or Friday"), at which time they'd fill out the necessary paperwork. Elder McLeod heard Josefina respond, but heard it distantly, something about how excited she felt, and how sorry for earlier, sorry for everything.

The elders walked home in the dark, passing loud, rejuvenated bars, but Elder McLeod heard everything as if through gauze. *Josefina is going to be baptized next Sunday, and what do I feel?* They passed the town square where a few people in jerseys still clung to the corners, their yellow shirts brown in the darkness, and the streamers on the sidewalk like so much garbage, and the confetti and the ribbons from balloons, all garbage.

Just before curfew that night, Elder McLeod followed Passos to the pay phone at the end of their street. Passos called each senior companion in the zone to collect the companionship's estimated contacts for the week, number of lessons, number of baptismal challenges (if any), acceptances (if any), baptisms (if any). He then summed these numbers and called the mission office, passing them along to one of the president's two assistants. Tonight Passos spoke to Elder Tierney, the American assistant, or so Elder McLeod assumed from his companion's formal tone, vaguely rivalrous: "Oh, yes, hello . . . I'm fine, thanks. You?"

McLeod stood a few feet to the left of the pay phone, not listening to Passos's report until he said, "But the zone did have one baptismal challenge this week . . . It was mine, actually. Ours. And it was an acceptance . . . Josefina da Silva . . . Yes, thank you. Well, we're very excited. I wanted to set up an interview while I've got you on the phone. When is good for the president? . . . Oh he is? Oh, I hadn't heard about that . . . In Santiago? . . . Well, that'll work out fine, then. We were hoping for late week . . . Friday morning is great . . . Great. Thank you, Elder . . . The same to you. Good night."

Passos hung up the phone and wandered over to him.

"What's up?" McLeod said.

"We're on for Friday morning."

"Okay. Is that all? You were talking about something else, I thought."

Passos looked distracted, his face far-seeming. "Huh? Oh. President Mason left tonight for a three-day mission presidents' conference. In Chile. All the mission presidents in the South American Area, apparently."

"Sounds big," McLeod said. "Was that Elder Tierney you talked to? What did he say it was about?"

"Something about raising retention rates among new converts."

"Ah, retention. I'm sure that'll be productive."

Passos came back to the present—the sudden creased brows. "Is that sarcasm, Elder? What did we talk about just the other day?" Then he softened. "We've done good work with Josefina. Let's not jeopardize it now."

The rest of the night proceeded uneventfully. The elders read at their desks—McLeod finished the second chapter in his new grammar book—and retired to bed. Just after lights-out Passos cleared his throat. "Elder McLeod, may I ask you a question?"

"Hmm-hmm."

"What do the Americans think of Elder Tierney?"

"What do they 'think' of him?"

"I mean is he liked? Is he very popular?"

"He is with the mission president, obviously," McLeod said. "Less so with us. Why do you ask?"

"No reason," Passos said.

McLeod shook his head in the dark. He pushed soft, inaudible air through his nose, and he closed his eyes.

———————

On Friday morning the elders picked up Josefina. She wore her Sunday best—that much McLeod could tell. Something white and loose on top, black on bottom. Elder McLeod didn't allow himself more than that peripheral awareness, the same strategy he used with the newsstands. The three of them traveled by bus to the main *rodoviária* in Carinha, from there to the *rodoviária* in Belo Horizonte, and from there to the big chapel downtown, in a taxi, and all of it at reimbursable expense. The Work did feel best at a dedicated pitch—Sweeney and Kimball had been right. The thought came to McLeod as he followed Passos and Josefina out of the taxi and onto the sidewalk in front of the church. Passos was reassuring Josefina that she had nothing to worry about in the interview, nothing at all. She really did want this, McLeod realized. She would be his first convert (he didn't count Zézinho), his first convert to justify the message.

"You're sure?" Josefina was saying to Passos. "What if the mission president asks me a question I don't know the answer to?"

"It's not that kind of interview," Passos said. "It's not a test. It's a conversation."

"It's just to make sure you know how important this step is," McLeod said. "Which you already do. You know so much already, Josefina. Trust us—you'll do great."

"Okay," she said, "okay."

Inside the ward building Elder Passos knocked at the bishop's office, which President Mason often borrowed for interviews. After a moment the president opened the door and his big round face loomed up in the doorframe like a rising moon. The face smiled at Josefina, then looked beyond her to the empty foyer, then looked to McLeod and Passos. "Can I speak with you for a moment, Elders?"

They all trailed smiles into the bishop's office, but as soon as McLeod pulled the door shut behind him, President Mason's smile dropped off his face, then Passos's and McLeod's, in quick succession, like shorting-out wires. McLeod and his companion sat on two padded chairs in front of a midsize dark-wood desk; President Mason sat behind it in a large black leather chair, a framed picture of the risen Lord glorying at his back.

"I should have confirmed with you two, but I didn't, and that's my error," the president said. "Elder Tierney had the interviewee's name down as 'Josef.'"

"It's Josefina," Passos said.

"An honest mistake," the president said.

The elders waited in silence for the president to make sense of his ashen look. He shifted in his chair—leather creaked and buckled. He shifted again, said, "Is your investigator married?"

"Josefina," McLeod said.

"Yes, Josefina. Is she married?"

"She is," Passos said.

"Well, that's good news then. That's good news." The president leaned forward in his chair—more creaking—and rested his forearms on the desk. He crossed his fingers in a loose weave, somewhere between relaxation and prayer. He sighed. "I think you heard I just returned from a three-day conference in Santiago, Chile. The theme of the conference was retention, and the South American Area is now committed to improving its performance in that regard. To this end, Elders, we've been instructed to only baptize families from now on, self-sustaining, celestial units. That's always been our goal, of course—our ultimate goal—to exalt families, to unite them in the eternities. But for now I'm afraid that means, in this case . . . well, you know what it means. I'm sorry, Elders. But tell me about Josefina's husband. Do they have any children?"

"Not yet," Passos said.

"She's pregnant," McLeod said. "And the husband isn't interested in the gospel at all. He's made that very clear. I'm confused, though. A few minutes ago you thought Josefina was 'Josef' and you were all ready for a baptismal interview, weren't you?"

President Mason pinched his eyebrows, and his companion, McLeod noticed out of the corner of his eye, did too. Another trip-wire effect—a puppeteer's trick, as if a string ran from the puppeteer's own bushy brows to the puppet's dark sleek *V*.

"Elder McLeod," Passos said, his voice low and chiding. He showed him his face from the day before—*I'll take care of this*—but this time McLeod ignored it.

He turned his eyes to the president. "Well? Weren't you?"

"Mind your tone, Elder," the president said. He nodded at Elder Passos as if to point out for McLeod the proper attitude before the mission president, the proper tonal posture. His companion stared at him sidelong, a pleading, angry stare. Whose side was Passos on, in the end? Josefina's? It certainly didn't seem that way. McLeod had almost forgotten this part of Passos, but now it came rushing back at him. His companion the climber! His companion the missionary careerist! All at once McLeod felt a physical revulsion for Passos, something coursing up through him like bile. He felt it float him up free of the respectable world: he could say anything now, do anything, if only to embarrass Elder Passos.

McLeod looked into the president's big foreboding face. "Why are you avoiding the question? When it's a man, you're all for it. It's green lights all the way."

"Mind your *tone*, Elder McLeod," the president said.

"Are you going to answer the question or not?"

"Elder McLeod!" Passos grabbed him hard, strangling his wrist as if to cut off circulation to his mouth. "The kingdom can't grow without priesthood holders. Isn't that right?" He turned to the mission president.

"That's the hard truth," the president said. "You ought to listen to your senior companion, Elder McLeod."

"We'll work with her husband more," Passos said. "We'll bring him around. She'll help us. I know she will. She really is golden, President."

"I'm sure she is. That's why we want her baptism to be truly meaningful. We want it to be an important step toward the ex-altation of her entire family. Our goal is to unite people in the eternities, not divide them. But that can only happen if a man and woman are sealed together in the temple. You both know this as well as I do, Elders."

"Where was this 'meaningful baptism' talk eight months ago when we called you about a ten-year-old?" McLeod said. "Do you remember that? Do you remember you okayed it? The kid went in the front door and out the back. And now when we bring you a *real* investigator—"

"That's precisely what we're trying to have less of, Elder McLeod. In one door, out the other. We're not asking your investi-gator not to be baptized—"

"Josefina. Her *name* is Josefina."

"We are simply asking her to wait for her husband so that her baptism can be *truly*—"

"Yeah," McLeod said, standing up from his chair, "yeah, yeah, yeah, yeah, yeah, yeah, yeah," and he walked out of the office and slammed the door behind him.

Out in the foyer Josefina said, "What's wrong, Elder?" She sat straight-backed at the edge of a floral-patterned couch, her knees together beneath her black skirt, shining with the light from the window like waxed fruit. Her white blouse hung loose over her stomach, much tighter over her chest. "What's happening, Elder? What is it?"

He couldn't look her in the face now, least of all now. He shook his head for her, slowly, and looked away.

Passos made no attempt to hide his anger at McLeod, made no gesture at reconciliation the next day or the next. He and McLeod knocked doors in the afternoons and evenings, speaking in short clipped sentences when they did speak, which was rarely, and almost always about logistics. Where to? What next? Which bus? Little more than this.

When Josefina failed to show up at church on Sunday, the elders took Rose with them for a drop-in visit that night. They needed Josefina's closest friend in the ward to help cheer her, help her put things in perspective, but they also needed Rose in order to comply with the mission's newest rule: missionaries must bring a third party when visiting a woman alone in her home. Elder Passos didn't like the rule any more than McLeod did, but he didn't intend to copy McLeod's idiotic strategy of shouting into the wind, spitting into it, then hanging his head when he got all hoarse and wet.

Head-hanging had become McLeod's default posture. He hardly looked up from the floor during the entire visit at Josefina's, his face dull, eyes vacant. He looked lobotomized. Worse yet was the way Josefina herself mirrored McLeod's body language. She sat on the love seat, her back hunched, hands crossed in front of her knees, her gaze angled down at the bowl of pebbles on the coffee table, the untouched plate of *biscoitos*. Passos talked and talked but he couldn't get through to her. Only when Rose opened her mouth to speak did Josefina even shift her position on the love seat. Rose hesitated.

"Please," Passos said. "Please."

"Well, I just wanted to say," she began, "and I'd meant to tell you this at the beginning, Josefina. I'm sorry Maurilho couldn't be here with us tonight, but he finally got a job, a janitorial position at the town hall, and he has to work nights now, even Sunday nights. I know he's a little embarrassed about it all. He's not a prideful man, my husband, but he's smart enough to run that town hall, and now he's pushing a broom there. The Lord humbles us sometimes, to make us teachable. He has to break our hearts before he can rebuild them better."

By now Josefina had looked up at her friend, her eyes sharpening slightly, and her posture too. When Rose finished, she nodded at Passos. He was searching for a particular verse in the Doctrine and Covenants to build on Rose's point, to add to the Spirit suddenly warming the room. Was it section 131? The word of the Lord to the Prophet Joseph Smith: how his afflictions would be but for a small moment, and if he endured them well, the Lord would exalt him on high. It was section 121, he remembered.

Passos turned to the section, but before he could locate the verse Elder McLeod opened his mouth for the first time all visit.

"Where's Leandro?" he said.

Passos looked up, startled to hear his companion's voice, and saw him staring intensely into Josefina's eyes.

"I don't know," Josefina admitted.

"When was the last time you saw him? Did he know we were coming here tonight?"

"I told him you were coming. I told him last night, but—"

"Was he sober?" McLeod said.

The visit ended a few minutes later. On the bus ride home McLeod and Rose exchanged a few polite words. Passos kept totally silent.

President Mason had been right about McLeod all along. The president was more clear-eyed about his companion, more blunt and honest. A difficult missionary. Arrogant. Stubborn. He needs a leader more than a friend, Elder Passos. The president had told him this in the bishop's office the other day, and not for the first time, after McLeod had stomped out of the room trailing his *yeah, yeah, yeah, yeah* like a little boy dragging his baby blanket. His junior companion was acting worse than junior now, worse than *juvenile.* For he threw loud tantrums at the realities he disliked, then walked around with his nose in the air as if convinced of his own purity, untainted by compromise, by facts. McLeod suddenly embodied for Elder Passos some of America's worst tendencies. He suddenly reminded him of Elder Jones: boorish yet haughty, naïve yet cynical, self-righteous despite such obvious cruelty.

These thoughts of Passos's coincided, and not coincidentally, with the news of America's buildup to war. Neither Passos nor McLeod had violated the missionary rules against reading newspapers or magazines, watching TV, listening to the radio. The talk of war with Iraq simply pervaded the air around them, like humidity before a thunderstorm. Already a unanimous vote in America's Congress. Troop movements in Kuwait. Refugees at the border. Signs of the times, Elder Passos thought.

On Thursday afternoon the elders knocked a door and an oldish woman answered it. Tracting had improved with the end of the championships, but the harvests still came in meager, and opened doors still rather surprised the missionaries. Elders Passos and McLeod straightened up as the woman tucked long strands of gray behind her ear, smiling slightly, straddling the threshold of the door. Yes? Could she help them? Passos gave the more extended introduction in which he anticipated common questions—"Elder" was a title; they came from Recife and Boston, respectively—then he asked the woman if they could come inside to share their message.

The woman hesitated.

"It won't take long at all," Passos added.

She opened the door a little wider, stepping aside to make room for the missionaries to enter her dirt courtyard.

"Oh, actually," Passos said. "Are you alone, ma'am? Is your husband or anyone else home with you?"

McLeod snorted, muttered under his breath, in English, "She's like sixty, dude."

"Shut up," Passos said. He too spoke in English. He turned to the woman. "I sometimes have to translate for him. Excuse us."

The woman nodded. "My son is here."

Inside the darkened living room the elders sat opposite the woman on a pair of chairs brought in from the kitchen. She called out to her son more than once as the three of them made small talk, waiting. After a minute more the woman shrugged and told the elders they might as well begin. Elder Passos hesitated a moment—did the rule require that the third party actually be in

the room?—and in that space McLeod started into the first lesson, reciting memorized lines on God as a loving Heavenly Father
who calls prophets, and so on. Passos took up the next two sections, providing his own variations on the themes of God's Son
and His atoning sacrifice and the original church He established
on the earth. The missionaries were halfway through the next section on that church's eventual apostasy—"saving truths were lost
or corrupted," McLeod was reciting—when a big shirtless man
stepped into the room, immense brown belly first. The man stood
generously proportioned throughout, but especially at his middle,
so bowed out and smooth as to look ceramic. No sooner had he
dropped down beside his mother on the couch than he leveled a
stare at Elder McLeod. "Are you American?"

McLeod gave a slow nod.

"How about that fucking president of yours?"

In the instant Passos felt McLeod straighten beside him, bristle.
He spoke quickly. "Sir?" he said. "Sir." He explained about the
gospel message they were sharing with his mother. They'd been
talking about the attributes of God. Would he like to tell them how
he imagined God?

"God is good," the man said. His eyes returned to McLeod.
"And God ain't greedy either. He don't want to bomb poor little
countries just to get their fucking oil. He don't want—"

Passos cleared his throat loudly. He stood up and shook the
woman's hand, then the man's. He thanked them for their time and
at the doorway exchanged a few last pleasantries, a few *God bless
you*s. McLeod kept notably quiet. He waited until they rounded a
corner away from the house before he said, sounding confident of

Passos's accord, "Talk about an ignoramus, huh? Anyway, thanks for sticking up for me back there. I appreciate it."

Passos answered in English: "I did not say I disagree with him."

A week more passed like that, two weeks. The elders visited Josefina several times, with Rose or Rômulo in tow. Most of the visits devolved into planning sessions, strategic brainstorms. How to get Leandro interested? How to get him to show up at all? What about a casual meeting one night, just a chance to relax and talk? What about a dinner at Rose and Maurilho's? They needed to reestablish their friendship with Leandro, needed to properly apologize for their run-in after the championships. Or what if they dropped by unannounced? A surprise visit?

Most of the suggestions came from Passos, some from Rose, some from Josefina herself. McLeod did little except to naysay, as Passos saw it. His companion took up each suggestion like a pawnshop jewel appraiser, holding it to the light and finding something to disparage: too transparent, too murky, too sneaky, and weren't they supposed to be missionaries first, friends second? Wasn't that another of the things they'd talked about?

Things between Passos and McLeod hadn't healed in the last weeks so much as scabbed over—they'd resigned themselves to each other's formalities—though on some nights Elder Passos's frustrations still rose to a boil, causing him to compose in his head long lists of McLeod's faults: *pride, negativity, hypercriticism, petulance, arrogance, self-absorption* . . . He even began to take private pleasure in the carfuls of men shouting out at them "Bin Laden,

Bin Laden!" or "Imperialists!" or "Warmongers!" Passos knew that many of these drive-by critics probably lumped him in with the whitey at his side, but he considered this a bearable price to pay for the sight of McLeod's jaw gripping, the flaring in his eyes. Of course Elder Passos did not hate his companion. Nor did he feel apathetic toward him. His feelings now lived in a shifting middle space, a place that could accommodate affection and hope—that the offer of a stay in McLeod's basement still stood, for example— but that could also make room for scorn, spite, bitterness, resentment, hopes of comeuppance.

On another day, toward the end of February, the missionaries tracted a rich neighborhood. To give them a chance, Passos thought, though he knew from long experience not to expect much from the worldly and vaunted. In the richer neighborhoods electric fences topped the property walls instead of broken bottles. On some of the walls, on the white glaring stucco, local vandals spray-painted looping insignia. Others left messages of protest:

FILHOS DA PUTA!

IMPERIALISTAS!

VIVA A REVOLUÇÃO!

The rich hardly ever answered their doors, championships or no championships, now or ever, and this neighborhood looked to Elder Passos like no exception. Then his turn came to knock a Spanish-style house, two stories, its tight-tiled roof like a scaly hide. A man in a crisp blue button-down opened the door and invited them in. The elders followed him up the courtyard's walkway, elaborate plants lining the sides, a red convertible shining in the open garage. The man led them into the house and invited them to sit at a large, lacquered table. Dark-haired, olive-skinned, he spoke Portuguese with an accent—not unlike McLeod's, Passos thought. An American accent. Had he moved here from there? Or returned from years abroad?

"Please be comfortable," the man said, leaving the room and returning with two glasses of filtered water. Passos noticed under the man's arm a thin spiral-bound book. The man placed it on the table: *How to Evangelize the Mormons.*

McLeod scoffed—that rush of air through his nose—and for once Passos matched it. They did it in synch. They took drinks of their water and rose to their feet. Passos cited an appointment they'd just remembered, they were sorry.

Out in the street McLeod said, "You think he was a pastor?"

"I'm sure of it," Passos said.

"I hate that crap."

"Yeah."

"And that book of his—right on the table in front of us? Talk about brazen, huh?"

"Brazen was that shiny convertible in the garage. Courtesy of tithe money, I'll bet."

" 'Lay not up treasures . . .' " McLeod said.

"Tell that to your countrymen," Passos said.

"What? What does that even mean? Where is this coming from?"

Passos kept quiet, kept walking. He slowed down to stop at the next door but his companion kept on, as he had some two months earlier, one of the first afternoons of the elders' companionship. As Passos watched McLeod march down the street, straight-backed, proud, he too remembered. His long search to find the open *padaría*. The Guaraná, one of the few things McLeod kept in the fridge. Their first argument, their first amends. He watched McLeod reach the corner of the street now and disappear around it, not looking back. Elder Passos didn't call after him, though he did feel a brief tug of guilt in his chest. Also the feeling of a strategic error, a potentially costly moment of excess. He thought of Dos Santos, and in that instant he decided—yes, exactly as Dos Santos would do.

Passos hurried to the corner and got out to the main street just in time to see McLeod boarding a bus in the near distance. The buses were running regularly today, which made for one difference from the last time. But let that be the only difference. Passos caught the next outbound bus and stopped at the market en route to home.

He found his companion at his desk in the front room, with the blue grammar book lying open. Passos stood inside the doorway, panting. He held a case of Guaraná like a dumbbell in his right hand.

"A whole case, huh?" McLeod said. "Is Guaraná your standard peace offering?"

Elder Passos held still for the length of his companion's deliberating stare.

"I've already got a case," McLeod said.

Passos crossed the room and placed the soda on his own desk. He removed two cans, held one out for McLeod. "You can never have too much, right?"

After a pause McLeod took the can and hefted it. "It's luke-warm."

"Are you worried thou will spew it out of thy mouth?" Passos said, smiling.

McLeod gave a little smile of his own. He went to the kitchen and came back with two cans from the refrigerator, icy to the touch, already beading. Passos sat down across from his companion as they drank—gulped, in McLeod's case. He finished in half the time as Elder Passos, tipping back his head and emptying the dregs in a quick practiced shaking motion, the can like a vibrato instrument. Then he brought the can down on the desk with a loud percussive violent *smack* that made Passos jump and McLeod smile, for another moment anyway. His companion's face settled into a look of expectation. Finally he said, "Well? Are you going to actually apologize? Are you going to at least explain yourself?"

Passos continued to sip his Guaraná. "Explain what?"

"Why you've been such a jerk lately. Why you've been after me with all this anti-American crap. I thought you were on my side."

"It's not about sides, Elder McLeod."

"What's it about then? Where did that line about the pastor even come from?"

"I shouldn't have said that. I am sorry about that. It's just . . . Well, I've been a little frustrated lately, and maybe that had some-thing to do with it. I've been frustrated with the way you've han-dled things with Josefina and Leandro. It seems like all you do is play the pessimist, all you do is criticize."

"What's there to be optimistic about, Elder? You threw Josefina under the bus with the president. Now we're waiting for Leandro, which means we're waiting for a miracle."

Elder Passos took a long, a very long, draft of his Guaraná. It had never been clearer to him why McLeod—despite his intelligence and experience, despite his diligence, for the most part—remained a junior so late into his mission. He actually believed that a heroic stand against the president's new rules could have made a difference, could have turned aside directives that the president had received from his superiors, who had received them from their superiors, and so on, all the way up to the General Authorities, all the way up to the Prophet himself. McLeod believed that a pair of foot soldiers could deflect the sheer tonnage of that institutional momentum. He knew nothing about leadership, nothing about organizations. He knew nothing of consequence about the church he put on the airs of an expert about. Elder Passos wanted to say this—he suddenly *ached* to say it—but he didn't. He thought of Dos Santos. Convivial Dos Santos. Conciliatory. *Cunning.* Beloved on the mission, then off to America, taking it for all it's worth, but no more.

Passos took a finishing gulp of his soda, then smacked the can down on the desk in imitation of McLeod. "You say we're waiting for a miracle with Leandro?" he said. "Well, we're not. We're *planning* for one."

Elder Passos took his weekly planner from his breast pocket and flattened it out on McLeod's desk.

Plan or no plan, apology or no apology, Elder McLeod felt shaky. He didn't know how to set his feet anymore. He was uncertain around Passos, unsteady, and often angry, an anger that swelled his other anxieties, an unsteadiness that unsteadied everything.

In the last few weeks he had regressed into ogling, a little more hesitant than before, and more furtive, but somehow that only made it feel worse. McLeod still made a conscious effort, despite his lapses, to avoid all but Josefina's pupils, but he had largely ceased such efforts with the newsstands downtown, the racy billboards, the pornographic call cards in phone booths. All the blurs resolving into images now. Or the women from Passos's magazine bubbling up like molten to the troubled surface of his mind. He had even started masturbating again: three times in the shower, twice into nests of toilet paper, always turned away from the Jesus pictures on the mirror, but still. Five times in two weeks —it worried McLeod. It made him feel dirty, atavistic. It made him feel out of control.

That night Elder McLeod got up to urinate, or so he told himself as he crept out of the darkened bedroom. He closed the door behind him, kept the light off in the bathroom as he sat on the toilet and quietly peed against the side of the bowl. When he finished, he sat in the dark, brooding, his undergarments pooled around his ankles. He began to work at himself with a sort of carelessness, as if conscious intention were the only path to sin. He didn't even know if he believed in sin. He moved faster. He thought vaguely of the insults he had suffered in the last weeks, the insults that God had *allowed* him to suffer, and underneath it all the images marshaled themselves—billboards, call cards, Passos's magazine—a ghostly mix of bodies, a ménage, spinning faster and faster as he neared his climax, and suddenly, and he was already going now, it had already happened: Josefina.

But it couldn't have been. McLeod refused to believe it. Josefina was the last person he would have admitted into such lurid imaginings. He wanted no persons at all, only bodies. He looked down at the wilted dark penis in his hand, the white bloom of toilet paper, and he shuddered.

———————

The next morning, a P-Day, Elder McLeod leaned on Passos to accompany him to Sweeney's ("I thought we agreed you'd go there less," Passos said), then he leaned on Sweeney ("Where've you been?" Sweeney said) to accompany him to the mission president's office in Belo Horizonte. On the bus ride up, and then over lunch, McLeod outlined the basic problems for his friend. A capricious companion. A stranded investigator. All the anti-American garbage. And a feeling of waste, still, and doubt, still.

"I mean . . ." McLeod said. "Do you know what I mean?" He looked up from his buffet plate to see Sweeney bearing down on a forkful of rice and beans.

Sweeney paused, ticked his eyes up. "You mean how you think too much? Yeah, I know."

"Don't you ever doubt? When things go wrong for you and you

look to those bedrock truths, don't you ever wonder where they are, or even *what* they are? Don't you ever listen to yourself teaching or street contacting and think, What in the *hell* am I saying?"

Sweeney put down his fork. "Why would I want to think that, McLeod? I've had a happy life so far, and I've got a beautiful girl waiting for me at home. We're going to get married in the temple, we'll have kids, and we'll give them happy lives too. Why would I want to jeopardize all that? Why would I want to mess that up? The gospel *works*, McLeod. That's what matters. And that's what I've been trying to tell you."

"That's *not* what you told me," McLeod said. "That night with you and Kimball, the night of our Slump Day party? Do you remember what you said? You said if I wasn't going to at least try to believe it then why the hell stay out here? Why even finish the mission? *That's* what you said."

Sweeney sighed, went back to his food. "I don't know if I have the energy for this anymore."

"The gospel might work," McLeod said, "or it might work for *you*, but that's not the same as it being true. That's not the same as actually believing it. Because for me, as far as I'm concerned, if I don't believe it, it doesn't work. I can't just act my way through it anymore, recite the lines. If I could do that, who knows, maybe I would. Maybe I wouldn't have all these problems. I wouldn't be on my way to the mission president to confess, you know, the capital-P problem . . ."

Sweeney looked up from his plate again, eyes brightening.

"And don't you smile at me like that," McLeod said, but he smiled himself. "Look at you—*now* you're interested. You are certifiable, you know that?"

"The capital-*P* problem?" Sweeney said. "You mean——" He started into the hand motion.

McLeod cut him short. "Yes," he said. "The very one."

"Yeah?" Sweeney's smirk grew wider, but he tilted his head. "You're not stashing girlie mags or anything, are you?"

"No."

"Well, okay, then. What's the big deal? Are you really going to town or something?"

"It's complicated."

"It's complicated?"

McLeod nodded, held Sweeney's gaze for several poker-faced seconds. He wouldn't give anything about Josefina. He couldn't. After a minute more Sweeney shrugged, and returned to his buffet plate.

———————

An hour later Elder McLeod sat in front of President Mason in the office he'd stalked out of two weeks earlier. He wanted absolution—he wanted a kind of cure—and there was only President Mason to play priest to McLeod's penitent.

"I know you're probably surprised to see me," he began.

President Mason's wide round face stretched tauter than usual, his eyebrows were raised. He wore a ready, almost open expression. He leaned back in his chair.

"I mean," McLeod continued, "I suppose I didn't, I don't know, acquit myself very well the last time I was here."

President Mason lifted his hand. "You certainly didn't, Elder, but this isn't necessary. It was a difficult situation. I know these new rules will help the work in the long run, but for now they're very difficult. I understand that. In fact, I'll admit that I admired the way you fought for your investigator." President Mason lowered his head a bit. "But what did you really come here to tell me?"

"I'm angry," McLeod said, and his words surprised him. He kept speaking, and the words kept surprising. He was listening to sounds from some other person's mouth. He confessed all the images and the masturbation, though he didn't mention Josefina by name. He confessed the stagnation he felt, the sense of waste. He even talked about his father, how he longed to be like him—he longed for that steadiness, that ruddered certainty—and yet he didn't believe any more than he had two years earlier, before he even decided on a mission.

"But why are you *angry*?" President Mason said. "You said you're angry. I don't hear that in these cases very often."

"I guess I feel like I should be changing by now," McLeod said, "but I know I'm not."

President Mason switched over to English. "It doesn't come like lightning, you know. It might not fully happen during your mission—it might not happen for years. A deadline wasn't promised. That wasn't written into the contract."

His father had said things like this, things just like this. McLeod looked down, trying to reset the thought, but he was already back in his father's office at the church. The stern assignments, the little pep talk. *You'll feel like you're falling, because you are.* A week after that McLeod had gone to Jen's house, a surprise visit, a sort of ambush. Jen in the lighted frame of her doorway, her form backlit at the edges but mostly dark. He couldn't make out her eyes. She wore a jacket and what looked like red pajama bottoms. Her parents were home, she said. Upstairs.

"I wanted to say I'm sorry," he said.

"Okay," she said. Then silence. "Is that all?"

"Can I come in, Jen? I want to apologize properly."

"I don't think coming in is a good idea."

On the other side of the cul-de-sac a rasping motorcycle started its engine. McLeod turned around to look, the close-set headlights like feral eyes. The motorcyclist revved loudly, then peeled out down the street.

"Nuisance," Jen mumbled, and when McLeod turned around again she was shutting the door.

Right in his face, he had told his father. But his father was unfazed. "She doesn't have to forgive you," he said. "It isn't a contract. It isn't about her—it's about you."

McLeod blinked several times in the mission president's office. He pursed his face to remember that the words in the air belonged to President Mason, the man bearing down on him with his watery blue eyes and his round, moony face. "A testimony *will* happen," he was saying. "You've just got to be patient."

McLeod's equilibrium returned. "Maybe it won't, though. Maybe it never will happen for me. Maybe some people can believe, and others simply can't. The ground is fertile for some but infertile—"

The president shook his head. "That's false doctrine, Elder. That's predestination. Everyone is *capable* of belief if they're worthy of it. To say otherwise is to deny our Heavenly Father's plan for us, and His love for us. The Lord will open your heart, Elder, but it'll happen on the Lord's timetable, not yours."

President Mason reached down to the black valise at the side of his desk and rooted around in it. He produced a small, yellow, laminated card. "Your testimony will come sooner or later, Elder McLeod. I know that. God lives and loves us and wants nothing more than for us to return to live with Him in the eternities. I know that too." President Mason held up the card. "And as for your other problem—read these tips and follow them to the letter." He stood up and moved to the door with the card. "They're just tips, as I said, but they've worked for others. The operative doctrine here is that God lives and loves us. He wants us to be worthy to return to Him. I'm glad you came in, Elder. I'm glad we talked."

The president pressed the yellow card into Elder McLeod's hand, gave him a perfunctory hug, and ushered him out into the foyer, where Sweeney slouched on the floral-patterned couch. Sweeney straightened up. The president showed him a tight smile. He said to the both of them, still in English, "I trust your respective companions are together today?"

McLeod and Sweeney nodded.

"Missionary exchanges are okay now and then," the president said, "but remember that companionship assignments don't end on P-Day."

Sweeney nodded again, sat up even straighter, in the same spot and the same position, McLeod realized, that Josefina had sat in two weeks earlier. President Mason turned from the couch and said to McLeod, "I never did ask how that investigator of yours is doing, did I? What was her name again? I'm sorry I'm so bad with names."

"Josefina."

"Yes, Josefina. How is she? How's her husband? Is he progressing at all?"

"Not really," McLeod said. "We're still trying, though. We've got a few ideas. We've got a tentative appointment this coming Saturday, actually."

"Good. Keep up the good work. Keep trying. The both of you. Goodbye, Elders."

After the president went back into the bishop's office Elder Sweeney sprang off the couch and snatched the yellow card from McLeod's hand. "I knew it," he hissed. " 'The Guide to Self-Control!' Ooooh, and laminated now."

McLeod put a finger to his lips and motioned toward the door. Outside, he asked for the card back. "I haven't had a chance to even see what it is."

"You don't know 'The Guide to Self-Control'?" Sweeney said. "Dude, this is a *classic* of Mormon literature! Anybody who's really going to town gets this card."

"And how are you such an expert?"

"I've been going to town my whole mission," Sweeney said. "A little different for me, though, isn't it? I'm thinking of Tiff, and that's practically kosher."

"Is that right?"

"T minus four months to homecoming," he said, handing over the card. "T minus five months to the wedding."

THE GUIDE TO SELF-CONTROL

1. Never touch the intimate parts of your body except during normal toilet processes. Avoid being alone as much as possible.

2. When you bathe, do not admire yourself in a mirror. Never stay in the bath more than five or six minutes—just long enough to bathe and dry and dress.

3. When in bed, if that is where you have your problem for the most part, dress yourself for the night so securely that you cannot easily touch your vital parts, and so that it would be difficult and time-consuming for you to remove these clothes.

4. If the temptation seems overpowering while you are in bed, get out of bed and go into the kitchen and fix yourself a snack, even if it is in the middle of the night, and even if you are not hungry, and despite your fears of gaining weight.

5. Put wholesome thoughts into your mind at all times. Read good books—church books, Scriptures, Sermons of the Brethren. Make a daily habit of reading at least one chapter of Scripture, preferably from one of the four Gospels in the New Testament, or the Book of Mormon. The four Gospels—Matthew, Mark, Luke, and John—can be helpful because of their uplifting qualities.

6. Pray. But when you pray, don't pray about this problem, for that will tend to keep it in your mind more than ever. Pray for faith, pray for understanding of the Scriptures, pray for the General Authorities, your friends, your family, but keep the problem out of your mind by not mentioning it ever—not in conversation with others, not in your prayers. Keep it out of your mind!

On Saturday morning the elders left the apartment after companionship study and prayer. It was now March 1, the worst of summer behind them, and McLeod could take heart at the sounds of birds beginning to chatter again in the standing-up sun, returned after the long weeks of swelter and animal silence. The world was just a little more balanced now, a little more calm.

They were en route to pick up Rômulo. He had agreed to

accompany them to Josefina's in accordance with the mission's newest rule, which Passos insisted that they keep, of course. Of course, if their surprise visit turned into an actual visit, a visit that featured Leandro, they wouldn't *need* a chaperone, would they? The very fact that they'd planned to take Rômulo along meant they expected the plan not to work. Elder McLeod tried to check these thoughts—tried. But the good money put Josefina at the front door as her husband escaped, slithered out the back. On some level McLeod didn't even *want* Leandro to be there. He didn't think of him as a problem to be solved, as he knew Passos did, so much as a problem to be avoided.

The elders passed the first bus stop, the Pentecostal church, the lumberyard and the empty lots beside it, and all the while Elder Passos made attempts at levity. "Elder White-*ee*," he chanted softly. "Your hair is invisible, your head is free . . . of visible hair . . ." These attempts carried the force of nostalgia, a nostalgia for the recent. They recalled a time not more than a few weeks past when the elders could joke with each other with impunity, without fear of awakening latent grievances or tripping one wire by its mere proximity to another. McLeod remembered the first time Passos had called him whitey, something only Maurilho had called him, and Maurilho did it with love.

So do I. Of course.

Today it annoyed McLeod to hear the word in Passos's mouth, but he swallowed his annoyance. At least his companion was trying.

"Or maybe I should call you Elder Blond-*ee*," Passos said. "Wouldn't that be more descriptive?"

"I think I prefer 'whitey,' actually."

"Elder White-*ee*," Passos began again.

They passed the other bus stop, and the paint store, approaching the side street that fed into the convoluted back way they sometimes took to get to Maurilho's. Passos started down the side street now, but McLeod called him back. They were going to pick up Rômulo, right?

"Yes," Passos said, "but let's go this way." He pointed down the strip of bleached asphalt that curved away behind orange-brick property walls.

"Maurilho's right off the main road," McLeod said. "This way's faster." He looked at his watch—half past ten—then turned out his wrist to show the time to Passos. "We can't afford the scenic route, Elder. We want to try to catch Leandro before lunch, don't we?"

Passos glanced behind him, then up ahead at the drive-through's unlit sign that rose high above the property wall.

"Is it the drive-through?" McLeod said. "Nothing's happening there now."

Passos still hesitated.

"You won't even walk past it during the day?" McLeod said.

"I'd prefer not to."

"It's almost ten thirty-five." McLeod held out his watch again.

"Fine, let's go," Passos said, and he caught up to McLeod and overtook him, now at a decidedly hurried pace.

They knocked at Maurilho's a few minutes later. Rômulo came to the front gate in his Sunday best: a short-sleeved white dress shirt, a blue tie, brown dress pants, neatly creased, and matching brown loafers that looked to have been polished, the leather dully shining in the sun. Rômulo also carried a shoulder bag with the strap running diagonally down his shirtfront and behind his tie, just as the missionaries wore their bags.

"Look at this guy," McLeod said. "All he needs now is a name tag!"

"You ready to go?" Passos said.

Rômulo nodded, blushing. He pulled the door shut behind him. Passos said they were short on time. Did Rômulo have money for bus fare? He did. At the end of the street Passos and McLeod turned left onto the main road. Rômulo called after them: "It's actually faster to backtrack to the bus stop there." He pointed right.

The elders stopped, exchanged a look. At length Passos nodded, then the three of them retraced their steps along the sidewalk that passed the drive-through on their right.

"What's in the bag?" McLeod asked Rômulo.

"Mostly my scriptures."

"Wow," he said. "Will you look at this guy? And on a Saturday morning too. I figured you'd have just rolled out of bed after another night of partying. All that wild partying you do, right?"

"Yeah, well," Rômulo said, and he gestured up at the drive-through sign just as the three of them passed under it. "I did get woken up last night, though it wasn't any party I'd ever go to. The noises from this place, man. You wouldn't think they could carry that far. I had to get out of bed and shut the window."

"What do you mean?" McLeod said. "Do they have loudspeakers or something?"

"Loudspeakers? No, I mean the . . . you know . . ." He raised his eyebrows, grimaced a bit. After a minute more Rômulo cocked his head at McLeod. "You know what a drive-through is, don't you?"

"I'm pretty sure," McLeod said, just as he wasn't anymore. He had first assumed that the lot contained a drive-through movie theater, a deserted one, or maybe an adult movie house that opened for business only after hours.

Passos scoffed. "I thought you knew what it was. It's not a drive-through like McDonald's, Elder. You don't buy your American burgers there."

"You buy sex," Rômulo said. "It's a brothel. Or I guess you could bring your mistress there in your car. I think they've got stalls where you can park, or rooms. I'm not sure. I haven't been, obviously. I can tell you all about those noises, though, especially on the weekends. Man are they terrible."

Elder Passos and Rômulo kept walking, but Elder McLeod stood moored a few yards beyond the sign. He couldn't even pretend to nonchalance. He had never actually seen a physical house of prostitution—he could hardly believe they really existed—and now here one stood in the broad bright daylight. It had been here the whole time he had been here, less than two miles from the apartment, hiding out in the open. Had it not been for the sign Elder McLeod would have assumed that the brown stucco wall enclosed an abandoned lot. All at once it made sense why his companion preferred to detour around this particular stretch of road. It was impossible to behold even the walls now without thinking of the sinfulness and impossible bravery of some men. McLeod ticked his gaze up the length of the sign like a mariner looking for directions, and a different sky wheeled into view.

His companion was saying something. He said it again. On the third time McLeod recognized his name. "McLeod! Earth to Elder McLeod!"

"What?"

"I thought we were hurrying for Leandro. What are you doing?"

"Nothing," McLeod said.

Elder Passos checked his watch as they turned onto Josefina's street. Quarter past eleven. If they were lucky enough to find Leandro at home, they'd have just enough time for a lesson before lunch. Though "lesson" was too formal a word for what Passos had in mind. He wanted a low-key conversation, a chat, really, which still managed to wind upward toward the spiritual, slowly, almost imperceptibly, like a graceful circular staircase. He planned to end with a scripture, not read aloud—again, too formal—but rather recited from memory, from a place of long and heartfelt conviction. *Therefore everyone who hears these words of mine and puts them into practice is like a wise man who built his house on the rock* . . . Then Passos would bear his testimony and then, if the moment proved right—if the Spirit indicated—he would invite Leandro himself to say the closing prayer. Maybe they would even kneel around the coffee table, all of them, in a gesture of added humility. And if Josefina invited the elders to stay on for lunch? If she insisted? Elder Passos already knew what he would say: They had another appointment, they were very sorry. It mattered less that this wasn't the strict truth; what mattered was that they leave the house while the Spirit was still a palpable presence, the air like a warm oceanic buoyancy to surrender to, to float away on.

They arrived at Josefina's door. Passos went to knock but his companion stopped him.

"Let the honorary missionary try," McLeod said. He brought Rômulo in between them, within knocking distance of the door.

"We don't have time," Passos said, rapping on the metal. The sound reverberated and fell away, and in the wake of it the silence felt accusing. "We've got forty minutes if we're lucky."

Yet again Passos startled himself by the tone in his voice, not explanatory but defensive. For a moment it seemed like Rômulo stood between them more to head off a confrontation than to accompany a missionary lesson.

They heard the front door scrape open, footsteps in their direction, the tread somewhat heavier than usual. The steps left off just short of the door.

"Who is it?" Leandro called.

Passos had expected Josefina to come to the door, if anyone did, and now in his surprise he let the question hang.

"Who is it?" Leandro asked again.

McLeod moved to answer but Passos warned him off with a sharp wave. He lowered his voice beyond recognition, and said, "Electric company here."

Elder Passos ignored the curious smile from Rômulo, the outright glare from McLeod. He didn't care about that; he couldn't afford to. The door latch clattered and the door swung open.

Leandro stood in the rectangular frame, confused at first, then darkening with recognition. He wore green soccer shorts, a white tank top, and the same thick goatee he'd had the evening after the finals several weeks ago. The muscles in his arms, his entire body, tensed as he looked from his companion to Rômulo to him, and back to his companion.

Passos said, "Leandro." He raised his hand like a footballer acknowledging his foul to the referee. "Leandro, listen, we just want to talk to you. We haven't seen you in a long time, you know? Do you have a few minutes before lunch? Just to talk?"

"Go away," Leandro said, his voice like gravel, rough and hard and loose. Elder Passos couldn't tell if the smell of *cachaça* carried on his words or if it came off his body, deep-down pervaded, seeped in over the course of weeks and months and years. The sweet-sour stench of too much alcohol. The body never forgets.

"Leandro," Passos said, "please—"

"I said go away. We don't want you here. *She* doesn't want you here either. She just can't say it. But I can. Go. Go!" He flung his hand out, pointing, barely missing Rômulo's face. Rômulo flinched.

"And who are you anyway?" Leandro said to him. "Are you supposed to be the electric man?"

"I'm Rômulo," he said. "Maurilho and Rose's son? I met you once in—"

"So there's three of you now? *Three* of you here for my wife?"

Elder McLeod took a sudden step forward. "Hey! Hey. Don't you start that."

Leandro took the same step backward, out of instinct, but he more than made up for it as he moved to within inches of McLeod's face, straightening, stiffening, nostrils flaring. McLeod held his ground on the stoop, returned the stare. Elder Passos felt suddenly disoriented, unprepared. He tried to interrupt the current that coursed between McLeod and Leandro; he put up both hands like a traffic officer. "Listen, listen, listen." He said it again. "Leandro? Leandro, please listen!"

The man slid his eyes, slowly, in Passos's direction. He kept his head straight, kept McLeod in front of him.

"We didn't want . . ." Passos said. "We didn't come here to upset you. We're your friends, okay? We just wanted to say hello again. We've missed you. That's all we wanted to say. Okay?"

Leandro's voice came even lower now, a growl. "We don't want you here. I don't want you here. Josefina doesn't want you here."

And just then Josefina stepped into the front doorway. She stood half in shadow, half in light, but Passos could still make out the beginnings of a stomach under her T-shirt. She called across the courtyard: "Is everything okay, honey?" She paused. "Elders?"

Leandro turned toward his wife as McLeod shouted past him, "Josefina, it's us. It's the Elders!" Again the over-intimacy in his companion's voice—even now Passos heard it—until Leandro turned back around and crowded that much more into McLeod's face, a stiff finger at his sternum. He pushed McLeod back—hard jabs, short, jabbing steps. "You don't fucking talk to my wife, Elder Gringo! You don't even fucking talk—"

Leandro doubled forward and made a sound like a lowing cow, his eyes screwed tight shut. Only then did Passos see his companion's arm buried elbow-deep in Leandro's stomach. McLeod reared back and drove his fist home again. The lowing renewed, ran down to a wheeze, then Leandro tipped forward and collapsed onto the stoop.

Josefina shouted, "Elders! What did you do? Get out of here!" She rushed to her husband and braced her hands on his back as he pitched and heaved for breath. "Are you all right, Leandro? Honey?" When she looked up she glowered to see them still backing away. "I said get out of here, Elders! Don't come back!"

McLeod turned and ran, and Passos and Rômulo followed after.

———————

Two, maybe three minutes later. Passos and Rômulo at the bus stop. Rômulo bent double over his knees, breathing hard. Passos too. He took great drags of air, his lungs burned. For all the walking he and McLeod did every day, Elder Passos lacked the stamina for full-tilt running.

He looked up at the sound of an outbound city bus rumbling onto the main road a few blocks away. The big rasping thing picked up speed only to slow down as it neared them, pushing up a wave of heat and sound. Elder Passos didn't even try to speak over it. He reached into his pocket for bus fare but Rômulo refused it, pointed instead down the street. "You saw him go that way?"

Passos nodded. Rômulo climbed onto the bus and from the stairwell turned around. He showed a weak, worried smile to Elder Passos. Then he disappeared behind the sun-dark glass of the bus's closing doors.

———————

Elder Passos found his companion at the corrugated rail by the riverbank, a familiar spot. McLeod sat with his gaze on the river, eyes vacant as a doll's, the water pulled and corded by the current. Passos sat down beside him, regarding him sidelong, waiting, waiting.

After a long time McLeod said, "What's there to say?"

"Nothing now," Passos said. "You made very sure of that, didn't you?"

Silence.

"*Didn't* you? You and your diplomacy of the balled-up fist. It's the American way, isn't it?"

More silence.

"Here we are trying to publish peace, but I should have known better, huh? Elder? Don't you think? *Huh?*"

Elder McLeod kept his eyes on the river. For a moment the sounds from the road faded to nothing and only the quick sleek burble of the water floated up to them.

"Peace," Passos said in English, as much to himself as to McLeod. He laughed. "*Peace*. Listen to the word in your language, Elder." He repeated it again in a nasal, sawed-off Yankee accent. "Peeeace. Peeeeeeeze. It doesn't even sound like English, does it? It's an impostor in your language. Peeeeeze. Peeeeeeeze. Peeeeeeeeeze." Elder Passos grated the word just inches from McLeod's ear. "Peeeeeze," he said again, louder, "*Peeeeeeeeeze*," like a crazed insect, almost shouting it, "*Peeeeeeeeeeeze!*"

McLeod swung around and took fistfuls of Passos's shirtfront. "Stop it!"

"Or what? Or what? You'll hit me too? Huh?"

Elder McLeod relinquished his grip, turned back to the river. But Passos kept after him, yelling at full voice, full up with righteous anger. "Do you have any idea what you did back there? You just beat up an investigator in front of another investigator—the investigator's wife! Do you know what that makes us? The both of us? Elder McLeod? I'm talking to you! I'm your senior companion and I am talking to you!"

"He was filth," McLeod whispered. "You said it yourself."

"So you clobber him? That's the only option? You don't talk about it, or walk away? You have to clobber him and ruin everything we worked for? Josefina, Elder! Did you hear what she said? 'Get out of here! Don't come back!' *She* said that, not Leandro. And because of you. *You* are the one who's thrown her under the bus. Do you hear me? Do you hear me!"

Elder McLeod didn't answer, didn't move. He just stared at the water, staring through it, and after a while Elder Passos started staring through it too. His worst anger gave out on him like a candle flame extinguished in its own melt. They sat there, the two of them, in silence. Twelve o'clock came and went. Twelve thirty. At one o'clock Elder Passos rose from the embankment guard and McLeod got up and followed after him. The elders walked to the nearest *padaría* and bought cheese sandwiches and ate them at a table near the open-air storefront. An afternoon rain came on, turning the sidewalks brown and muddy and the streets slate gray. The speckled line between dry and wet came right up to the threshold of the storefront's little eating space: rain greased the metal track of the roll-up gate, then inched past it as the drops got thicker and a beaded curtain dropped down from the awning, started spraying the table's legs. The drops began kicking up a floor-level mist; it coated McLeod's shoes, Passos noticed. At one point a wind gust blew a scrim of wet all over them. Passos scraped back his chair, shucked his pants. McLeod sat motionless, holding his hard roll in front of him for a long, absent minute. Then he took a soggy bite.

The sky cleared half an hour later. The elders left the *padaría* and walked through downtown with no particular purpose or direction, the streets still wet from the rain, dull mirrors, and the sun in them now, a strange effect. Cars passed by and dragged shallow wakes of whitewater after them, each one like the sound of paper ripping. The sidewalk dust-turned-to-mud formed a thin brown paste on the pavement, forming a collage of footprints in turn. Elder Passos tried to fit his steps into steps that had gone before him.

Finally McLeod spoke. "I want that Dr. Seuss book back that I gave you. It was a gift from my mother. I'm taking it back when we get home."

Passos laughed, said, "Fine by me," like he didn't care at all.

"Good," McLeod said, "and we'll cut out the English practice too, all right?"

"Fine by me," Passos said.

"And maybe I'll just write my parents and tell them you changed your mind about wanting to stay with them? You wouldn't like being around all those violent Americans."

"You can do whatever you want—" Passos felt a catch in his throat, then a surge of private anger. He didn't want to feel venal, dependent. Not on McLeod. Not today. "It turns out I don't need your charity anyway. You or your family's."

"It's not charity," McLeod said, "and whatever it is, it's not mine. It's mostly my mother's offer, but then again she is my mother. She values my opinion. Maybe I was wrong about you. Maybe I'll tell her that. I thought you wanted to go to America, but I guess I was wrong. It sounds like you'd really hate it there."

"Well," Passos said. He only hung back for a second. "Well, Elder McLeod, maybe you're right. With you around the house— yeah, you're probably right."

"Oh I wouldn't be around," McLeod said. "Is that what you thought? I'll be long gone by then. Away at college, and a good one too, and with my own room, I'll make sure of it. And reading great books, lots of them, and not burning a single one—books that don't begin every sentence with 'And it came to pass' or 'Verily, verily, I say unto you.' And all the rest of this? Brazil? The mission? You? You'll all be a memory, a little *speck* on the horizon."

Passos made the same laugh as before, a little snort. He watched the sun pass out of the puddles in the street into another drift of clouds.

That night at the apartment Elder Passos dropped the Dr. Seuss book on McLeod's desk as he read there. The book made a loud, sharp smack against the wood.

"I've got most of it memorized anyway," Passos said.

"Oh you do?" McLeod said. "Is that so? Because I do too. What's your favorite part? Recite it for me, Elder? Please?"

Elder Passos turned back for the bedroom without a word. " 'Thou shalt not bear false witness,' " his companion called after him. "You and your false witness, huh? But don't worry, Elder Passos. 'Don't worry, don't stew. Just go right along, you'll start happening too. Oh! The places you'll go . . .' "

The next morning Elder Passos found on his desk the blue hardcover grammar book, *Vocabulário e gramática avançada*. A handwritten note bookmarked the first page: *You can have your gift back too. Only fair. I've got most of it memorized anyway.*

Passos had barely finished reading the note before he crumpled it and started, with the book in hand, for the kitchen trash.

At church that day the elders waited through sacrament meeting, Sunday school, a joint Priesthood-Relief Society meeting, waited through the full three hours of church, hoping against hope that

Josefina might just be late. After church they met Rose and Maurilho in the hallway. Rômulo stood behind his parents. He nodded at Passos and McLeod, a little sheepish, then studied the floor.

"Josefina wasn't here today?" Rose said. She brought the corners of her mouth up in a wincing half smile, a comforting, sympathetic look meant for the both of them. But Passos turned to his companion and cocked his head, determined that the sympathy, and the blame, should belong to McLeod alone.

"No, I guess she didn't come," McLeod said. "We had a problem yesterday with—well, I had a problem with—"

"Rômulo told us," Maurilho said. "But listen, we had an idea. What do you say to this? You let things cool for another few days, then you come over to our place on, say, Thursday for a big dinner, and we invite Leandro and Josefina to join us. What do you think?"

Elder Passos turned back to McLeod, his same head-cock as before, his faux-solicitous stare. He watched with satisfaction as his companion's face flushed, his jaws gripping, ungripping.

Rose spoke up to fill the silence. "Also, I was thinking I could go over there and personally invite them. At least Josefina. Since it's at our house, you know? If you thought that would be helpful, of course."

McLeod turned to face him now. "Well, companion? Senior companion?"

"No, no," Passos said, "you decide. I'm delegating this to your discretion."

"Fine," he said to Rose. "Let's try it. It can't hurt to try, right?"

"I could even pick them up," Maurilho said. "And you guys too if you wanted. I'll be downtown already. I've got day shifts this week. And I finally got the car fixed, did I tell you?" He addressed McLeod more than Passos, as usual, rubbing his thumb back and forth against his index and middle fingers. "I'm flush now, did you hear?"

McLeod smiled a little. "How is the new job?"

"Ah, you know, mop here, sweep there. It's a job. A stopgap, really."

"It's a blessing from God," Rose said.

"So we're on for Thursday?" Maurilho said. "I get off at seven. I could pick people up a little after that. Sound good?"

McLeod looked over at Passos again. Passos held to his mask of false cheeriness.

"Okay," McLeod said. "That sounds good."

"Great," Maurilho said, and he clapped a hand on Elder McLeod's shoulder, leading him down the hallway ahead of Passos. "Let's just hope that the world doesn't end before Thursday, what with that loon you've got in the White House . . ." and so on into a gentle diatribe that Passos didn't join in on and that McLeod, for a change, didn't seem to mind.

On Thursday afternoon the elders detoured around the drive-through en route to Rose's house. They talked to her outside on the front stoop since Maurilho was already at work and Rômulo was still at school. They asked how the personal invitation had gone. Rose dropped her head, said no one had answered. Three times she went to the house, and every time the same.

"Did you say who it was?" Passos asked her.

"Yes," Rose said. "Every time."

"What did you say?"

"I'd knock on the door and call out 'Hello, Josefina? It's Rose.' I'd try that two or three times, and I'd wait a long time between each try."

Elder Passos sighed, just slightly, and shook his head, his hands on his hips, arms akimbo. He noticed his companion out of the corner of his eye, head hung and sad-looking too. They had both been hoping against hope.

"I'm sorry," Rose said.

"It's not your fault," McLeod said.

"I know, but I still feel sorry. The two of you will still come tonight, though, right? I'm making *feijoada*. We won't be able to eat it all by ourselves."

"Of course we'll come," Passos said. "We're grateful to you."

They shook hands with Rose and started back across the courtyard. Rose called after them, "Oh, and Elders? Maurilho said he still wants to pick you up downtown tonight, if that's where you'll be working? At around seven? I'm supposed to find out exactly where."

"Tell him we'll be knocking Rua Branca," Passos said. "And tell him thanks."

Passos noticed the flash of annoyance in his companion's eyes. He had made the decision about Rua Branca just now, and he'd done it despite the fact that McLeod had told him about his and his last companion's fruitless slog up that long, hilly street. But Passos knew nothing about McLeod's last companion, and he could imagine McLeod dragging his feet to various degrees of success. And he didn't mind annoying him either.

On the inbound bus the late sun slanted through the windows,

strobing the passengers in light and dark as the bus passed buildings, open lots, more buildings, overpasses, more open lots . . . A
few minutes later Elder Passos caught sight of Rua Branca through
the broad flat frame of the bus's windshield, the bus slowing down
for the last stop before the river. Rua Branca meant "White Street,"
though most of it lay in shadow now, dark gray against the gilded
orange houses and property walls. The street climbed up the sudden steep rise of the far bank, looking to Passos like the seam of a
giant basketball.

The bus came to a stop. Passos stood and moved to the middle
door.

"There's a closer place to get off," McLeod said. "On the other
side of the bridge."

"We're getting off here," Passos said, and started down the
stairs as the hydraulic doors sighed open.

In the street Passos turned away from the river and began
walking in the opposite direction. A moment later he heard his
companion behind him. Not a word of protest, no air through his
nose. He must have sensed where they were going.

"I figure we've got time," Passos said. "It's not even six yet.
Then we'll do Rua Branca."

The elders turned onto Josefina's street a minute later, both of
them slowing their pace. They took the last hundred yards to her
door in silence, walking at half speed, lightening their footfalls, as
if the house might spook and run away. At the door Elder McLeod
lowered his voice to ask Passos what he planned to say if someone
did answer.

Passos hovered his fist a few inches from the metal of the outer
door. "I'll say what the Spirit tells me to, Elder."

He knocked and waited. He knocked again. Waited. Nothing at all moved on the street, or on the main street behind them. The sound of the river came up. A few birds. Nothing at all from the house. After another minute Passos felt his companion's eyes on him. He turned and saw a look of apology on McLeod's face.

"Do you think she's heard us?" McLeod said.

"Hold on."

Passos knocked the door one more time, and hard, a loud series of raps that stung the air like gun reports. He waited again—a full minute, two—until something clacked from inside the courtyard. A door handle. The sound of the front door scraping back across the threshold and onto the poured-cement floor. The elders perked up, held their breaths. They heard a few staccato scrapes on the dirt of the courtyard. Then Josefina's voice in the air: "Who is it?"

Passos hesitated a moment.

McLeod said, "It's us, Josefina. The elders. We've come to apologize. We want to apologize to both of you. Josefina?"

The silence stretched out like something living, a dense, coiling, spring-loading thing. Passos stared straight at the door, steeled. But after a minute more his companion called out again, "Josefina? Please. Please let us apologize."

The steps in the dirt started up again, steadier now. They changed pitch, hitting cement, it sounded like, slapping once, twice, three times. The sound of sandals on the entryway floor. The sound of the front door clattering shut.

Passos stopped to check his watch again. Eight six-teen. He blew air through his mouth, turned around. Not half-way up the steep Rua Branca and the city below already looked miniature, the web of streets and alleyways radiating out from downtown like tiny tidy spokes, the kinks in the roads ironed out by distance. The rows of orange boxy houses, too, improved from this height, looking more like concerted complexes of houses, like freight cars running parallel to the roads. The whites on the teeming clotheslines shaded blue, and the river, dark brown since the sun had set, kept traces of the afterglow, warm seepages, like gold dust at the bottom of a prospector's tray. The scene was tranquil, quiet, and utterly at odds with Elder Passos's mood. Most of the people on Rua Branca weren't home, or at least didn't answer their doors; the few who did begged off in short order. It was an ordi-nary stretch of tracting, in other words, but tonight it was almost unbearable to Passos. The only solid presence in their teaching pool had sunk, and who could take her place on this street? The man who'd closed his door as fast as he'd opened it, saying "No, no, no, no—"? Or the woman who'd frowned at McLeod's Portu-guese, then at *his* Portuguese? "But I'm Brazilian," he'd said. The woman held out her palms, shook her head, shut the door. Or the little girl who'd peered through a gap in the gate, conferred with a parent back in the house, then returned to report that no one was home? "But *you're* home," Passos had said.

None of this should really have rankled Elder Passos, but all of it did—every no-show, every evasion, everything that reminded him of the drawing board they were back to, blank and black as a void. On top of it all, he was hungry: Maurilho was late. More than an hour late. Passos checked his watch again. Eight twenty. He lowered himself down onto his haunches, rested his arms on his knees, rocking at intervals, checking his watch.

"I've never understood how you guys can sit like that," McLeod said. "Doesn't that hurt your knees?"

Passos ignored him. "We're sure Maurilho didn't say another time? We're sure he said seven?"

"I'm sure."

"Has he ever stood you up before?"

McLeod shook his head.

"Well where is he then? I'm hungry."

McLeod stood behind him and a little farther out in the road. He squinted at something in the distance. "Is that his car?"

A small blue two-door was turning onto the avenue from a side street just above the bridge. The car hitched, then started accelerating up the hill, the whine of the engine mounting. As it got closer, Passos could make out Maurilho's face through the windshield, brows furrowed. The car skidded to a stop a little too close to them. Passos jumped to his feet, jumped back. His companion too.

Maurilho cranked down the car window. He glared at McLeod, said, "You see the news tonight, Elder? Huh?" There was violence in his voice.

McLeod pulled back his head on his neck, turtle-like. He studied the big man as if for clues. Then he turned to Passos, his face an appeal: Maurilho knew the missionary rules as well as anyone. What was he getting at? What were they missing?

"They're attacking Baghdad," Maurilho said, his eyes deadbolted on McLeod. "Your country, Elder. They're actually doing it. People are dying as we speak." Then he said, "Come on, get in the car. Come on!"

Elder Passos climbed into the backseat; McLeod got in beside him, leaving the front seat open. Maurilho whipped the car around and raced down the hill through downtown and the area beyond, the sights of the city blurring past. He kept up a torrent of facts, indictments, laments. He shot looks at McLeod in the rearview, the whites of his eyes flashing in the glass. Massive air strikes. The entire city on fire. Three hundred thousand troops on the ground. Thousands of refugees already, thousands dead. The oil fields closely guarded, of course. Did McLeod know what the Americans were calling it? Operation Iraqi Liberation. Maurilho slurred the abbreviating letters in English: "O-I-L. Do you recognize that word, Elder McLeod?"

It kept up all throughout dinner. Maurilho held his fork like a weapon, wielding it, stabbing it in the air at McLeod to accentuate his strongest words about "that warmonger president of yours": ". . . *bloodthirsty . . . lying . . . thieving . . . maniacal* . . . And *this* is why people hate America—this murderousness, this complete disregard for life! This is why they'll blow themselves up, why they'll fly planes into buildings—just to scare you!"

McLeod no longer looked to Passos for appeal, though Passos wished he would. He too felt angry about the invasion, but more than that he felt taken aback at the sheer force and duration of

Maurilho's tirade—the eyes boring into McLeod as if it were all his fault, the fork a silver blur. At first Elder Passos had felt *Amens* welling in him, more surges of satisfaction at the look on McLeod's face, the jaw muscles doing their furious contractions. Maurilho could outright excoriate America in a way that Elder Passos simply couldn't, or wouldn't, for fear of burning bridges with McLeod, or, if they'd been burned already, for fear of spoiling his chances at the assistantship by provoking an explosion in his companionship. But now even Passos felt to wave the white flag. What invisible satisfaction he'd taken in Maurilho's performance in the first act disappeared under the pilings-on of the second and third. "The United Blood-Spattered States of America! Belligerent from its very inception: one hand on a silver spoon, the other on a gun! A country *of* the violent, *by* the violent, *for* the violent! And I haven't even mentioned all the CIA killings—in Brazil, all over Latin America, all over the world! And all the coups you've incited, all the dictators you've installed, the blood money you've traded in . . ." and on and on.

The other faces at the table, like Passos's, tipped forward in helpless chastened expressions. They'd hazarded their appeals into the maelstrom—"Okay, let's change the subject," "Dad, come on," "Honey, *please*"—but to no effect. Elder Passos himself had broken in to say, "You know, this just reminds me how lucky we are to have the gospel as our guide, an authority *above* any earthly tribunal."

"A lot of good it'll do the Iraqis tonight," Maurilho had said, and right back on the warpath. He seemed to have narrowed his vision and focus until Rômulo and Rose and Elder Passos all melted away, and only he and McLeod remained—he, leaning forward across the table into his points, and McLeod, leaning back, a spreading smile on his face. Just then McLeod shifted in his seat. He rested his cheek in the cradle of his fingers as if to strike the dreamy listener pose.

Maurilho paused. "You think this is a joke? You think this is all some damn *joke*?"

Rose scraped back her chair in the tiny silence that followed and retrieved from the kitchen counter a molded *dolce de leite*. None of them had made any progress in their meals, the black beans and rice and pork parts heaped on their plates beside potatoes and carrots—a fancy dinner, a sign of changed fortunes. Rose placed the dessert in the center of the table like a peace offering. "Please. I made it special."

Maurilho said, "I just can't believe . . ." and he trailed off. He watched as his wife cut into the dense brown mold.

"You're not done, are you? Oh no, Professor," McLeod said. He spoke in a grand voice, an orator's voice. "Oh Professor, please don't stop! You mustn't! What other searing insights have you been hiding from us? All this time with a genius in our midst! What other pearls of wisdom has your eighth-grade education endowed you with? Was it eighth grade, Maurilho? Or did you get as far as ninth? All the more reason for you to continue! Tell us your secrets that we too may have a chance to one day become a *janitor*. Please, Professor, I beg you. Please go on."

Maurilho stiffened in his chair, turning hard, magnetic. He drew all the silence in the room to him, and the wide-eyed stares. Elder Passos, Rômulo, Rose, holding a butter knife just above the flan—all of them turned from McLeod to Maurilho.

"Well," the big man said. He chuckled. He placed his hands

palms-down on the table, and a smile, every bit as false as McLeod's, distorted his face. "Well, I can tell you this much, Elder McLeod. The country you come from is evil. Are there any questions?"

"No, Professor. No questions." McLeod stood up and walked out of the kitchen and out of the house. Passos stood too—out of reflex.

"I'm so sorry," he said.

"Go on," Maurilho said. "Go after him. That child."

———————

Elder Passos found his companion at the bus stop a few streets beyond the drive-through. The sight of McLeod sitting alone under a cement awning was familiar now, almost comical, a bad punch line that earns its groaning laughs through purposeful repetition. He kept quiet beside McLeod on the bench. On the bus itself, McLeod waited for Passos to sit down, then chose a seat across the aisle from him. At one point the woman sitting to McLeod's left craned her head to read his name tag.

"Are you some kind of salesman?" Passos heard her ask.

"Not tonight."

McLeod stood up and moved to the pole nearest the middle door, staring out the darkened window at the night. Elder Passos could study his companion's face in the reflection, as well as the woman's across the aisle from him, by pretending to gaze out the window himself: the faces looked ghostly, unreal in the glass, especially the woman's. She tilted it at McLeod, frowning, transposed over the moving streetlights and walls beyond the bus like a spirit observing its body. The entire day seemed unreal as Passos thought about it: the last-ditch effort at Josefina's, the tiny blue car growing larger as it sped up the hill, the worst words spoken in the calmest tones, and the thought of a city being bombed, the shocks of light, the huge tearing of afterburners.

He thought back to a time and a mood not unlike tonight's: the last days before his departure for the MTC. The news channels were still replaying the footage from New York (those red-orange bursts, and all that smoke) nearly a week and a half after the fact. On the day of Passos's farewell talk at church one of the wealthier members of the ward had hosted a little party for him: finger foods, quiet conversation, a few gifts. The TV ran in a back room and at one point Passos followed the crowd in to see it. On the screen an American fighter jet idled on the runway of an aircraft carrier, its black turbine suddenly lighting up like the tip of a giant cigarette.

"They're saying three thousand died in the attacks," someone behind Passos said. "How many do you think they'll kill in return?"

Yet Passos's thoughts in those days bore striking resemblance to his thoughts—his real thoughts—tonight. What did it all mean for *him*? For his chances at America? For a student visa? His attempts at the deep indignation of Maurilho felt dutiful, abstract. The only things he really felt were the things he experienced. The tense silence on the bus. The silence walking home. The silence in the apartment as the elders separated to their corners—McLeod to the bedroom, Passos to the front room.

Elder Passos read for an hour at his desk, or tried to. The Bible in English, as it happened. He kept a note card and pen close by to jot down vocabulary he meant to look up, and any spiritual thoughts or impressions he might use in his address at the upcoming zone conference. "The noise of the world," he wrote down. He noticed the Seuss book bunched upright in the corner of McLeod's desk; it looked awkward there, its spine much taller and thinner than the other volumes', a lone skyscraper amid one-story flats. The arrangement lacked his companion's normal symmetry; it called too much attention to itself. Passos wondered if the book hadn't been placed there for that very purpose—to catch his eye, make him jealous somehow. Had the book been on McLeod's desk before he gave it to him? Or loaned it to him? Or whatever he'd done? Passos couldn't remember.

His eye drifted to the black-and-white picture of McLeod's family. The mother and sister showing white wide smiles, the rose blush of their cheeks showing as a darker gray. Then the father with an exaggerated, mock-serious look (McLeod had said that his father, for all his patriarchal gravity, loved to kid around). And the dog, serene-faced, fat. All in all, a handsome, friendly-looking family. Passos imagined he could get along with each person in the photograph. He already liked the mother. McLeod had showed him the pictures she'd sent of the spacious, carpeted room in the basement: a bed, a bedside table, a little lamp, a desk, another lamp, a small window high up on the far wall that showed a cross-section of soil and grass and sky, and in the near corner, at the edge of the picture, a white door opening onto a white, tiled floor. "That'd be your bathroom," McLeod had explained. His companion turned the photograph over to show him his mother's note—*1 bed, 1 bath, 0 occupants, for now . . .* —in graceful, confident cursive. Another photograph of the room bore the inscription on the back: *Le Chez Passos?*

Clever, then, and generous. Passos read these qualities into the mother's face in the picture. Nothing bloodthirsty about her. Maurilho had been wrong to focus his anger on McLeod, make a scapegoat of him. He should have acted better. But then he wasn't a missionary. He wasn't an ordained representative of the Lord.

Passos got up from his desk and walked into the bedroom to see his companion laid out like a body in state. McLeod stretched out fully dressed on his bed, arms at his side, feet together, his eyes on the ceiling. He didn't acknowledge Elder Passos as he came into the room, or as he sat down on his own bed, or as he said, "Elder."

The word startled in its clarity, like struck crystal, a sound made huge in the wake of so much silence. A moment later Passos said, "Elder McLeod."

His companion got out of bed and went to his dresser. He gave his back to Passos, loosening his tie with deliberate slowness, undoing his shirt down to the last button.

"Elder McLeod!" Passos said.

The reply drifted back to him like a wisp of incense, lazy and thin. "Yeah, companion?" At length McLeod turned around. "My companion, right? My succorer? Have you got something to add, companion? Something Maurilho might have missed in his lecture? You're a bit of a lecturer yourself, you know."

"I am sorry Maurilho got so out of hand, but—"

"But what? But not enough to say anything? You were supposed to be on my side."

"It's not about sides, McLeod."

"It *is*, Passos—" McLeod's voice wavered, cracked. "You're supposed to be on my side. You're supposed to stick up for me."

"Elder," Passos said. "It's not *about* you. And the fact is . . ." He paused. "Listen, I'm sorry. I should have said something. I tried to—I tried—but I should have tried harder. Okay? I'm sorry, Elder."

McLeod's face was still hard and withholding.

"But the fact is," Passos continued, "that Maurilho is not a missionary—you are. You represent the Lord and His church, and you're going to have to apologize to Maurilho for what you said to him."

Elder McLeod shook his head at this, wagging it, snorting. He let the head hang down, let it swing side to side as if he no longer controlled it, a mere pendulum. After a moment he lifted his face and showed the same amused smile he had shown to Maurilho. "All you lecturers. All you foreign-relations experts. One on every corner, right? Right next to the glue sniffers. Right next to the drive-through customers. Or no, no—they're experts themselves! I just wish I knew as much about your country as you all know about mine. Even the janitors, huh? *Especially* the janitors. Even the filthy shirtless little kids. And of course the drunks. We can't forget about the drunks. And what about all the favela dwellers? The people living in places even the cops won't go near? They must know too. The falling-down shack builders, the thieves, the drug traffickers. Even the dead dogs rotting in the streets must know. So many lecturers. I should feel grateful, I guess. I do feel grateful. And for you too, Elder. How did I get so lucky to get you for a companion? How can I ever thank you?"

Elder Passos felt a smile on his own face now, an irresistible impulse, it seemed. He had meant to rebuke, then show an increase in love, as the scripture counseled, but now, and instead, Elder Passos heard the unmistakable voice of his former companion.

"Did you know Elder Jones?" Passos said.

"I knew of him," McLeod said. "Sure."

"May I tell you a story about Elder Jones?"

"Sure."

"He was my first American companion, as I think I've told you. Very obedient. Very curious. For example, one day he asked me if Brazil had a Fourth of July. Just like that. 'Do you guys have a Fourth of July here?' 'A Fourth of July?' 'Yeah. Do you?' I said I wasn't sure I knew what he meant. He said, 'You know, a Fourth of July!' So I told him, yes, we did have a fourth day in our month of July. Was that what he meant? He said, 'You know what I mean! A Fourth of July!' But he couldn't explain it. He just kept saying, 'Fourth of July! Fourth of July!' I think he might have been the most ignorant person I've ever known. And you remind me of him, Elder McLeod. You really do."

"Oh," McLeod said, more a sound than a word. He lifted his hands up in the air like a faith healer, and said in English, in a singsong, "Are you ready, then? My last words to you, Elder." He hesitated, mouth ajar. "Fuck you. Fuck. You. All right?"

Elder McLeod turned around and continued undressing. A minute later Passos moved to his own dresser. He undid his tie, his shirt; he removed his socks. He changed out of his dress pants into a pair of mesh shorts.

"All right," Passos whispered.

That night McLeod went into the bathroom and mas-
turbated out of anger—anger more than lust. Succor me, Lord, for
I am compassed about by assholes. But the Lord didn't answer. Of
course he didn't. After twenty-one months he had gone away for
good, dissolving through McLeod's grasping fingers like sand, or
the *hope* of sand, and leaving him Passos instead. And Maurilho.
And Leandro. The big-bellied men in the dark houses. The idiots
shouting from their cars. And now Josefina too, and the hardness
of her silence, the finality. What more did he need?

He conjured the images from the newsstands, the call cards, the
racy billboards, the spectral train of bodies. He accessed the silo
of stored stolen glances—women in the streets, women on buses,
women who bared their breasts for infants, and secretly, he imagined, for him—and now, on the topmost layer, the image of women
in the nearby drive-through. *Those noises,* Rômulo had said.

Afterward he tore down the Jesus pictures from the mirror. He
crumbled them into balls and flushed them down the toilet one
by one.

The next morning Elder McLeod canceled his alarm and slept
in. He missed breakfast, personal study, companionship study. At
a little past nine o'clock he finally got up. He showered, dressed
in the bedroom. Then he went into the entryway/living room and
sat in his blue chair, taking his shoes out from under it and lacing
them in silence. Elder Passos sat at his desk in full dress. From the

slope of his shoulders he appeared to be reading. A minute later he stood up from the desk, letting the soft leather cover of his scriptures slap shut. He came over and knelt with his arms on the chair beside McLeod, waiting, his head bowed. McLeod went to the door and opened it. Passos looked up at him, a long blankness on his face, then he stood up too and led them out into the street.

For the rest of the day the elders looked everywhere but at each other. They spoke to door contacts, street contacts, bus drivers, but never to each other. That was Friday. On Saturday McLeod started dropping from his door introductions even the mention of his companion's name. No longer "Hi, I'm Elder McLeod, and this is my companion Elder Passos, and we're representatives of the Church of Jesus Christ of Latter-day Saints," but rather "Hi, I'm Elder McLeod, and we're representatives . . ." and so on. Elder Passos took to using the same technique on his turns. They became invisible to each other, closed off by degrees, each on either side of a chasm that widened, deepened by the day. Saturday. Sunday. Monday. Tuesday.

On Wednesday, McLeod and Passos boarded a crosstown bus bound for Sweeney's apartment—McLeod in street clothes, Passos in uniform. McLeod and his friends had agreed to meet up for a P-Day powwow, something they hadn't done in two months, more. It would be a chance to relax, to let down their guards, and a chance for McLeod to escape nearly a week's worth of silence. He felt weak and dull, trapped in his own head. When he'd called Sweeney last night en route to home, he'd simply said, loud enough for Passos to hear, "I need to hang out tomorrow, Sweeney. Tell Kimball."

And Passos had gone along with it. He didn't have to. He could have refused. He could have planted himself in the apartment this morning, effectively stranding McLeod at home, since for a missionary to cross an entire city alone, leaving his area in the process, he needed a store of insubordination and bravery that Elder McLeod couldn't quite muster, even now. To sleep in was one thing; to skip personal and companionship study, companionship prayer, was one thing. Even to stalk away companionless, in anger, was one thing. But to be truly alone was another. Twenty-one months of conjoined living and moving had instilled in McLeod, as it did sooner or later in all missionaries, a distinct separation anxiety from his missionary companion, no matter who or how awful he happened to be. Elder Passos must have known this, but he hadn't exploited it, hadn't dared McLeod to overcome it and commit an actionable offense. He had followed him out to the bus stop instead, taken a seat across the aisle from him, taken out his scriptures to read.

Which meant that Passos too must have been eager for a reprieve, desperate even, for a break from the silence. He too must have pined to talk to someone, even if that someone happened to be Sweeney's junior companion or Kimball's. Jokesters, Passos called them. Unserious, unimpressive, immature. But at least they came from a non-evil country, right? Passos could commiserate with Nunes and Batista about the boorish Americans and their imperialist, blood-spattered ways. He could reprise all the slanders from Maurilho's diatribe that Passos had endorsed with his willful silence. More than once since that night at Maurilho's McLeod had started letters to his mother—"I was wrong about Passos," he wrote in one draft, "and I don't think you should help him"—but each time he gave up. *I don't think you should help him.* It sounded so blunt, so sudden, so unlike the voice of charity and calm that he had cultivated for his family in his previous letters. How could he act out of spite for Passos without betraying the fact of his spite? He decided to let things be.

McLeod could see the finish line anyway. He was in the home-stretch. Just yesterday he'd received a letter from the mission office asking him to "please indicate which release date you prefer—May 14, or a transfer later on June 25." Which did he *prefer*? McLeod had laughed out loud, a joyful, giddy laugh. Less than two months to go, then. A transfer and a half. Which meant less than two *weeks* to go with Passos, since McLeod would demand a new companion in the upcoming transfers. He'd make the appeal directly to the president in the personal interview after next week's zone conference.

Elder McLeod snuck a furtive glance across the bus aisle—his ogling glance, returned to its old form—and in an instant his bilious revulsion to Passos surged up again. Look at him. The sad, frescoed face, more yellow than brown. The eyebrows diving in concentration, an open book of scripture on his lap, the rigid posture. Everything about him suggested self-seriousness, soberness, *righteousness*, so-called. Is this what everyone wanted McLeod to become? Is this the life his father envisioned for him?

One night in the spring of his senior year, a few months before his nineteenth birthday, McLeod walked into the living room and saw his father rapt in the blue-white light of an old home movie. "Your mother found a place that converts these to DVD," he said, and motioned for his son to take a seat beside him on the couch. On the screen, two white-shirted teenagers, one of them a younger version of his father—the same lank parted hair, the same hair *style* even, unchanged across thirty-five years—stood in an open field below the Eiffel Tower. Then, as if at a director's prompt, the young men started running around in circles, crossing and recrossing each other's paths. They moved in jerky, stop-time strides, and the film was grainy, swarming with dust motes, but McLeod could still make out his father's face, and his big, carefree smile.

"That was a Preparation Day, you understand," McLeod's father said. "We weren't usually like that." He laughed through his nose. "But look at us. We must have thought we were making a Beatles movie. One of our friends from the ward had a camcorder— they were very expensive in those days—and he gave us this as a present. That's Elder Nielsen there beside me, doing the handstand now—oh my. Well . . ." He clicked off the TV and turned on a lamp beside the couch. "I'll finish watching that some other time. I don't want you to get the wrong impression about the mission. It's hard work, you know. It's not all sightseeing and games. It's hardly ever like that."

"I know," McLeod said. "I know that."

"Where are you in your reading now?"

"First Corinthians thirteen."

"Well, tell me about it."

"'For now we see through a glass, darkly; but then face to face: now I know in part; but then shall I know even as also I am known.'"

"You memorized that?" his father said.

McLeod felt sudden tears rimming his eyes. "I'm going to try it, Dad. The experiment. I'm going to go on a mission."

His father put his arm around his shoulder and pulled him into a sideways embrace. "I knew you would, Seth. I knew you would."

———————

The bus let the elders off into a new-sprung rain, the sky above them quickly closing, darkening, the undersides of the clouds stained the color of eggplant. McLeod and Passos walked at pace. Sweeney's building—a narrow three-story walk-up that put McLeod in mind of a vertical desk organizer, one apartment on top of the other on top of the other—loomed up ahead as the rain thickened. They took the last several hundred yards at a run, took the stairs that wrapped around the building two at a time. Sweeney's companion, Elder Nunes, answered the door in proselytizing clothes. He had his poncho on already, a large umbrella at his side. He glanced up and down the dripping pair of them and laughed. He handed an umbrella to Passos, stepped out into the awninged hallway to join him. Passos tilted his head at Nunes, then up at the emptying sky. "Trust me," Nunes said. Then to McLeod: "Well?" He swept his arm toward the open front door.

Elder McLeod entered the apartment and gave a nod to Elder Batista, Kimball's junior, who crouched in the dim gray light of the entryway, fitting on a pair of rubber overshoes.

"Where is everybody?" McLeod asked Batista.

"Hiding, man."

"Huh?"

Batista worked a corner of the overshoe around his back heel, but the rubber snapped back. "Come on," he muttered. Elder McLeod looked around the apartment. All the doors were shut, all the windows closed, except one, in the kitchen—a small frame on a big hardening sky. The window light gave onto the long counter-top that separated the kitchen from the entryway/living room; it imparted a shine to that surface that cast the other surfaces in the apartment in dark relief: the small wooden dining table, its drop-down flaps like giant ears, the desks, the taped-up pictures on the walls, and the stacks of teaching pamphlets and Books of Mormon teetering in the shadowed corners.

McLeod heard whispered voices conferring outside in the hall-way. He turned around just as Nunes leaned his head back in the door. "Batista, you coming or what?" He looked up at McLeod. "Oh, and hey, tonight we want you guys to come pick us up at Passos's apartment, okay? Well, your apartment too."

"Who's 'we'?" McLeod said. He laughed a little. "Yeah, okay."

When Batista finally got out the door and shut it behind him, the apartment was that much darker. McLeod searched for the light switch on the wall. The naked bulb (why were the bulbs always naked?) filled up the room with a harsh thin light that reminded him of old black-and-white police dramas, the bad guys lurking in boiler rooms or languishing in holding cells while detectives leaned into their questions. The bulb should be hanging, though, swinging, making me feel like I'm in the underdecks of a ship. McLeod noticed on the wall one taped-up sheet of paper in par-ticular: a map of Sweeney's area, taking in a slice of west Carinha, and all of the smaller, neighboring city of Borém. Had the map been there the last time he visited? McLeod didn't think so. He would have noticed it. Was it Nunes's idea, then? Or Sweeney's? Some symbolic stand against the usual slacking off that marked the waning days of a missionary's service? Elder McLeod felt a pinch of comparative shame at the thought. He called out in English, "Hello? Where is everybody? Sweeney? Kimball?"

The only answer came from the rain sounds through the open kitchen window. McLeod walked toward it, saw a checkerboard of orange-tile roofs and sooted white satellite dishes, brown alleyways, gray side streets—all of it tipping up at him, pushing half of the sky out of the frame. The water buzzed in the puddles in the street below, and for a moment McLeod couldn't be sure if he'd heard the toilet flushing from the bathroom or some sudden rush from outside. Then Elder Kimball emerged from one of the closed doors off the entryway/living room, looking pale and pained, seasick, and barely altering his drained expression at the sight of McLeod standing behind the kitchen counter. "Oh, hey," Kimball said weakly. "Wait. I thought you'd sworn off P-Day clothes— even on P-Days."

"Times have changed," McLeod said. "What's with you?"

"Green bananas."

"Yeah?"

"It's all I can figure. Ate them at lunch yesterday. Those things hold a grudge, man, let me tell you." He put a hand in his dense helmet of P-Day hair, frowning, looking like he'd forgotten something. "Remind me where you've been for the last two months?"

"Yeah, I know. It's a crappy situation. I'm just glad to be away from it for a day."

"You mean Passos?"

"There are words for him, but none of them Bible."

"I thought you said he wasn't as bad as the hype."

"He's *worse*," McLeod said, and a silence filled the room. He changed the subject, remembering. Had Sweeney gotten the letter from the mission office? About their group?

"May fourteenth," Kimball said, a sly spreading smile. "Less than two months until I get to play with my Blondie."

"You and Sweeney both, right?"

Kimball's smile went lopsided. He shook his head in stiff quick jerks.

"What's up?" McLeod said, suddenly hushed.

Elder Kimball spoke even quieter. "Sweeney got a Dear John from the girlfriend. Not even a Dear John letter, actually. She sent a wedding announcement, her and some dude named Corey—who marries a Corey?—and there was this little Dear John *note* inside the envelope."

"I thought they were practically engaged."

"Who knows, man. The note said she'd tried to tell him sooner. That old story. It looks like a BYU romance to me. Three weeks and they're soul mates, you know? Agreed to marry in the pre-existence, all that. My brother said you see it all the time there."

"Wait. He showed you the note?"

"Well, he just sort of dropped it on the floor. He tore it up, actually, then he dropped the pieces on the floor. I was with him when he opened it this morning. Here." Kimball motioned for McLeod to follow him, on tiptoe, to the little trash bin at the far edge of the kitchen. It stood mere feet from Sweeney's bedroom door. Kimball picked the several pieces of the announcement and the note out of the trash and assembled them on the kitchen counter. Elder McLeod inspected the announcement first: a black-and-white photograph of a square-jawed letterman type holding the pale pretty girl in his arms, her ringed hand on display against his chest. And on a separate piece of card stock, the following:

Dr. and Mrs. Jeremy Ledgewood
are pleased to announce
the marriage of their daughter
Tiffany Anne Ledgewood
to
Corey Bruce Jensen
on Saturday, the second day of August
Two thousand and three
in the Salt Lake City LDS Temple.
You are cordially invited to attend a
reception held in their honor.

Then the note. It filled half a page with tiny looping words about how sorry she was that she hadn't told him sooner, how she'd tried but she hadn't known what to say, how it had happened so fast, though of course the Spirit had confirmed it. "I still don't know what to say. I guess I just hope you'll be able to understand someday and I hope you'll still finish your mission with honor. I know you might not want to hear this right now but I'll always consider you a friend, Andy. I'm so proud of you." The next line had been scribbled over. McLeod could just make out "I never . . ." The note concluded: "Affectionately, Tiffany."

McLeod looked up from the kitchen counter to the closed bedroom door, then to Kimball. "What's he doing in there?"

Kimball shrugged his shoulders.

"And he's been in there since this morning?"

He nodded.

Elder McLeod took eggshell steps across the kitchen, opening cupboards in search of food. He found a box of imitation Cocoa Puffs in one cupboard and took it to the threshold of Sweeney's bedroom door. He held up crossed fingers to Kimball, then he knocked once and entered.

The room was dark and very still. The blinds shut. The fan turned off. The sound of rain drummed distantly on the roof. The air thick and close with heat. Elder McLeod waited for his eyes to adjust, then he crossed the room, stepping on stiff pieces of paper from the sound of it. Sweeney didn't move. He lay facedown on his bed, his arms stretched up above him, his legs in strict unnatural parallel. He looked like a victim on the rack.

A narrow shaft of gray light broke through the gap where the metal blinds met, making a halfhearted partition of the room. McLeod sat down to one side of it, on Nunes's bed. He picked up one of the stiff pieces of paper and examined it in the shaft of light: a torn Polaroid of the lower half of Tiffany's cross-country stride, the long white legs amputated just above the knees, one of them straight, the other bent. Other shreds showed faces with no bodies, a group of headless girls on horseback, an oak tree split right down the middle. Sweeney stood just off-center in the latter picture, extending three-quarters of his arm to a rude white tear.

"What are you doing?" Sweeney said.

McLeod shook the box of cereal. "I brought you some lunch."

"McLeod?"

"Yeah."

"Oh, McLeod."

Sweeney settled his head in the crook of his elbow, let out a quavering sigh. McLeod shook the box again and opened it. He pulled out a handful of dark, vaguely sticky spheres, extending the handful toward Sweeney's face, holding it out the way you hold out feed to horses. After a time Sweeney rolled over to face him; he propped his head up on his fist. He looked at Elder McLeod's outstretched hand for a long minute, then reached out and overturned it. The little spheres made hollow reports on the linoleum, rattling as they came to rest. McLeod reached into the box and produced another handful, which Sweeney overturned again. McLeod laughed a little.

"Do it again," Sweeney said.

McLeod did it again. Sweeney flung McLeod's hand up, or slapped it up, a loud, echoey uppercut of a slap that sent the imitation Cocoa Puffs flying. McLeod and Sweeney laughed together.

"Just give me the fucking box," Sweeney said. "And don't you dare tell me to keep it Bible. Not today."

Elder McLeod handed over the box of cereal. "Today is an exception."

"You're fucking right today is a fucking exception."

Sweeney plunged half of his arm into the box, then shoved the puffs into his mouth, making loud rapid crunching sounds. He repeated the process half a dozen times, coming up for air every two or three handfuls.

"I figured you were hungry," McLeod said.

"Did you bring anything to drink?"

"I can get something for you."

"No," Sweeney said. "I'll get it."

Elder Sweeney let the box fall to the floor, swung up out of the bed, crushed his way across the room. He opened the door and staggered out into the gray light, his arm shielding his eyes. Elder McLeod followed at a distance. In the kitchen Kimball stood before the tatters of the announcement and the note, studying them. He sipped a glass of chocolate milk. He looked up as Sweeney and McLeod came into the room, tried to cover up what he'd uncovered. Elder Sweeney pushed him aside and stared at the announcement, his mouth open—wider, wider—like he'd just had the wind knocked out of him. Again. His eyes began to fill. Kimball made an apologetic wince at McLeod, then looked down.

Elder McLeod went to the fridge and filled a glass of water and brought it over to Sweeney. He pulled him away from the counter, turned him. He pressed the glass into Sweeney's hand the way he'd once pressed contact cards on strangers: *Dear sir, dear madam, this can help. We promise.*

Kimball swept the pieces of the announcement and the note into his hand and dropped them in the trash, though not without Sweeney noticing.

"In the trash is where it belongs," McLeod said. "The best thing you can do is ignore it. And drink your water."

Elder McLeod stepped back against the wall beside the window, leaning there, and Elder Kimball joined him. The two of them watching Sweeney as if from an observation room. The front of Sweeney's corkscrew pate matted down, his eyes red and unfocused. The absent sips from his glass of water. "You disappeared again, McLeod," he said, not looking up. "Where'd you go this time?"

"Stuff with Passos again. But it's almost over. Next week at zone conference I'm demanding a transfer from the president. Then no more of the vanishing acts. The last transfer of our missions will be the best one yet."

"Oh sure, sure, sure . . ." Sweeney said, trailing off. He laughed. "And I'm sure President Mason will give you exactly what you want, McLeod. Since he loves you so much, right?"

Sweeney laughed again, a loud uninhibited laugh that cut off as if caught in a reversal of wind. He drank down the rest of his water in one long, breathless gulp. Then he held out the glass and let it slip from his hand; it bounced once and shattered on the linoleum. McLeod and Kimball looked at the shimmering mess, then at Sweeney, who was looking beyond it. Sweeney took two quick strides to the drying rack and got out another glass that he also dropped, a neat, almost dainty gesture. He dropped another glass, then another. Elders McLeod and Kimball watched in grim recognition. A porcelain cereal bowl hit the floor and radiated shards. A dinner plate cracked in half on impact. Neither McLeod nor Kimball said anything, and neither moved, but then Sweeney finished the drying rack and went to the cupboard, started raking the dishes from the shelves, a guttural roar building in his throat. A heavy mixing bowl smashed into pieces at Kimball's feet. He jumped back. "Hey!" Another smashed too close to McLeod. He and Kimball ran for the living room. Sweeney followed after them, flipping the wooden dining table, kicking out the four drop flaps with as many shouts. He swept the desks, toppled the stacks in the corners, kicking books and pamphlets across the room as he tore down the pictures from the walls, the map of the area, the monthly calendar—none of it mattered anymore. Sweeney moved Kimball and McLeod around the room as if by opposing magnetic force. He finally slowed near the front door, pausing there, his breathing loud and ragged, his eyes wild. Then, as if to avoid taking stock of the futility now littering the room, he sprinted headlong for the bedroom door, just short of which Elder McLeod checked him into the wall. McLeod held on to Sweeney, lowering him down to the floor, saying, "I'm sorry, okay? But come on. Are you okay?"

And Sweeney just gasped and gasped for breath until he caught it on a choking sob.

The rain kept up. It thickened and bowed. It swept the streets in gusting scrims, making a mockery of all umbrellas, as the three elders descended at the stop near the drive-through. The crosstown bus went no closer to home. Elders Passos and Nunes and Batista would have to take the rest on foot. The bus pulled away, sprouting thick crescents of water from the wheel wells. Passos and Nunes stepped back under the awning. Batista stood planted in the coursing gutter, pushing little wavelets up and over his rubber overshoes. "Oh, are my feet in the water?" he said. "Didn't even notice, brethren. Didn't even notice."

He laughed, and Nunes laughed too, but said how ridiculous Batista looked in those things, like a circus clown. They spent several seconds back-and-forthing the pros and cons of overshoes until Passos put an end to the conversation. "I've only ever seen Americans wearing them. Come on."

Elder Passos led a spirited run-walk for several minutes as Nunes and Batista tittered behind him. They kicked up puddles at each other, like children, some of the water splashing the backs of Passos's pant legs, which were already soaked. At moments he almost regretted being rid of McLeod in exchange for these child-ish greenies—child*ish*, not child*like*.

They reached the bus stop closest to the apartment, paused under the awning to catch their breaths. The rain on the cement slab above them sounded like TV static at full blast. Elder Nunes raised his voice almost to a shout and Passos still couldn't quite hear what he said.

"What was that?" Passos shouted.

"I said I sure hope you didn't leave your laundry out in this."

Elder Passos slumped his head into his palm, remembering.

"Did you really?" Nunes said. "I was just kidding."

"Great," Passos said. "Some P-Day."

"You didn't know it was going to rain today?"

"How would I have known that, Elder?"

"You just feel it, man. You're Brazilian."

"He's from the northeast," Batista said. "They're all Bedouins up there."

More tittering from Nunes and Batista. More soaking rain as they made the final dash for home. They turned off the main road onto the elders' street, running along the rivers that gushed at the curbsides and deposited trash and mango leaves at the eddying flooded drain grates. Passos jumped the river onto the sidewalk as he neared his front gate. He thrust his hand into the mail slot, came away with a clutch of envelopes. In the courtyard the rain boiled in several centimeters of standing water. Passos and Nunes, and even Batista with his overshoes, started stepping and stepping like flamingoes, trying to keep their feet dry as they tore down the morning's laundry from the clothesline. Elder Passos had a mind to leave McLeod's laundry out, but Nunes and Batista had already grabbed indiscriminate handfuls of garments socks shirts pants ties, mixing the just with the unjust. Inside, the laundry took over the apartment, laid out to dry, or re-dry, on chair backs, tables, desks, countertops, doorknobs, door edges, anything and every-thing. An hour later a dank fungal stench suffused the air and the elders had to push through still-dripping clothes as if through jungle brush just to move about the apartment. Elder Passos spent the first part of the afternoon reading the letter Nana had sent, responding to it, then encouraging Nunes and Batista to do the same. Had they already written their letters home? he asked. Didn't they have people worrying about them, wondering?

Passos spent the second half of the afternoon cutting out pictures of Jesus from church magazines and redoing the mirror, making it thick with images. Jesus in the manger. Jesus in the temple. Jesus with the woman at the well, with His disciples. Jesus with the little children, *heirs of the kingdom of heaven*, He said, and also *Allow them to come to me*. Allow them to be childlike, not child*ish*, not inane, laughing at who knows what in the bedroom, swapping wisecracks, just like McLeod and his set of jokesters. They should be writing their families to let them know they're alive, to bear testimony to them, to be *missionaries*. Why was he so surrounded by idiots? Why did they all think they were here? To tell stupid jokes? To win popularity contests? Jesus at the Last Supper, the washing of the feet. Jesus atoning in Gethsemane, the agony on His face, His betrayal by Judas. Elder Passos arranged each picture so that it just overlapped the one beneath it, so that he could fit as many pictures in as possible. He looked at all of the cutouts so far, the mounting sweep of them, one image bleeding into another into another, a sort of kaleidoscopic montage of His Life and Passion.

Passos's grandmother still ailed. This was the word she used. "I am still ailing, my little son. Unfortunately." She said she'd thought enough time had passed, but after a day behind the counter her ankle had swelled up again, even bigger than before, round and dark as an avocado. The pain laid her low for another week.

She couldn't even think anymore. Felipe and Tiago had to all but carry her onto the bus to go to the doctors. White-coated scoundrels, all of them. The endless waiting rooms, the flat-faced receptionists. And then, adding insult to injury, they kept her there, said she ailed from more than a sprain—an ill-healed fracture, they said. Had to break it again to set it right. Could he believe it? She was writing him from the convalescence ward now. She'd be there a week, they said, maybe more. Tiago visited often, even Felipe. They were both good boys. She ought to sue the city. They'd promised pavement more than a year ago, and now the scoundrels said she'd need to use a walker for six weeks—either that or some motorized cart, probably some old golf cart from the States. Ha!

Nana bucked up for him, he knew. She tried to make a joke of things—"Ha!"—but it wasn't funny. Elder Passos could see the writing on the wall. On the mirror. Jesus before Pilate, before the Pharisees and Sadducees, fattened snarling men. Jesus amid the jeering Roman soldiers. *To this end was I born*, He said. It was not a funny message. Elder Passos could see into the mirror and beyond it, could see through the glass, for a moment, clearly. Tiago and Felipe visited Nana often, which meant that neither of them went much to school or church. It had been this way for two months now, more. They took turns behind the counter during the day, one bringing in what little business the street offered while the other played pickup football games. At night they helped Nana, or now visited her in the hospital. In two months more, maybe longer, Nana would start walking again, tending the store again—a trickle of customers, a river of bills. The street would stay dusty and unpaved, the life meager. There was nothing there for them. Jesus at Golgotha, on the cross. Jesus risen up on the morning of the third day. *Touch me not,* He said, *for I have not yet ascended.* Then Jesus with the apostles before his final ascension, and the commandment to *go into all the world and take the gospel to every creature.* Jesus beside the Father, in the clouds of glory, and the promise that He will soon come again. From birth to death to rebirth, the whole story, and all of it staring him in the face, a premonition.

He knew his companion couldn't be trusted, couldn't be counted on. The silence meant the end of the basement apartment—he felt sure of it. Passos couldn't untell the lies McLeod had no doubt told his parents about him. He couldn't undo that damage. He needed the assistantship, the BYU scholarship. Elder Passos thought of the opening talk he would give at Tuesday's zone conference—a standing assignment, the talk, that in the hands of many zone leaders became little more than a précis for the president's longer address. The president had assigned Passos to discuss the new rules about family-oriented teaching from a practical, missionary standpoint. But Passos would do much more than that. He would get President Mason's attention; he would *convert* the missionaries of his zone to the procedural by way of the doctrinal, by way of the spiritual. The noise of the world. The shelter in inspired rules. The small means by which great things come to pass. Elder Passos removed a note card from his breast pocket and jotted down another idea. The great and eternal blessings of obedience, which is all the Lord asks of us, remember—obedience: no more or less than that.

Passos repeated this last phrase aloud, slowly, and with oratorical emphasis, in the finished bathroom mirror: "Obedience: no more or less than that."

———————

At a little after nine o'clock that night Elder McLeod arrived with his friends in tow, the three of them ashen and funereal, Passos saw, at the prospect of reuniting with their assigned companions. He ought to address companionship unity in his talk as well. He ought to stress that.

Elders Batista and Kimball and Nunes and Sweeney filed away into the night a few minutes later, leaving the apartment to descend back into its pall of silence. But Passos felt confident he could handle it. If things went according to plan, he'd only have to deal with McLeod for two more weeks. True, they hadn't been together for very long, not even two transfers yet, but in order for Passos to serve as an assistant for any significant length of time he needed to move up to the mission office soon, and why not this transfer? He might even hint at this to the president in his upcoming interview. That and the BYU scholarship. He could mention how he'd always dreamed of going there, but of course the money and the distance and all that bureaucracy . . . Let President Mason reassure him. Then let Passos respond with a well-turned bit of English, something very American, something to demonstrate his growing mastery of the language.

The next day the elders were more tentative in their silence. They gestured to each other, made occasional eye contact. More than once Elder Passos thought McLeod might just say something. He would have welcomed the change, any move toward reconciling, if only for the purpose of the interview with the president. He hadn't yet figured out how to describe the silence in terms that would absolve him, as the senior companion, of all blame.

They lunched unceremoniously at a *padaría* downtown, eating cheese bread, sitting on a pair of folding chairs. Leaving the store, Passos saw Josefina studying the wares in a shop window on a nearby corner. A woman about Josefina's height, in any case, in a loose-fitting blouse. The same posture, the same dark hair—or was it? Passos quickened his step, and McLeod beside him. When they were half a block away the woman glanced in their direction, made a face, her pinched features not at all like Josefina's, and hurried into the shop. Passos and McLeod slowed down together, nearly stopped, as if they'd entered a slower, thicker medium.

By Friday the silence had hardened again. On Saturday it seemed more impenetrable than ever, though it also seemed to float free of the elders, independent of each of them, a poisonous gas that flushed up from depths neither had anticipated or really intended. At times Elder Passos felt he could almost see it, sense it staining the air around them like squid's ink. Sunday passed like that. Then Monday. Passos felt himself start to resent even the sound of McLeod's breathing. He thought McLeod probably resented the sound of his too.

At seven o'clock Tuesday morning Elder Passos stepped into the bathroom and closed the door behind him, making sure of his privacy, though his companion was still very much asleep. Passos took out the three-by-five note cards he had prepared for his talk at zone conference that afternoon. The cards were filled to the bottom edge with tiny, tidy script. He read aloud through the first card, practicing pace and cadence. He read through the second, too, and only on the third—he looked up into the mirror for brief, meaningful eye contact—did he realize that McLeod had torn down all his Jesus pictures again. He must have done it sometime during the night. *To anger me. Try to throw me off-kilter for the talk he's watched me prepare, hour after hour, night after night. It won't work. It won't.*

And it didn't. That afternoon at the conference Elder Passos mastered his concentration as he moved through the cards with a calm, unhurried, confident air, addressing the twenty or so missionaries, and of course the mission president, who had gathered in Belo Horizonte to receive instruction and edification. Passos first outlined the zone's numbers as compared with those from two months ago at the last zone conference. They had fallen off rather precipitously, "though not alarmingly," Passos pronounced. For consider how the new emphasis on family-centered teaching had caused retention numbers to rise mission-wide. He transitioned into the doctrine, saying, "And consider how every great move toward progress—eternal progress—encounters opposition, especially at the beginning. Consider how the Evil One tried to overwhelm the young Joseph Smith when he first prayed to His Heavenly Father aloud, in the earnestness of his soul. 'Immediately,' Joseph wrote, 'I was seized upon by some power which entirely overcame me, and had such an astonishing influence over me as to bind my tongue so that I could not speak. Thick darkness gathered around me, and it seemed to me for a time as if I were doomed to sudden destruction.' And consider, too—and this is the take-home—how the Prophet freed himself from this Enemy of All Righteousness: 'I exerted all my powers to call upon God to deliver me . . .'

"My fellow missionaries, let me be as clear as I can. Our inspired leaders have told us to focus on teaching and baptizing
families, self-sustaining celestial units. This is an effort that matters, and matters everlastingly, and the Everlasting Enemy knows
this. We will therefore have to work harder than ever to call on
God to help us. We will have to *exert* ourselves more than ever to
be obedient and worthy of the Lord's helping hand. The noise of
the world, indeed, can be deafening. We need shelter and protec-
tion from the world. We need a place where we can hear ourselves
think, a place to present the gospel in the bright light of simple
truth. And where can we find this shelter? Where *do* we find it? In
the rules and regulations of our inspired leaders.

"You all know the new rules to which I refer. I have communicated them to you myself, many times. They are simple and easy
to follow. They are small things, truly, but truly, as the scripture
says, 'by small and simple means do great things come to pass.' I
testify that if we follow these new rules, if we focus our teaching
on families, and if we call upon the Lord through the exertions of
our hands and hearts, we will reap such great blessings 'as there
will not be room enough to receive them.' This is the promise of
the Lord to the prophet Malachi, and this is His promise, today,
to each of us. The Lord requires of us not impossible sacrifice,
remember—not inhuman feats of strength or deprivation. What
does He require of us? Simple, saving obedience. Obedience, my
friends: no more or less than that."

———

Two hours later Passos sat before the president in the bishop's office. The president smiled. "That was some talk you gave."

"Thank you," Passos said in English. "I worked hard on it."

"You sure did," the president said, also in English. He chuckled a bit. "You went above and beyond, stole some of my thunder. Do you know that phrase? To steal someone's thunder?"

Elder Passos shook his head.

"Well, that's okay. Idioms are hard."

"You don't have to talk so slow," Passos said. "I can understand English well now. Elder McLeod and I have been practicing."

"I can tell. Your grammar is very good. How is Elder McLeod?"

"He's okay. He is difficult, but okay."

"He goes home after one more transfer," the president said. "You probably knew that? Anyway, I wanted to tell you that I do appreciate the challenges you face with him, and I do notice the way you handle those challenges. You're a good missionary, Elder Passos, a good zone leader, and I don't mind telling you that I can always use good missionaries in the office with me."

"You mean assistants?" Passos said.

The president chuckled again, and Elder Passos cringed at what he assumed had been his over-directness. In English he still lacked the nuance, the necessary euphemisms of educated speech. He formed an apology on his lips.

"Obviously I can't make promises," the president said. "The Lord is the head of this mission, not me. But I don't mind saying that I could use a good missionary like you, a resourceful missionary, as my assistant. If you can keep up the good work you're doing with Elder McLeod for one more transfer . . . Do you think you can do that?"

Elder Passos slowly nodded. The president returned the nod.

He dropped his eyes—to his wristwatch?—then returned them to Passos. A formal smile, a tiny pause. Passos knew the afternoon had been long for the president. He must want to be done with his interviews. Passos couldn't afford the lead-in; he couldn't afford the English. He said in Portuguese, "President, may I ask one more question?"

"Shoot," the president said, still in English.

"Ah, yes, 'shoot,' " Passos said. "That one I do know." The president smiled politely, waited. "Well, I wanted to ask, is it true that assistants to the president are offered scholarships—I've sometimes heard this around the mission—scholarships to BYU? Some of the missionaries in my zone have asked me, which is why I ask. Some of the Brazilians have asked. Many of them would like to go to BYU, of course, but it's very expensive to travel and very difficult to get a visa. They say the scholarship helps."

"And are you one of those Brazilians, Elder Passos?"

"I'm sorry?"

The president was laughing again. "I've never heard the rumor quite like that," he said, "though it is true I have many contacts in Utah. My younger brother is on the admissions board at BYU. Maybe that's how the rumor started, I don't know. I know BYU likes foreign students, though—they like diversity—and I'll bet a smart, resourceful missionary like you would make a smart, resourceful student. I might be able to write a recommendation to that effect, Elder. But don't start worrying about that yet. How much time do you have left?"

"Five months," Passos said.

"Well, you see my point. That's a long time. For now just

concentrate on that companion of yours. Then we'll see what we can do for you, okay? Is there anything else?"

"No, President. Thank you."

"Thank you," President Mason said, and half rose to shake Passos's hand. "Tell your companion to come in next, please."

Passos came out of the bishop's office, caught eyes with McLeod, briefly, then nodded at the door. McLeod stood up and crossed the glowing foyer: late-afternoon sunlight pushed through the window shades, translucent pulled-down sheets that looked to McLeod like backlit flypaper. He carried some of that orange light in with him to the bishop's office. President Mason sat at his desk, the picture of the risen Lord shining behind him, the president shining too, if only for a second, his face lit up like a harvest moon. He smiled and shook McLeod's hand. Elder McLeod sat down on a chair half as big as the president's leather recliner.

"I liked your talk," McLeod said, lying. He wanted to start on a positive note even if it meant a servile untruth—a Passosesque gambit. In truth the president's zone conference address had been worse than usual, soaked straight through with his business-speak. At one point he'd interrupted himself to ask the group, and not rhetorically, "How do you say 'deliverables' in Portuguese?" But McLeod felt he had an end, for once, that could justify any means.

President Mason smiled again, acknowledging McLeod's compliment, then started into the language of the personal interview. How did he feel about his progress as a missionary, as a disciple and representative of Christ? How did he feel the Work was going? How was he coming along on the Problem? This last question was a slight deviation from the script, but McLeod didn't let it distract him from his own: *I feel better about it . . . It's going better . . . Much better.* President Mason didn't challenge McLeod or ask any follow-ups. He shifted in his deep leather chair, creaking, shook his watch out of his shirt cuff. "Good. I'm glad to hear it. Is there anything else, then?"

McLeod realized his mistake. Late in the afternoon of a long day, late into the lineup of missionary interviews, the president was too tired to probe on his own. "Well," McLeod said, stalling for time. He said the word again, through a quavering sigh ("Well . . ."), letting the tone of his voice begin the disclosure.

The president leaned back in his chair, showing a knowing half smile. He laced his hands together in his prayerlike way, rested them on the desk, said, "What's in that 'well,' Elder? I know that 'well' very well."

"Well, I don't think the Work's going that great, actually," McLeod said.

"Work harder then, Elder. Apply the principles that I covered today, that your senior companion talked about as well. The Lord will reward your obedience."

"I haven't stopped masturbating either."

"When was the last time it happened?"

"Last night."

"Follow 'The Guide to Self-Control,' Elder. Pray. Take short, cold showers. Wear blue jeans at night if that helps. Follow the Guide."

"I haven't spoken to Elder Passos in two weeks. I want a new companion in the next transfer. I need one."

President Mason lifted his eyebrows. "Two weeks. Wow." He let out a chuckle. "The best I ever managed was a day and a half of the silent treatment. I never had the patience for it. Well, how is your companionship scripture study going? How about companionship prayer?"

"You don't understand, President. We haven't talked at all. Anything that involves talking to each other, we avoid."

"Literal silence?" President Mason said.

"Literal silence."

"And why didn't your senior companion tell me about any of this?"

"You'd have to ask him that."

The president's eyebrows furrowed, his face darkened over. He gestured for McLeod to go on.

Which he very much did. He had come prepared. He catalogued every offense, every trespass, every passive aggression of the last month, of the entire companionship. It wasn't just the anti-American jabs, the anti-Americanism in general; it was everything, everywhere; it was as pervasive as God. The belligerent big-bellied man in the first lesson. *I did not say I disagree with him,* Passos said. Or the pastor with the red convertible—purchased, they'd both assumed, with tithe money—and McLeod's harmless comment to lay not up treasures. *Tell that to your countrymen,* Passos said. McLeod felt like he lived on a minefield. He walked down the street and the Brazilians did double takes—blond hair, blue eyes, must be American, right?—and *Hey, Bin Laden! Hooray, Bin Laden! Tell your president this, tell your president that!* As if McLeod could just get him on the phone, just dial in to the White House and say *President! Urgent memo from the third world!* McLeod could count on something like that every day now—he could practically set his watch to it—and he could tell that his companion enjoyed it. He smiled sometimes. He laughed! Only it wasn't even laughter—it was this amused little smirk he always did. The son of a bitch was a walking smirk!

President Mason put a hand up. "I'm sure your companion would give a different version of things."

"I'm sure he would," McLeod said. "I'm sure he'd lie. The son of a bitch is a walking lie!"

"Watch your language, Elder. And listen. Listen. I understand what you're saying. I've experienced some of it myself. But you can't let it get to you so much. And you can't feed into it either. This isn't the third world. This is the vineyard the Lord has called you to work in. Right?" The president paused, leaning forward. He lowered his voice. "Elder McLeod, are you praying for the success of your companionship? Are you praying for a testimony? Are you doing the simple things the Lord asks of you? Are you doing the things I asked of you?"

Elder McLeod sighed a long, quavering sigh, and this one unaffected. "I need a new companion, President. Please. I don't think I could take another transfer with him."

President Mason said, "Okay, Elder. Elder McLeod? Look at me. I'm up here." McLeod looked into the president's round large face, even rounder and larger at this distance. The man half bowed his head; he spoke at a near whisper. "I think I can work something out, all right? I'll have to ask the Lord first, of course. He is the head of this mission, not me. I testify of that. But I'll try to work something out. Now," he said, "let me tell you a story. When I was a missionary, I served with an Elder Donson. We didn't get along for a number of reasons, none of which were political, but of course it was still a problem. One morning I woke up and he'd shined my shoes. It was a dusty area and we did a lot of walking. He'd shined my shoes and I knew it and yet I didn't say a word about it, and neither did he. The next morning I got up early and shined his shoes. Then the next day he did mine, and the next I did his, and so on. It went on like that for more than a week. Something had changed. We both felt it. We both felt grateful for it. We were never bosom buddies—don't misunderstand me—but now we could work together. We could concentrate on the Work. Do you understand what I'm saying?"

––––––––––

Elder McLeod understood but he didn't care. He didn't have to now. He and Passos rode the bus back to Carinha in the same silence, stark and heavy and imperious. At a few moments that night, granted, and during the next several days, McLeod thought he might have sensed the silence softening, lifting. At a few moments he felt his companion's eyes on him, though he couldn't be sure if they implored him or bored into him. Perhaps Passos wanted to regain McLeod's goodwill in regards to his parents' basement. Perhaps he wanted to make his peace before transfers, play conciliator on the eve of his ascension to the assistantship, which he'd all but clinched with his ass-kissing performance at the zone conference. Or maybe he just wanted McLeod to look at him as he broke into one last smirk. In any case, McLeod never returned the gaze.

On the following Tuesday night, Transfers Eve, McLeod trailed his senior companion to the pay phone nearest their apartment. It had been nearly three weeks of silence and by now the elders had perfected their system for communicating *at* each other on matters of logistical import. McLeod had first used the system on the Monday after their silence began, calling to inform Rose (and, more to the point, Maurilho) that they wouldn't be coming to their house for lunch. "Something's come up," McLeod said in a loud, flat voice. Rose had merely asked, "Are you sure?" The week after that she merely sighed, and so on.

Elder Passos used the system less frequently, since as the senior companion he already exercised the prerogative to call the shots more or less as he pleased. But now, as McLeod stood beside him at the pay phone, it became clear from Passos's voice that he intended McLeod to hear every word of his conversation. Passos spoke at full volume into the receiver: "Elder Tierney, is that you? . . . Fine, fine. I'm ready when you are . . . Yes, of course. At your convenience. Thank you." He hung up the phone and waited.

Elder McLeod had only witnessed this particular process once before: on the eve of the last transfers, standing not far from where he stood now, overhearing Passos's conversation with the assistants. Prior to that, he had always been on the blind end of the zone leaders' calls, the information hot in their hands, the thrill of a power trip in their voices. You're going here, or there—get packing. You're getting a new companion—make sure the place is ready for company. And sometimes—nothing. No change at all. The next day a P-Day like any other. The sense of anticlimax, the leadenness, as if syrup ran in the veins. But was that really worse, McLeod thought, than the feeling of being jerked around like a pawn on God's chessboard? Transferred missionaries barely had enough time to pack their things and get a few hours' rest before they were due the next morning at the local *rodoviária*. No goodbyes to the people they'd befriended or taught, those fireworks already fading in the dark. No sense of a proper resolve at the end

of three months, six months, more—no period to end on, only a
dash. The irreducible strangeness of the mission.

And strange, too, that in McLeod's present circumstance, where
he felt sure that one or both of them would be transferred, he *could*
have made the time to say goodbye to friends and investigators,
except that he had none to say goodbye to anymore. No more Josefina. No more Maurilho. Rose and Rômulo: collateral losses. And
no more Passos, of course. What shoots of friendship had grown
up between them had long since withered and returned to the
ground. The thought of Dr. Seuss, or his nickname, or any of the
things they'd joked about, laughed about, practiced English on—it
all made Elder McLeod cringe. The very sight of Elder Passos, the
peripheral *blur* of him, raised McLeod's hackles in a way he could
no longer control; it had hardened into reflex. Such that now, as
McLeod waited along with his companion for Elder Tierney's return call, he actually stood a few feet *behind* the pay phone's blue
plastic shell. All he saw of Passos were his legs.

Up above, McLeod could see the last holdouts of evening giving way before the first muted stars of the night. The top of the
sky looked cobalt, the sides blue, the bottom gray. Not enough day
remained to power the tunnel of refracted light along the tops of
property walls; the jagged teeth rose instead in darkened silhouette. The phone rang out in the silence. Once. Then again. On the
third ring Passos picked up and said, "Hello? . . . Yes, fine. I know
how busy you must be." His voice sounded falsely companionable,
falsely cool. "So, yes, go right ahead. Pen at the ready . . . Yes,
okay . . . Yes . . . Got it . . . To Pampulha, got it, yes . . ." Then he
said, "Kimball gets a new companion? Okay. So he stays, then. Got
it. Keep going."

Elder McLeod noted what he took to be a gesture on his behalf—repeating aloud the news about a friend—but then, not thirty seconds later, Passos said in a buoyant voice, "So Sweeney's going to Sete Lagoas, you say? He's getting transferred way down there? Okay, got it, got it . . . And what about De Freira? . . . He stays? Okay. And Álvarez? . . . He stays too. Got it . . . And you didn't mention Elder McLeod. Does that mean he stays? . . . McLeod stays in Carinha, got it. And so do I. One more transfer, then. Okay. Good night to you—"

McLeod rushed around to the front of the pay phone just as Passos ended the call. He pushed his companion aside, grabbed the receiver. "Hello? Hello?" He pulled a contact card from his breast pocket and dialed the mission office's number on the back. Elder Tierney answered the office phone. "Yes, Elder Passos? Is there something else you needed?"

"This is McLeod. Did you say I'm *not* being transferred? I'm staying with Passos? Did I just hear that right?"

"Elder McLeod?" The voice on the line paused. "Elder, we have a longstanding system set up for relaying—"

"I want to talk to President Mason. Put me through to him right now."

"Elder McLeod, do you have any idea how busy we are tonight?"

"Put me through to President Mason."

"It's out of the question, Elder. We have a system in place."

The line clicked dead. McLeod choked the receiver, bowing his head in a surge of rage, feeling dizzy with it. After a moment he lowered the phone back to its cradle, a conscious, forced-gentle gesture. Then he stepped away from the pay phone and noticed his companion at his left. Passos opened his palms to him, his mouth, but Elder McLeod warned them shut with one hateful look.

He sat in the blue chair in the entryway/living room, considering the sight of his shoes before him. Elder Passos was undressing in the bedroom, though McLeod didn't hear him, didn't even notice the light. McLeod felt furious and calm at once, numb and adrenal, resigned and scared. His body pulsed, yet strangely relaxed away from him, at the very thought of what he might do. If I take my shoes into the bedroom, he thought, that commits me. Then I'll have decided to do it. Elder McLeod didn't think about the money, or what he might wear. He didn't think about the consequences, immediate or otherwise. For now he thought only of the shoes. They sat deflated and sad, side by side, several inches in front of him. He could simply slide them under the seat, as Passos had done, and as he normally did at the end of a day. He could treat tonight like any other. Dear God, if you exist at all, dear God, if you *are* in fact . . . He supposed this wasn't what President Mason had in mind. He wasn't kneeling. He wasn't even closing his eyes.

McLeod tried again. He pushed his shoes aside—not under the chair but beside it—and he kneeled to pray, resting his elbows on the blue concave seat. The floor felt hard underneath him, unforgiving. His knees began to throb after only a minute or two—he had barely cleared the preliminaries of the prayer, the *I thank Thees*—and he wondered how he'd ever managed the long pleadings he offered almost nightly at the beginning of his mission. *Please God. Now. Make yourself known to me,* he used to pray. *I'm keeping up my side of the bargain. Keep yours.* One night in the MTC

Elder McLeod spent a full hour in prayer, mostly listening, mostly waiting, and at the end of it a repeated phrase, like a water drop gathering weight, released into his mind: *It's enough, it's enough, it's enough* . . . But now it wasn't. He prayed with a sterner, gamier heart. He offered less a plea than an ultimatum, a sort of threat: God, if you really exist, if you are at all, then you will stop me, you will protect my virtue . . . McLeod listened and waited, waited and listened.

He opened his eyes and saw the shoes. Why did their positioning matter anyway? It was because of the windows. The entryway/living room window was chest high and gave out onto the hard concrete, the *loud* concrete, of the outer courtyard. The bedroom window, waist high, by contrast, gave onto a strip of soft loamy earth to the *side* of the courtyard. Where McLeod put on his shoes mattered less—or it mattered, but only because he had already decided to leave from the bedroom window. Tonight. *Tonight*, McLeod decided.

Elder Passos lay in bed with his English Bible open on the mattress in front of him. He read the book often lately for English practice and inspiration, though mostly for English practice. First Corinthians 14 sat under his gaze now, but it went unread as the events of the night drew his mind away into roiled reflection. Of course he hadn't expected McLeod to take the news *well*. He hadn't expected an instant change. But Elder Passos had expected at least something—some recognition, some acknowledgment of his vulnerability, or of the fact, at the very least, that this hadn't been his fault any more than McLeod's. Passos had probably wanted this even *less* than McLeod. But now here they were— another six weeks—and since there was nothing at all to be done about it, they might as well adapt to it with a measure of grace.

After the call with the assistants, Elder Passos had contacted all the senior companions in his zone, passing along the transfer news as McLeod paced back and forth behind the phone, adapting to his own transfer news with all the grace of a mental patient, kicking at the dirt, hurling rocks against property walls, erupting from his low steady mumble into guttural shouts.

"What was that noise?" Elder Sweeney had asked.

"My companion is upset," Passos said.

"Is he still your companion?"

"Yes."

Sweeney sighed. He laughed and sighed at the same time. He muttered in English, "Poor bastard."

"I can understand you," Passos said.

"Yeah, well, go easy on him, Passos. He's having a pretty hard time of it."

"And what about me? I'm not? Huh? He should go easy on *me*, Elder Sweeney! Elder Sweeney?"

But the line had gone dead.

In the bedroom now, Elder Passos readjusted the pillow propped up under his chest. He trained his eyes back on the verses in 1 Corinthians, and after a time his attention followed. The passage continued on the subject of love, or "charity," as the King James Version had it. Passos turned a page with great care, wary of tearing it. Most of the pages were already brittle, some of the edges serrated like paper knives, though less from use, he gathered, than from brittling serrating time. Elder Passos had found the Bible a year or so earlier in the closet of his second missionary apartment, the book abandoned, apparently, by an outgoing elder. The missionary must have received it or inherited it many years earlier—a faded ink inscription on the front cover read *To our son: Herein you shall find the words of Life*—and he must have read it only once in a great while. Passos could find very few fingerprints on the pages, oils, smudges, grease stains; he could find no marginalia of any kind anywhere; and he found only a few colored pencil underlinings of the most obvious verses: Genesis 1:27, Amos 3:7, John 3:16 . . . In 1 Corinthians 13 someone had underlined Paul's famous words about the need to put away childish things. Elder Passos tried to recall the exact language in English, though his effort lacked conviction. He turned back two pages and reread the

verse in question: *When I was a child, I spake as a child, I under-*
stood as a child, I thought as a child: but when I became a man, I put
away childish things.

He thought of McLeod. How could he not? Passos, after all, had
started reading the King James Bible in earnest after McLeod had
taken back his cartoon book *Oh, the Places You'll Go!* Passos didn't
miss the book at all: it had never really challenged him, and what
little affection he'd had for the story, he had since put away and
felt much better for it. He thought of McLeod, too, because of the
chapter the verse came from. He happened to know that 1 Corinthians 13 was his companion's favorite section in the Bible. McLeod
had volunteered this information early on in their companionship
in the casual, almost forgetful way that Passos hadn't yet come to
recognize as vain: "Oh, First Corinthians thirteen? Love it. Probably my favorite chapter in all scripture. Just beautiful, beautiful
language. Memorized most of it I like it so much. That's one place
where nobody does it better than the King James."

In retrospect it seemed inevitable to Elder Passos that McLeod
should say that, and just that way. Of course he loved 1 Corinthians! All the tentative believers did, the worldly wise! To their
minds Paul said nothing about obedience or devotion or actual
literal belief except to say, Hey, don't worry about that—just love,
man. In general Passos knew to be wary of such feel-gooders,
apostates defining love as lawlessness. Why hadn't he been more
wary of McLeod? Why hadn't he seen through him all along? To
think that all of McLeod's flaws—his shallow-roots faith, his arrogance, his false superiority—all of them hid out in the open in that
statement. McLeod loved 1 Corinthians 13, he and every other so-
called Christian. And why did he love it? The beautiful language.

The undemanding surface of things. And why was the language so beautiful? Why was it, in fact, the very best? Because a group of aristocratic proto-Americans had written it. Because some English king hundreds of years ago had rammed it down the throats of half the world, made an imperialist weapon out of it. Because it trucked in obscurity, difficulty, in so-called tradition, in "hath" instead of "have," "doeth" instead of "does," "giveth" instead of "give," and even "charity" instead of "love."

Love: even the most unmistakable word got substituted out lest the uninitiated gain admittance to the club, lest they prove themselves equal to the club members and complicate their plans to continue raping, pillaging, plundering, exploiting, *bombing* the uninitiated. But Passos, now more than ever, understood the implicit challenge, understood the stakes, and he refused to be turned away by all the *thees* and *thous*, the moneyed diction, the unspoken rules. Turned off, certainly, but not turned away. Elder Passos had determined to finish the English New Testament—at least that much. He was halfway there. Then he could go back to the New Life Portuguese translation he had read since his early youth, a translation of the Bible in which Jesus sounded less like an overcareful Englishman, adjusting his powdered wig as he cast out the Devil—*Get thee hence, Satan*—and more like the Son of God, a carpenter, a workingman, a man of strong words. *Get out of here, Satan! Get out of here!*

———————

A few minutes later Elder McLeod finally came into the bedroom. He carried his shoes in his left hand, placed them on the floor beside his bed—an odd change of precedent, as if he feared that

Passos might steal or vandalize the shoes and wanted them closer to him to protect them. McLeod stood at the dresser, his back to Passos; he seemed to be undoing his tie. He left his shirt and dress pants on. When he half turned from the dresser Passos snapped back to his Bible. He sensed out of the corner of his eye a long, hard stare from his companion, who at length lay down on his bed, on top of the covers. McLeod didn't move from that position for the next twenty minutes.

At ten thirty exactly Passos turned out the bedroom light. He kneeled at his bedside for personal prayer, tried to ignore his sarcophagal companion behind him. He prayed for a change of heart for the both of them, and he meant it, or at least he thought he did. When Elder Passos opened his eyes again he felt like he was underwater: blue light on the blue-green floor, a baptism by moonlight. The moon itself, silver and round, hung in the window like one of the Christmas ornaments that used to fascinate Passos. Christmas globes, his mother called them. He loved how they caught the light and held it, magnified it, and how they magnified and seemed to age a little boy's face as he leaned in close. Elder Passos was still on his knees at the bedside, and he hardly felt a solid floor underneath him. His memory of an early Christmas was another of the pearls he didn't share with anyone, much less the McLeods of the world. He himself hadn't thought of it since the previous Christmas. He and his mother and brothers all there, even his father— Passos and Felipe little boys, Tiago in diapers. In the center of the memory, a conical green tree hung with bright shining balls, some red, some green, some silver. The green of the tree against the red of the throw rug underneath it, and the porcelain crèche on a nearby table. Under the tree, three matching soccer balls, white with black pentagonal tiles. Tiago's ball rivaled him in size, a useless toy for an infant, but now Passos felt he understood it: a sign of relative largesse, along with the modest Christmas tree, the rug, the crèche. The husband has work for a change, the wife has her sons—three of them, a respectable number. She sits on the floor in front of the tree, cross-legged, her hair swept back, smile wide. At one point she holds up her own gift, a bright white sweater, to pose for a photograph. Then she widens her arms to take in all three of her boys, her embrace encompassing them together, like a mother hen gathering in her chirping young. Who could deny such a woman her right to happiness? Who could believe that life for her would ever be anything but full and new?

Something about this and other memories, granted, seemed too perfect to Elder Passos, too composed, as if the scenes had reinvented themselves out of the photographs meant merely to mark them. Sometimes the photographs moved in his memory, his mother and brothers, even his father, moving as if in the wash of a strobe light. Sometimes they appeared to be moving backward, back toward that Eden around the Christmas tree, but they never made it. They never would, of course. The only hope lay forward.

Elder Passos felt this familiar piece of knowledge alight on him like a sudden revelation. *The only hope lay forward.* He sensed it moving down his body like a warm draft of drink. He felt it in his heart and in his mind: a chance. For him. Maybe even for him and his companion. Why pray for a change of heart in McLeod if he didn't believe in at least the possibility of that change? Give him a little time, Passos thought. McLeod wasn't ready tonight, but who knew about tomorrow. The future slept unformed and void, and only God knew what could be made of it.

Passos rose from his knees and got into bed. He looked over at McLeod. His companion still lay motionless atop the covers and still mostly dressed, from what Passos could tell. He wore his dark socks (or were his feet just in shadow?), his dark pants, and his white shirt, palely blue in the moonlight. Give him time, then. Give him a little more time. Maybe as early as tomorrow, Passos thought, turning over and starting the slow drift toward sleep.

He opened his eyes and checked his clock again, checked his companion: 1:28 a.m., and Passos displaying the clear signs of deep, oblivious sleep, his chest rising and falling at slow steady intervals, a small snore even, a wheeze, like the breathing of an old man. Elder McLeod slowly brought his feet around to the side of the bed, and stood up, even more slowly, into his pre-tied shoes. He transferred his weight from his arms to his legs, an exchange of burdens, and another commitment. On the floor just past the elders' beds lay a pane of bluish, cloud-mottled moonlight. McLeod stepped into it and turned to see his face in the dresser mirror across from him. He looked gaunt, deliberate, suffused in blue, like a man in a Picasso painting. He felt his reflection was of a kind to make a noise, almost, a low, ancient moan. Quickly, then, but very quietly, he climbed out the bedroom window and into the night.

───────

The outer door presented the first obstacle. Elder McLeod had never noticed how loud the catch sounded, how sharply the door hinge creaked, until just now. He shut the gate behind him carefully, so carefully, but then he wondered at his care. And what if Passos *had* heard him? So what? He could have made a run for it if he'd had to, and he would have. He did. He started into a jog. Down their street under a remote perfect moon that held off the clouds and stood directly above him no matter where or how fast he ran. Onto the main street and past the bus stop, past the darkly silhouetted husks of the bank, the supermarket, the post office, the second bus stop—until the drive-through's blue neon sign loomed up suddenly, too suddenly, and McLeod stopped. He heard the breath inside him, like wind in a cave, as if he'd covered up his ears. Why had he run, and had he really run so fast? They lived nearly two miles from the drive-through, yet here he stood already. McLeod felt it should have taken longer to get here. He should have had more time to prepare. He felt as if God, whom he did not believe in, had cast a net over the world and hauled it in, drive-through first, dropping it squirming at his feet. To force the issue.

Elder McLeod moved to within a few hundred yards of what he took to be the drive-through's walk-in entrance, a small metal door halfway down the stucco perimeter wall. An automatic gate beside the door opened up to let cars enter, as one did in the time McLeod stood waiting, a young Jonah under low, luminescent clouds, feeling the cool night air prick his skin, insinuate itself between the gaps of his white button-down. This was the only style of presentable shirt Elder McLeod owned. He needed to feel presentable. He didn't know why. He had left his tie behind, though, and his missionary name tag, as well as his undergarments and any form of identification. In his pocket he carried a hundred reais, and twenty American dollars for good measure.

His breathing had calmed by now—from the running, anyway—though he still looked around as if someone or something might see him. He scoured the street for security cameras, though McLeod had never seen one during his entire time in Brazil. Still: the thought, the mere *thought* of embarrassment, of being caught out in his sins . . . McLeod moved closer to the walk-in gate, if only to gain shelter from the street. "Just go, just go, just go," he mumbled under his breath. The metal door appeared before him. He took a pair of deep breaths and arranged his face in an expression of nonchalance, and before he could stop himself he stepped in off the street.

Some fifty feet inside the door was a tollbooth-like structure, its windows yellow against the darkness, and sitting in the booth, a dark-haired woman. Beyond the booth stretched a low-lying series of curtained stalls. Elder McLeod thought of a row of outsize voting booths, or a stable. He started forward, startling as the pitch of his footfalls changed: the pavement had turned to small white gravel, bluish in the moonlight and the glow of the neon sign, the ground like the floor of a fish tank. The crunch of McLeod's footsteps alerted the woman in the booth, who looked up to see him hesitating. She slid open a glass window and nodded at him. McLeod strode forward with sudden feigned purpose.

"Good evening," he said, forcing a smile.

"Good evening," she said, a smile of her own. She looked thirty-ish, maybe fortyish. The skin of her face, stretched smooth across her cheekbones, bore no signs of makeup and only a few lines that gathered at the corners of her large eyes and mouth. She wore a simple red tank top. Her arms were firm. Her cleavage ample.

"You know I could charge you for this," she said.

"What?" McLeod said, looking up.

"What'll it be?"

"I'm sorry?"

"Are you here with someone or are you looking for someone?"

"I guess I'm looking."

"How much time do you want?"

"How much time?"

"How much time. You pay up front."

McLeod gripped the narrow counter protruding from the tollbooth, looked at his feet as if he'd dropped something. A moment later he bent down ("Sorry, just a second") as if to pick that something up. It was curious: Elder McLeod, after so many years of moral training, was utterly empty of moral concerns in this moment. Only practical considerations, cordiality, proper procedure—only these things clamored in his mind. What was the language for such an occasion? What was the Portuguese for "escort"? He didn't know. For "prostitute"? He couldn't think of it. He was sure he knew the word, but he couldn't make himself remember it. The only word he could call to mind came from his reading of the Portuguese Book of Mormon. He had needed more time to prepare. He didn't have a condom. He had never actually used one. What was he doing here? Was it too late to back out? He could just turn around and walk away, couldn't he? Run away, *flee*, like Joseph from Potiphar's wife.

"How much time?" the woman said again. She seemed to be losing her patience.

"I am . . ." McLeod said. "I'm not from around here."

"I noticed," she said. "You want fifteen minutes? Thirty minutes? How much time?"

"You mean with a harlot, right?"

The woman paused. For the first time she really took McLeod in, up and down. He felt conscious of his close-cropped hair, probably too close-cropped, his freckled face, forced smile, overformal attire.

"Where are you from?" the woman said.

"The United States."

"I'll give you fifteen minutes for fifty American dollars."

"I only have twenty. I have a hundred reais, though." Elder McLeod produced the fold of bills from his pocket and passed it across the little counter. The woman stood up and took the money and stuffed it in the back pocket of her short jean skirt. "Okay," she said. "Follow me."

"You?" McLeod said.

"I'm your harlot," she said.

Elder McLeod followed the woman into one of the middle stalls, a dim-lit, oversize cubicle of a room: three cement walls and the fourth, a curtained partition, which the woman stopped to Velcro shut. She took McLeod's hand and led him to the edge of a small bed, sat him down on it, then stepped back and peeled off her tank top with both hands. She did it in one fluid motion, more efficient than seductive, but Elder McLeod still thought: I can never unwatch this, even if I want to. I can never undo this, worlds without end.

The woman unclasped a pink bra and let it fall away. She caught it, placed it with the tank top on the small lamp table beside the bed. The room could fit little else: the table, the bed. The lamp shed a harsh yellow light that cast half-moon shadows beneath the woman's pendulous breasts. The breasts contoured down just so at the nipple, McLeod noticed. The woman slid her jean skirt and underwear down together. She stepped out of them. Her naked hair at eye level.

"Aren't you going to undress?"

The woman looked down at him like a puzzled god.

"But I don't . . ." McLeod said. "How do you say?" He pointed at himself. "I don't have anything to cover me . . ."

"Ah," the woman said, and she took two steps toward the lamp table and opened a small drawer, giving her back to McLeod. He tried to undress in that interval, tearing at buttons, belt, zipper. By the time the woman faced him again, an opened condom in her hand, he had his dress pants down at his ankles. He sat hunched over his erection, half covering it with his hands, but then he noticed her noticing—her puzzled expression deepened—and he allowed himself to be totally exposed.

"How old are you?" the woman asked.

"Twenty," McLeod said. "Twenty-one."

She gestured with the condom. "Do you want me to do it?"

"Please."

McLeod felt the sudden urge to look at the floor, but he resisted it, holding to the woman's eyes instead. He imagined he saw a trace of amusement on her face, but it slid away quickly.

"It's okay," the woman said. "Here." She sat down beside him on the bed and rolled the condom down. The feel of another's fingers on his penis offset the strange chilling sensation of the condom, if only for a moment. He felt greasy and ridiculous. He felt embarrassed. The woman took him by the hand again and led him to the center of the bed, waddling on her knees. She turned to him. "Do you know which way you like?" He hesitated. "Here," she said. She lay on her back, breasts spread to either side, and pulled him over her, and took him into her. "Okay?" She moved her pelvis against him to demonstrate.

"I . . ." McLeod started to say. *I know that much.* He felt flooded with embarrassment now; he burned with it. No other sensation anywhere in his body could compete with it, and soon he began to soften. He shut his eyes and for several seconds tried to block out all thoughts, all sounds. The woman said, "Is that okay?" He opened his eyes and saw her watching him, wondering, adjusting her rhythm to heighten his. After a moment more she said, "Are you close?"

For the second time that night Elder McLeod's mind emptied of all but strategy, a desire to salvage his situation, a desire for *less bad.* He had always imagined that sex would be easier than masturbation, easier to get where he needed to go, but now he felt himself ebbing inside the prostitute. He hated himself for it. He redoubled his movements, flexing the arms he braced on. The woman wore a dutiful expression on her face, dutiful yet somehow concerned, which only made things worse.

"Close?" she said again.

Elder McLeod shut his eyes and conjured up images in a panic—women on billboards, newsstands—nothing—women in Passos's magazine—nothing—women in the drive-through—the absurdity of that, the sudden absurdity of everything, his whole life—until only the thought of Josefina, the thought of *her* under him, only that could sustain him through the last desperate moments. He grunted, pleasure-pain shot through him, and he collapsed on top of the woman. Her body tensed.

"Sorry, sorry," he said, but he didn't move. She wriggled partway out from under him, half sitting up in bed now, and he came face-front with her breasts, pendulous and full, the undersides still in shadow. The nipples turned down just slightly, he noticed again. These were the first breasts presented for his touch. The body of a total stranger.

"You done?" she said, trying to guide him off her. "Was that okay for you?" She gripped McLeod's shoulders with either hand, pushing gently, but she stopped as soon as his shoulders began to jog. She tensed again. "Why are you laughing?"

"I'm not . . ."

The woman paused. "You're crying?"

He wandered the streets of Carinha for the rest of the night, the city reduced to a sort of miniature: the blacked-out storefronts along the main street, the occasional cars, their tail-lights blurring orange-red, the wan yellow halos of streetlamps on the sidewalks, and the moon, always the moon overhead. The glowing disk grew larger as the night wore on, sinking into a haze of thin, disconsolate clouds. The cloud cover broke for minutes at a time and the streets became ghostly in the darkened light, the city all but abandoned at this hour. Elder McLeod had expected many people about, even at three, three thirty in the morning—he had imagined a great licentious nocturnal host, shadowy but real, bristling—but instead he saw only a handful of people, and most of them asleep. He passed forms wrapped in patchworks of dark coarse blankets, like mummies. One of them lay under a bus-stop bench, another in a recessed store entry, another on a bench in the park downtown. McLeod sat on the bench opposite this last bundle, to rest, feeling unafraid for several minutes until he saw the sepulchral form roll over. McLeod got up and lurched away as if he were alive among the dead, but only barely: he felt numb, emptied out—of chemicals, of everything. He tried not to think of what he'd done. He tried not to think at all, tried not to know anything, and for a stretch of an hour, two hours, he largely succeeded. He only knew that he didn't want to go back to the apartment, back to Elder Passos and the life of a missionary.

He drifted away from downtown into the residential neighborhoods, stopping again to rest on an unoccupied bus-stop bench. It
must have been four in the morning. The slab of concrete felt cool
underneath him, chilly. The chill deepened and broke through his
thin layer of dress pants and gathered in the undersides of his
thighs. Elder McLeod couldn't have rested, really, if he'd wanted
to. Alone on a bench in the middle of the night, not sleeping—
for fear of what?—but not wanting to go home either. Trapped,
liminal, purgatorial. And his mind waking up now, returning in
spite of himself to another cold, restless bench. He returned to
Joseph of Egypt and the Sunday school lessons he'd received as
an early teenager, and to the times he snuck to the woods behind
his house where his neighbor, an older boy of fourteen, kept a zip-
locked stash of *Playboys*. The young McLeod must have repaired
to the tiny clearing in the pine boughs too often, or often enough
to arouse suspicion, for one Saturday afternoon his father followed
after him at an unseen distance.

McLeod remembered sitting cross-legged in the clearing, flipping breathlessly through the pages, freezing at every rustle, every
soughing crack, and pushing down the erection that never seemed
to leave him now, that never stopped clenching his stomach like
a fist. He remembered his father crashing through the trees like
a warrior god, catching him with the magazine in one hand, his
penis in the other, but just holding it, just pinning it down, not
knowing what else to do with it. "What great wickedness is *this*?"
his father shouted, an allusion to Joseph with Potiphar's wife that
McLeod recognized, even then. He had learned the verse in Sunday school and, later, alone, in puberty's thrall, had fleshed out
the story in his mind: the indentured Joseph serving Potiphar's

wife, who drops her robe one day—her naked breasts, stomach, legs—and commands, *Lie with me.* Joseph stumbles back at the sight of her, at the suggestion. *How can I do this great wickedness?* Joseph says as McLeod's father rips the magazine out of his hand. His father stands over him now, *looms*, holding the magazine away from his body like a beshitted diaper. "Young man, you had better . . ." he says, but his stern voice falters as McLeod struggles to cover himself up, to get himself back into his jeans. He can't get his pants up fast enough, and suddenly he's crying. "Get out of here," McLeod shouts, "get the goddamn fuck *out* of here!" He finally manages to fold the erection into his pants and stands up, crying in earnest now. "Dad, just—just *leave* . . ."

But something has changed in his father's bearing. All of a sudden he leans down to hug McLeod, the offending *Playboy* still in his hand. McLeod punches the embrace away. He punches his father for the first and last time in his life, a glancing ineffectual blow to the chest. Then he tears out of the woods with his father calling after, "Seth, wait! Seth!" and the pine boughs whipping his face. He keeps running, running, the breath burning his throat, until he reaches Memorial Park at the center of town, the park with the pond where he and his father used to feed the ducks in springtime, but now it was fall. He spends a sleepless night on a park bench, his heart catching, again, at every rustling branch, every windy moan.

In the morning, more tired than he'd ever been, McLeod returned to his house. His father had stayed up too, all night, worrying about him, angry, he would tell McLeod later, but angry at himself more than anything. He must have been watching at the big bay window as McLeod appeared at the edge of their property.

He must have seen him while he was yet a great ways off, like the father of the prodigal son, for he ran out into the front yard and fell on McLeod's neck and kissed him. "I'm sorry," he said, "I'm so sorry. I love you, Seth. I'll always love you."

McLeod had never felt his father so close to him before, so urgent. His voice was strange, and his embrace too. They stood in the wet morning grass like that, not moving at all.

In time the rows of teeth on top of property walls started casting their silhouettes more sharply against the night. Elder McLeod watched the dark drain from the sky in the reverse order that it had filled it up the night before: from the bottom first, then the sides, then the top. At the first pink underblush on the clouds he stood up from the bus-stop bench and started walking again. He repassed the storefronts along the main street, passed by Maurilho's street completely, made a giant buttonhook of a detour around the drive-through. McLeod didn't fear temptation so much as reminder, though of course the detour itself reminded him. The very fact that he tried not to think of what he had done betrayed a certain hubris. He was Jonah again, trying to hide from the God he doubted. Trying to hide himself from himself.

McLeod turned toward home, and it loomed up even faster than the drive-through had. So be it, he thought. So be it. He opened the front gate, crossed the courtyard, then opened the front door, not caring if Passos heard him. Elder McLeod stepped into the front room at exactly five thirty, though he, watchless, thought it must have been closer to five. The room was dark. The air through the open window was warm.

McLeod took a seat in the blue chair and began to remove his shoes as if he had returned from a day of tracting. The force of habit. He had to laugh, or half laugh, a single push of air through his nose. As if nothing out of the ordinary had happened. As if his life had not changed forever. But he took off his shoes, still, and placed them back under the blue chair. He was like a man arranging chess pieces—just so. He noticed his companion's shoes, a few feet from his own, slumping there in the darkness. Passos's shoes looked like things grown up from the floor, like blackened roots protruding from the ground and retreating back to it, repenting their mistake. In the instant a rush of remorse and embarrassment, profound embarrassment, came over McLeod. It felt like a swooping chill, a sickness. The thought of repenting his own mistake—the thought of confession, or forced confession—brought to McLeod's mind a terrible scene. He didn't imagine God, or hellfire, or eternity. If he could have believed in these things he might have taken comfort in them—at least in the fact of their remoteness from him. But the scene McLeod imagined now had the hard feel of reality, time-bound, earthbound, the earth rushing up at him as in his falling dreams. He saw his mother and father at the airport, there to pick him up two months early. A dishonorable release, a ruined son. He saw the dead eyes in his father's face. He felt his mother's hug, too eager to comfort. And he wished in the depths of everything he was that he could repent everything he'd done, undo it.

As if nothing out of the ordinary had happened. Elder McLeod became aware of his body in the room, of what noises it made. For a long moment he listened for movement from the bedroom, not moving at all himself, barely breathing. Maybe Passos hadn't heard him. Not going out or coming back. And just maybe—the idea occurred lightly, almost jokingly.

After a minute McLeod stood up, taking soft stockinged steps across the tiny room. He slowed his movements as he reached his goal—the light switch just to the left of the bedroom door. He paused, considering the room behind him: the desks, the chairs, the shoes underneath them. Something began to loosen in McLeod, to move. He willed it to move. He reached for the nub of the light switch for the entryway/living room, but he reached for it slowly, very slowly. He didn't want the *click* to sound.

For the moment he existed in that liminal space between subconscious and conscious, dreaming and waking. Something had drawn Elder Passos up toward the surface such that he felt he could almost control the dream, as if he were an actor in a scene he had written himself, and yet he worked to stay asleep so he could learn what would happen. He and his mother walked hand in hand in green woods, a winding trail of the kind he had seen in pictures, but never in person. The trail was soft from accumulated pine needles, and somewhere a stream ran down among rocks. The water burbled in a playful vein that belied the soberness in his mother's voice. "If you go there, of course you'd need to take your brothers too."

"Of course, Mom."

"They look up to you."

"It's not forever, anyway."

"You have to promise me you won't forget about them."

"Mom, come on."

"Promise me, son. You're a good boy, but promise me."

"I promise you."

The trail widened out and the water slid away and the dappled light through the trees undappled, got steady and bright until it filled the vast green field that opened up in front of them. In the far corner of the field, two trees. They stood a good fifty meters apart. Passos and his mother crossed to the first tree, a towering mango, in a matter of steps. They plucked lunch from the reachable branches and ate it in the tree's expansive shade. Passos in bed could almost taste the sweet syrupy pulp on his tongue, feel it in between his teeth, gritty and reassuring. His mother laughed at him—"My little pig!"—and cupped her chin to show him what she meant. Passos wiped the same spot on his face and came away with an orange-red slime.

"So," his mother said, and she stood up and produced two homemade kites for them to fly, slanted boxes made out of grocery bags and balsam. The sun shone even brighter now. The wind picked up. The kites lifted and shrank to the size of postage stamps in a scrubbed blue sky. Toward evening Passos tired and sat down against the tree trunk. He read from his scriptures—his Bible in English—and only then did he notice the missionary clothes he wore. He looked over at his mother as she reeled in the kites, first hers, then his. She smiled mysteriously, as if thinking some private little thought. Then she turned her head, sensing his eyes on her, and her smile widened. "My little scholar," she said.

Passos smiled too, though a bit unsurely.

"What is it, son?" his mother said. "You're not in a hurry, are you?"

He shook his head.

"Good." Her voice rebounded, light as a song in her throat. "Good, good. We'll wait for the fireflies."

Passos nodded. He felt content and secure. He read for a minute more, then closed his eyes, leaning against the trunk of the mango tree. He remembered the second tree, some distance away, and he opened his eyes to study it. He picked up a wind-fallen mango and stood up and threw it as far as he could toward the tree. It fell well short.

He heard footsteps behind him. His mother gripped a green, spotted mango in her right hand. "Watch what your old mother can do," she said. "Are you watching?" She cocked her arm far back behind her head, hopped once, then twice on her back leg, then whirled around like a discus thrower and sent the mango flying through the air. The oblong fruit described a rainbow arc until it thunked against a low bough, dropping what sounded like large pinecones, loosing a shiver of white fuzz. The fuzz—a snowy scrim—updrafted and eddied on the breeze. It finally settled on the ground around the tree, coating its exposed, prodigious roots.

Passos tilted his head. "What kind of tree is that?"

His mother looked surprised. "You never played Brazilian snowstorm, my little son?"

"I don't think so."

"Why, it's a snowstorm tree. Here." She led them to the squat twisted tree base. Against the trunk, its bark gray and papery, his mother put out her hand to steady herself. She reached down and retrieved from between two roots a small green pod, cleanly burst down the middle, with its white fibrous insides showing. "These sides peel back," his mother explained, "until it's just the fluffy seeds, you see?" Then she lofted the pod straight up into the canopy of dark impenetrable green. Some leaves wafted down before another cloud of white, like an annunciation. Passos's mother bent down for more pods and he followed her lead, collecting a handful and unloading it, one by one, into the tree. The snow shook down in successive waves. It fell on his hair, his neck. It tickled his skin; it made him chuckle. He was chuckling with the sensation, then suddenly he was laughing, then suddenly, *boyishly*, he was spinning around. He put his arms out, gathering speed, spinning, making the white stuff coat him, making it swirl all around him in the darkening air. Over the *whoosh* of his movement he heard his mother laughing too, a bright, clear, girlish laugh. They laughed in chorus, mother and son—they didn't know why they laughed, only that they did, as if in defiance of the dream that was dimming away now, bleaching out, the surface approaching in spite of Passos's best efforts to stay under forever, to live there and breathe there, away from the world of waking sights, waking sounds.

The bedside clock said 5:34. He heard a subtle *click* in the hallway outside the bedroom. A band of yellow light appeared under the door. He listened for footsteps, thought he heard them: shuffling steps, soft as sails. Elder Passos jerked upright out of bed, caught in a sudden breathless clutch that breached the chrysalis of sleep once and for all. He pressed his ear to the wall. He heard a metallic scrape against the linoleum, the scrape of a chair leg, it sounded like. He heard the hollow knock of rubber against the floor. Was someone taking off his shoes? Or stealing theirs? He looked across the room for the first time. McLeod's bed was empty, still made up. Of course, he thought. Of course. What kind of intruder turns on the light, anyway? Passos released his breath. Why had he rushed to the thought of an intruder? McLeod had gotten up early before. Not lately, but still. Nothing else made sense.

Passos lay back down as if to enforce a calmness of mind. He closed his eyes in an attempt to get back to sleep, a futile attempt, he suspected, but he tried anyway. He tried to rejoin the dream with his mother—a pair of trees, a kind of snow, his mother's laughter—but as he struggled to conjure these images again, another set of stimuli recurred to him with the sudden force of memory: the key in the front door, the scrape on the linoleum, the clatter of the outer gate before that. Hadn't these been the very sounds to bring him up from his dream in the first place?

Elder Passos sat up again, trained his gaze on the glowing strip of light under the doorway. For a moment the strip seemed to waver, seemed surreal, and so, too, the idea of his companion leaving the apartment in the middle of the night. But what else could the sounds mean? Outer door, front door. The key in the lock, then footsteps inside. Passos rubbed hard at his eyes, sitting up all the way now, making sure he had left the dreaming state. But to wonder about a dream is to have left it already. Passos suddenly felt certain that his companion had left the house, alone, and in the night, a gross violation of missionary rules. He remembered McLeod's shoes strangely placed at his bedside. Exactly when had he left? For how long? For what purpose? Passos didn't know, but he didn't need to know. I hold a trump card now, he thought.

Then he thought of his mother in the dream. *You're a good boy, but promise me,* she'd said. That "but"—it pierced all the way to the bone. But what other options did he have? Should he pretend he hadn't heard his companion coming in the front gate at five thirty in the morning? Should he turn a blind, uncaring eye? In the event of a companion's serious misconduct—serious *sin,* potentially—a missionary did best to turn the matter over to the presiding priesthood authority. President Mason, in this case. Perhaps Passos had been handed a gift, he and McLeod both. It might not be too late for a change of transfer plans—Passos to the office and McLeod to another companion, or home early if necessary, however the president saw fit to handle him. It could be as simple as a phone call: an apology to the president for calling so early in the morning and an expression of concern for his junior companion, who had finally gone beyond Passos's ability to control, who needed more guidance than he could provide.

Elder Passos heard another short scrape of a chair readjusting under his companion's weight. What was he doing out there? Why had he left the apartment? What had he done?

He couldn't exactly go strike up a conversation about it with McLeod. Never mind that they hadn't spoken in three weeks—to even go out into the front room would be to acknowledge what he knew, to tip his hand. Much better to make a private phone call to the president, give him and McLeod the out they both wanted. Elder Passos didn't need McLeod's parents, anyway. He only needed a recommendation from the president, a student visa, and the rest, he felt confident, would take care of itself. And of course, *of course* he would remember his brothers. He would bring Nana over too, if she could ever be persuaded. If not, he would return after four years, maybe less, with an American degree in hand, and the world that much wider, that much better for him. Elder Passos knew now to build his house on two foundations— the spiritual and the secular. He knew his mother would be proud of him. He was a good boy, she'd said. But what did she mean by that "but"?

Passos heard another sound from the front room, a different sound, a sort of scratching. Tapping and scratching. He tried to ignore it. He covered his ears. Then the scratching noise stopped and a long silence followed. Elder Passos stiffened in his bed. If McLeod tried to sneak back into the bedroom, let him. He closed his eyes now, pretending to sleep. But the noise in the front room resumed. What was it? Where was it coming from?

Passos knew he couldn't afford to wonder. He started praying, to distract himself as much as anything. It was a sort of reflex, but soon he meant it. Elder Passos's thoughts rose up into genuine prayer the way the mind slips down into dreaming—in an act of ungovernable grace. His God-led thoughts led from his mother to his brothers, Nana, the mission, all of it, the whole purpose—and then to McLeod. He stopped on McLeod. Something stopped him there. A feeling of warning. What had Passos decided just last night? What had he resolved to do just hours earlier? Give him time. Give him a little more time. It implied a chance, a chance, at least, at explanation. Maybe McLeod had gone for a walk in the moonlight—a serious mistake but not mission-ending, not enough for a dishonorable release. How could Passos be such an unjust judge? If *he* expected a chance from the president, if he expected a chance from BYU, then didn't he owe one to Elder McLeod? Didn't he owe him at least the question? *You're a good boy*, his mother had said, *but*.

The feeling of warning still hovered like a fog in Passos's mind, though little by little it lifted, breaking altogether when a resolution took its place. Give him a little more time. Give him a chance. Never mind the call to the president. He'd get to the office soon enough. The president had all but promised him the assistantship next transfer. *For now just concentrate on that companion of yours.* He owed him the question at least.

Passos opened his eyes. The glowing yellow band at the foot of the door glowing softer. The rising warmth in the room. This way, besides, he could still call the president if he needed to—it would be trickier, but he could do it—and he could also satisfy his curiosity, growing more intense by the second. Where had McLeod actually gone? What had he done? Why? And what was he doing now? What was that noise—Passos heard it again—that tiny, insistent tapping and scratching, tapping and scratching, tapping and scratching. It sounded like mice in the walls. It drove Passos to his feet.

Elder McLeod looked up from his work to the window, still mostly dark. The bare bulb overhead cast overlapping shadows on the ceiling, a sort of flowering out from the center. The bulb, as always, gave off little light, but enough for McLeod's present purpose. He held Passos's left shoe in his left hand, sole up, taking a retracted pen tip to the packed-in dirt between the grooves, scraping at the dirt, then trying to tap the remainder free. Scraping, then tapping. Taking action. Elder McLeod thought of President Mason, who had given him the idea, but he thought of his father more. In the car at Logan Airport, not two hours before takeoff. His father's warm blessing hands on his head. And his assurances. *You wouldn't be doing this if you weren't going to do it well. That's one of the things I most admire about you.*

McLeod thought his father would be proud of him now, seeing him at work on his companion's shoes. The gospel of doing. Faith as a principle of action. Saint John's litmus test. The old tropes. If he could will himself to care, he could will himself to obey. If not out of love or belief, then out of fear. Maybe *that* was the whole game.

In any case, Elder McLeod felt a strange excitement as he carried out his good deed, tapping and scratching, tapping and scratching, the rhythmic energy of his hands imparting energy to his heart such that his *feelings* began to align against his thoughts in an almost exact counterpoint. I have set both feet, he felt, on a course that will restore my companionship to good faith, that will provide the impetus for a strong end to my mission, a triumphal end, and that will trigger God's grace in my heart, a permanent testimony. McLeod smiled at himself. He pulled back to his thoughts.

At the very least he could say he had tried something, and who knew? He might surprise Passos with the sheer suddenness of the gesture, the unexpectedness, as Passos had surprised him that first day with the Guaraná. *Did you do this?* he would say, and to him, audibly, unmistakably, the sound of a cease-fire. Holding up the shoes, like dull mirrors, and saying, *You did this, Elder McLeod?*

And McLeod would nod and say, *I'm sorry, Elder Passos. Not about*—gesturing to the shoes—*not about that, obviously. That I meant. I'm sorry about everything else. You know?*

Passos would nod too, or maybe not, but in any case McLeod would cross the entryway/living room to his desk and lever out the Seuss book he'd demanded back. He could hold it out to him: *Here, take it. This is another thing I'm sorry about. It was a gift, and it's yours.*

Passos would accept the return of the gift, with thanks. Then he would cross the room to *his* desk, digging through the drawer and retrieving the blue grammar book that Passos had given him as a birthday present and that he, McLeod, had returned out of spite, leaving a spiteful note in the pages. He really did regret that. He felt a sea of regrets welling up in him, huge crashing waves. He could tell that to Passos—the shoe-cleaning could occasion it— and maybe he really *could* restore his companionship to good faith.

Maybe. Could. Would. Might. The very language of his hope spread over McLeod's thoughts like a sedative, a check to keep his expectations in balance. He had felt this sense of performance before, this sense of personal history-making *in situ*, of doing something and knowing already how he'd describe it months, even years, afterward. One afternoon in his first area he had spotted a little girl with big hungry eyes. Gaping eyes, McLeod had thought. "Gaping" was just how he would describe them. He bought an ice-cream cone and motioned for the girl to come over and help herself. She moved to the cone and took it from his hand and looked at him flatly and walked away. A few months later he had stayed up half the night composing his homecoming talk; he hadn't been eight months into his mission at the time. The talk began: *I wasn't eight months into my mission when I started composing this homecoming talk* . . . The next morning he read over his too-clever effusions of the night before, and threw the pages away.

And he was doing it again now—on some level he knew that. The way he took breaks from cleaning Passos's shoes to observe the room, frame it for memory's sake, for posterity's. The entryway/living room in a dim yellow light. Shadows clinging to the corners. The air warm, the floor cool underfoot. In a gesture of charity—*It never faileth*, Paul said—he had taken up his companion's worn and dusty shoes to clean them, including the soles. Of course McLeod hoped something good might come of it. The heart is a hopeful, incorrigible thing.

McLeod finished Passos's left shoe and took up the right, making a fist of his hand and using it as a shoe horn. He brushed the dirt clods off with his free hand, removing the loose earth preparatory to the thorough treatment: the old toothbrush, the tin of shoe black, the small felt buffing rag retrieved from the recesses of his desk drawer. In the absence of a drop cloth, a loose circle of dirty precipitation had formed on the floor in front of McLeod's chair. He planned to sweep up before Passos awoke, which he figured would be in an hour or so, a little under. He didn't feel rushed, but he wanted to have time to spare. He took out his pen again, tip retracted, and started working at the stubborn tracks of dust that crusted into the grooves along the side of the right shoe, scratching at the dirt, then tapping at it, then scratching at it again, and so on. Elder McLeod had never cleaned his own shoes so thoroughly, much less a companion's shoes. He went at the cracks and veins of dirt with the avid, improvisational élan of a novice. Much of the dirt would take up residence again, by midday that day, in the very crevices he cleaned. The essence of the gesture lay not in utility but in ceremony, old as forgiveness itself. I am doing this for you, Passos, McLeod thought, not because it is practical but because it is impractical. I am doing this for you because you—

He looked up at the sound of bare feet slapping the linoleum.

Elder Passos, in shorts and garment top, stopped just past the hallway. He looked at McLeod, squinting. He visored his eyes, still squinting. "What are you doing?"

McLeod froze, pen in one hand, shoe in the other, as if he'd been caught in a shameful act. His companion's words confused him. Their tone confused him: rough, abrading. The first words to him in more than three weeks and they sounded like an accusation. A threat.

Passos's brows suddenly snapped all the way to the V. "Is that a pen? Hey! What are you doing to my shoe?"

McLeod opened his mouth to respond—"Wah . . ."— but only a wordless noise came out. He watched his companion's posture change, spring-load, and he tensed himself.

McLeod tried again. "Wait. No." The words felt leaden, slow on his tongue, as if three weeks of silence and the night's exhaustion had combined to atrophy his very ability to speak. The words labored up like a pair of wounded birds in the space between the two elders, the space Passos was suddenly closing as he glowered across the room. McLeod dropped the pen and took up Passos's shoe instead, cocked it back at his ear. Passos hesitated a beat, then another, and rushed, nose-first, into the airborne shoe. The collision made a sharp, wet *thwock*. The shoe fell to the ground and Passos followed it and McLeod saw dark blood forming up in his companion's nostrils. Passos looked dazed, blinking rapidly, touching his fingers to the blood, coming to a number of realizations. Elder McLeod crouched in a wrestler's stance in front of the chair. He felt the other shoe gripped in his hand now, and he came to realizations of his own.

This was not the way it was supposed to go. This was the little girl taking him in flatly, walking away instead of smiling, thanking him. This was the homecoming talk that fell dead on the page, too self-conscious, too *hopeful*. This was God resurrecting long enough to throw Jonah to the whale, then dying again, and consigning him to the dark reeking bowels forever.

This was McLeod's bloodied companion suddenly lunging for the fallen shoe. This was McLeod rushing forward and kicking it out of his hand. This was McLeod trying to fall astride Passos's chest only to feel Passos's knee instead, hard as a beam against his groin. This was the airless howl McLeod made, the feeling of drowning, of pain like the end of the world, the feeling of Passos falling astride *his* chest now, trapping his arms under bony knees, and landing hard, stiff, repetitive punches on his nose, his cheeks, his temples, his eyes.

This was not the way it was supposed to go.

After a time Passos felt McLeod's body slacken, felt him go heavy underneath him. His companion stopped bucking, stopped struggling altogether. He lay still and just accepted the sidelong blows, eyes closed, though softly, the soft eyelids of the unconscious or close to it. The eyelids startled Elder Passos, brought him back to himself. He arrested his fist halfway to McLeod's cheek, sharply rouged already with jags of skin-trapped blood. The entire right side of McLeod's face looked lurid with darkening spots, like bruises on a pear. The skin broke across his eyebrow and lower lip, leaking red. A thick streak of blood ran down from either nostril.

Passos rocked off his companion's chest and slid back along the floor several feet from McLeod. The breath had gone out of him suddenly; he hugged his knees. He had never fought like this before, never exchanged more than a few halfhearted blows with his brothers. The adrenaline coursed through his limbs, felt dangerous, like it might overflow the banks of his body.

Passos felt a wetness on his upper lip and tongued the tangy flavor with realization, relief: blood. His own blood. He had nearly forgotten.

"You made me bleed," he said to McLeod, as if to justify himself, and make sure McLeod could hear him. "McLeod? You hit me first, remember. You made me bleed first."

After another moment McLeod rolled onto his side, facing away from him. He let out a moan, then a sort of watery laugh. McLeod got to all fours, dripping blood onto the linoleum underneath him. "I can't even tell where it's coming from—my nose or my lip." He spoke his words as if through a mouthful of food, but when he spat nothing came out except a glistening web of pink. "Fucking . . ." He laughed again. " 'You made me bleed first.' "

"Well you did. You did. You had a pen to my shoe—you were vandalizing my shoes!—and I tried to stop you and you . . ."

Passos heard the craven desperation in his voice and stopped. His companion, as if reading his thoughts, said, "Save it for the president. Save your story."

McLeod struggled to his feet, then staggered into the bathroom. For several minutes—it seemed like seconds to Elder Passos— McLeod ran the faucet in the sink.

Passos used the time to rifle desperately through a rolodex of stratagems. He could claim self-defense, but how to explain McLeod's face? He could blackmail McLeod's silence, but how, with what? Maybe he should run to the pay phone now and pre-empt the conversation with President Mason. His companion had come home from who knows where this morning and he'd come in like that, all bloodied and swollen. Someone must have done it to him. He'll tell you otherwise, President, he'll say I did it, but you know him, you know how he is . . . But each idea was riskier, less plausible than the last. He didn't feel confident at all in his ability to lie at this magnitude, to bear up under the inevitable doubt-ing looks, the cross-examinations. Besides, hadn't the president told him to *help* McLeod, or at least to contain him? Hadn't he expressed his confidence in Passos? *I do appreciate the challenges you face with him, and I do notice the way you handle those chal-lenges.* Passos could read between the lines. His fate interlocked with McLeod's; he had become his companion's keeper. He had to keep President Mason from finding out anything: a new transfer period, six weeks for McLeod to heal . . . It could work. He just needed to keep it from the president. But how? And how to deal with McLeod in the meantime? Even if he did keep the news of the fight from getting out, how could he survive another *day* with McLeod, much less another transfer? Passos half expected his junior companion to burst out of the bathroom and barrel for his head.

At the thought of this Passos stood up from the floor, moving several steps deeper into the room. He had no desire to fight anymore, but neither did he feel any hope for an armistice. He felt nothing but the coppery mounting panic closing up his throat, burning in his eyes. If he could only change positions with McLeod, if he could only be the bloodier one, the obvious victim . . . But nothing was obvious anymore. Nothing had gone the way he'd hoped. McLeod had poisoned everything for him, everything.

The bathroom faucet stopped and the sound of the pipes cutting off moved through the apartment like a shudder.

———————

Elder McLeod stood before Passos with swollen eyes, a wad of toilet paper in either nostril, another patch of paper, soaked red already, sticking to his lower lip, and another to his eyebrow. Flecks of blood ran down his shirtfront. His hair was wet and dripping. When he spoke, he sounded like he'd just returned from the dentist, but his tone carried a surprising amount of calm, almost warmth. "I was trying to clean your shoes, Passos. I don't know why—it was probably stupid of me—but that's what I was doing.

I was cleaning them." He paused. "Well, anyway, I don't think this"—McLeod motioned to his face—"is very becoming of an assistant to the president, do you?"

"You hit me first," Passos said, trying to mirror McLeod's calmness. "I was just acting in self-defense."

McLeod gave a brief, grimacing smile. "I'm going to the mission office this morning. In just a few minutes, actually. And I'm not sure that version of things will hold up."

"If you go," Passos said, "if you do that, I'll tell the mission president about this morning. I heard you come in before sunrise. He'll want to know where you were."

"In the drive-through," McLeod said. "I was in the drive-through with a prostitute."

Elder Passos went quiet, thrown back by the words. Before he could fully process them McLeod brushed past him to his desk. He picked his shoulder bag up off the chair and slung it over his chest. He started for the front door.

"I'll tell him that!" Passos shouted. "If you go, I'll tell him that—you'll be sent home for sure. A dishonorable release, for sure. If you go, I'll tell the president what you just told me."

McLeod turned to him, said, "I'm going to tell him myself, Elder." He moved to the door and opened it.

"Your father! What about your father? Do you want *him* to find out about this? McLeod, listen to me. Just listen for a second." McLeod turned around, not quite looking at him. "You can't go outside like that. You can't . . . Look, I'm sorry, okay? I'm sorry."

McLeod stared at a spot just beyond Passos's shoulder, his eyes red and unfocused. After a moment he crossed the room to his desk again, taking up the framed black-and-white picture of his family. He held it gently in his hands. "I'll tell him too," McLeod said, more to himself now. "He needs to know about me. He needs to know."

Elder McLeod put the picture in his shoulder bag. He opened his desk drawer, raking papers around. He closed the drawer without removing anything. He ran his finger over the spines of his books tucked into the corner of his desk, passing all but the Dr. Seuss book, which he pulled from the row and held out to Passos. "Here."

Elder Passos stood still, arms stubborn at his sides. After a moment his companion shrugged his shoulders. He went over to Passos's desk and dropped the book there. "In case you change your mind."

Passos looked at McLeod, though not to acknowledge what he'd said. He watched him hesitating at Passos's desk, watched him lay a tentative hand on the desk drawer's handle.

"What are you doing?" Passos said.

"I don't suppose you'd want to re-gift that Portuguese grammar book."

"I threw it away. Weeks ago."

"Ah," McLeod said, a little sadly, Passos thought.

McLeod crossed into the bedroom. Passos didn't move. He heard a rasping dragging sound, heard the squeal of a heavy-duty zipper. He heard dresser doors opening, the chime of metal hangers, soft thuds. The sounds of shuffling, shuffling, then the heavy-duty squeal again. Elder Passos felt a catch in his breathing as McLeod emerged from the bedroom seconds later, pulling his large roller suitcase behind him, looking directly at Passos, as if he knew he'd been listening. McLeod came to within striking distance of him, then gestured down at his suitcase. "Save myself the trip back here." He put out his hand to Passos. "This is it, companion. Shake on it?"

Elder Passos looked at the hand and felt a sudden rage, but it acted to calm him, compress him. "No." He shook his head. Once. "No. I don't want to."

"Well, suit yourself." McLeod walked to the front door, opened it, lifted his suitcase down the stoop, and disappeared. He returned a moment later, sticking his head in the doorframe. "Oh, and just in case there was any doubt, I can tell you that the stay in my parents' basement is not going to work out."

"Good," Passos whispered.

McLeod hesitated, looking like he wanted to add something, but he didn't. He closed the door behind him. Passos heard the high-pitched buzz of McLeod's roller suitcase moving across the cement courtyard. The buzzing stopped as McLeod unlatched the outer gate—"Did you hear me?" Passos called out. "I said that's good!"—then it started up again on the other side of the property wall. It moved down the street, dropping in pitch, in volume, until it dropped off to nothing.

"Good!" Passos shouted. "Good!" He sobbed it now. "Good! Good! Good! Good! Good! Good! Good!" He went to his desk and fell into the chair, taking great drags of air until he had recovered himself. He thrust McLeod's book into his desk drawer, unable to even look at it. The walls started to reel around him; he closed his eyes. He tried to concentrate, calling on his deepest reserves. He could feel something else—persistent, underneath. At the top of each breath he held the air in a fragile, crystalline suspense. He heard the sound of his shouts still echoing in the room. A ringing in his ears, a low building hum, like the after-sound of a giant bell clap, the room pervaded with something so powerful, yet invisible. Like God, he thought. Yes, like God. The Rock. He is here already. Passos held to Him, suddenly, like the last thing in the world. He is here. He is Here. And she—she is too, even now. They are near me, both of them, even now. Passos shut his eyes tighter, took another deep breath, and once again set his mind, and his aging heart, to the solution.

I owe particular thanks to the Stegner Fellows at Stanford University, and to Alice Elliott Dark, Jayne Anne Phillips, Tobias Wolff, PJ Mark, Zachary Wagman, and Sharon McIlvain—readers, ghost writers all. I also wish to thank the editors of *Dialogue* and *The Paris Review*, where portions of this novel appeared in earlier form.